"Isabelle, I can... you something...

A sense of foreboding settled over her. "Scott, I don't think..."

"Hear me out. We've always been best friends. We know each other inside and out. I want us to move forward with our lives." He squeezed her hand earnestly.

"We are moving forward," she said reflexively.

"I mean together. I realize that writing articles for the local paper is not going to make a difference in this world. But I can change the future for these kids. I can take something horrible and make it happy. It's my hope that you'd do that with me."

All Isabelle could do was stare at him. "You just got through saying we were best friends, but you don't know me at all. I just won the chance of my lifetime. A shot at a gallery show! The one thing I've worked for since high school." Her voice cracked. Her palms were sweating and her heart rammed against her chest. "You are not asking me this right now."

"Oh, but I am," he replied quietly.

Dear Reader,

If you have read all of the Shores of Indian Lakes books, you will be familiar with Scott Abbott and Isabelle Hawks. Scott has had a crush on Isabelle for years. However, Isabelle has been hyper-focused on her art.

From the get-go I wanted Isabelle to be that kind of painter who is truly gifted, but the world hasn't discovered her yet. Her intuition and inner guidance have told her that if she simply keeps trying, working and believing, she will make it someday.

The problem is that Scott wants to begin his life with Isabelle. When she turns him down, choosing her art over him, Scott takes matters into his own hands and becomes a foster parent to two small children.

Isabelle is the oldest of six children and because her mother became a widow at a young age, Isabelle had to mature fast and be a parent to her siblings. Isabelle's thwarted childhood is one reason she pursues her portraits of faeries and water sprites—and motivation for embracing her freedom now.

What Isabelle hasn't realized is that she's been avoiding living her life all for the sake of art. Through Scott's growing relationship with his foster kids, Isabelle comes to see her choices with a new palette of colors. Finally, she must learn that without love in her life, her art will never flourish. Neither will her heart.

I hope you like *Family of His Own*. Please contact me on Facebook, Twitter (@cathlanigan), www.catherinelanigan.com and heartwarmingauthors. blogspot.com. Look for chapters on Wattpad.

Happy reading!

Catherine Lanigan

HEARTWARMING

Family of His Own

—

Catherine Lanigan

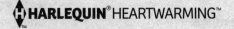 HARLEQUIN® HEARTWARMING™

Recycling programs
for this product may
not exist in your area.

ISBN-13: 978-0-373-36845-7

Family of His Own

Copyright © 2017 by Catherine Lanigan

All rights reserved. Except for use in any review, the reproduction or utilization of this work in whole or in part in any form by any electronic, mechanical or other means, now known or hereinafter invented, including xerography, photocopying and recording, or in any information storage or retrieval system, is forbidden without the written permission of the publisher, Harlequin Enterprises Limited, 225 Duncan Mill Road, Don Mills, Ontario M3B 3K9, Canada.

This is a work of fiction. Names, characters, places and incidents are either the product of the author's imagination or are used fictitiously, and any resemblance to actual persons, living or dead, business establishments, events or locales is entirely coincidental.

This edition published by arrangement with Harlequin Books S.A.

For questions and comments about the quality of this book, please contact us at CustomerService@Harlequin.com.

® and TM are trademarks of Harlequin Enterprises Limited or its corporate affiliates. Trademarks indicated with ® are registered in the United States Patent and Trademark Office, the Canadian Intellectual Property Office and in other countries.

Printed in U.S.A.

Catherine Lanigan knew she was born to storytelling at a very young age when she told stories to her younger brothers and sister to entertain them. After years of encouragement from family and high school teachers, Catherine was shocked and brokenhearted when her freshman college creative-writing professor told her that she had "no writing talent whatsoever" and that she would never earn a dime as a writer. He promised her that he would be her crutches and get her through his demanding class with a B grade so as not to destroy her high grade point average too much, *if* Catherine would promise never to write again. Catherine assumed he was the voice of authority and gave in to the bargain.

For fourteen years she did not write until she was encouraged by a television journalist to give her dream a shot. She wrote a six-hundred-page historical romantic spy thriller set against World War I. The journalist sent the manuscript to his agent, who then garnered bids from two publishers. That was nearly forty published novels, nonfiction books and anthologies ago.

Books by Catherine Lanigan

Harlequin Heartwarming

Shores of Indian Lake

Love Shadows
Heart's Desire
A Fine Year for Love
Katia's Promise
Fear of Falling
Sophie's Path
Protecting the Single Mom

MIRA Books

Dangerous Love
Elusive Love

Harlequin Desire

The Texan

Visit the Author Profile page
at Harlequin.com for more titles.

This book is dedicated to my late husband, Jed Nolan, my hero and best friend. I will love you to the moon and back, and throughout all the galaxies and universes.

Acknowledgments

This story is all about family. The ones we were born into and the ones we come to create. My years with the entire staff at Harlequin Heartwarming, as well as my Heartwarming author sisters, have woven a strong bond of family between us.

For an author, working with an editor should be the best expression of our thoughts and art. I have again had the extraordinary pleasure to meld ideas with my editor, Claire Caldwell, and together we have extracted the deepest desires and dreams from both Scott and Isabelle about what they truly want from life.

I greatly appreciate Victoria Curran's guidance in keeping our stories filled with enough heart to warm our readers. Our characters, stories and uplifting style are needed now in the world like never before. Kudos to you, Victoria, and all the team for all your hard work, genius and the long hours it takes to make Harlequin Heartwarming an exceptional line of romance novels.

And to Lissy Peace, my agent, always: I love you and honor our decades of working together.

CHAPTER ONE

THE SOUND OF gunshots cracked through snow-dusted tree branches and split the brittle December air. A flock of honking Canada geese veered away from the blasts, their wings thudding amid the rippling echoes.

Scott Abbott reloaded his GLOCK, aimed and fired at the paper target in the shape of a person a hundred yards from the plexiglass-protected shooting stand. His shots were all over the place. Only one came close to the heart. Still, he was vastly improved over last month when he stood here in the icy rain shooting through pea-soup fog. Night-vision gear wouldn't have helped. Scott needed more practice if he wanted to be as good as his friends.

"Good thing my life doesn't depend on your skills," Trent Davis, Indian Lake Police Detective, teased as he pulled on a pair of military-issue, noise-canceling earphones and aimed his Smith & Wesson M&P45 and easily squeezed off six shots dead into the target's heart area.

Scott grimaced at his best friend, Luke Bosworth, whose cool gaze was devoid of mirth. Luke had been a navy SEAL. His new semi-automatic 1911 Colt .45 plowed the target with eight shots, the paper flying off like escaping butterflies.

Scott blew on his freezing hands. "My aim is off. The cold." He shrugged.

"Yeah, tell it to the judge." Trent laughed and reloaded.

Scott pulled the sheepskin collar of his scarred leather bomber jacket around his neck. "How do you do it? I'm freezing and you're not even wearing your parka."

Trent rammed a new magazine into his gun and without taking his eyes from the target said, "This isn't a game for me. Never was. Never will be. That's not a paper man to me. That's the man who nearly killed my fiancée." Trent aimed and fired his gun.

Scott, who claimed a byline at the *Indian Lake Herald* newspaper, knew every last detail and then some about Trent's brilliant and dangerous plot to bring down the leader of the Le Grande drug ring in Indian Lake only a few short weeks ago.

Trent had headed up the Indian Lake PD's drug task force for nearly two years, resulting in many arrests, but it was the capture of Brad Kramer, AKA Raoul Le Grande, that brought

national attention to their small Indiana town—
and to Trent. He'd denied all interview requests,
though, except Scott's. Trent had many reasons
to avoid the press. Accuracy was one. Trent had
trusted only Scott to report sensitive details
about the intricate sting he'd set up to catch Le
Grande. Cate Sullivan, Le Grande's ex-wife,
had been at the center of the plan. Scott had
met Cate when Luke hired her to sell his home
after his first wife died of cancer. Cate was a
private woman and had kept her personal life
quiet. When Scott learned that Cate had been
living in disguise in Indian Lake for the past six
years, Scott was as surprised as everyone else.

Le Grande hadn't only wanted to use Indian
Lake as a way station for trafficking drugs
from Chicago up to Detroit and eventually to
Toronto. The drug lord had wanted his ex-wife
and six-year-old son, Danny, back.

Trent had convinced Cate to act as bait to
smoke Le Grande out. The plan was well orchestrated, yet even Trent had not calculated
the extent of Le Grande's twisted, maniacal
mind.

Thanks to Trent's Special Forces military
training and his exceptional perceptive genius,
Cate and Danny survived, and Le Grande was
now in prison awaiting trial.

Scott had been at the Christmas Pageant

at St. Mark's school when Le Grande had attempted to kidnap Danny, and he'd managed to capture the entire, harrowing scene on his iPhone. His eyewitness reporting, along with his photos and videos, were still getting attention across the country.

Not since had Scott worked for the *Chicago Tribune* right after graduation from Northwestern University had he dared to dream of prizes and awards. Now those possibilities seemed once again in reach.

"Hey!" Luke shouted over the blast of Trent's final bullet. "Back up there, buddy." He put his hand on Trent's shoulder. "Did you just say *fiancée*?"

Scott also did a double take. "What? You and Cate?"

Trent's half smile grew into a full-blown grin. "Yeah. Can you believe it? She said yes!"

"No," Scott said, feeling an odd sense of disbelief and disquietude. "I don't. You've only known her—what, a couple months?"

Scott stared at Trent, who had a goofy look on his face. Trent had just become the town hero. He could outshoot and outsmart master criminals. But when he talked about Cate, he turned to mush. It had been a long time since Scott had felt that way about Isabelle. Come to think of it, he'd never seen her get dewy-eyed over him. And if she had, he'd missed it. Maybe that was a good reason to rush into marriage. Grab the feeling while it was new and fresh, like a spring sapling. Let it grow over time.

Trent's laughter broke through Scott's thoughts.

"Yeah, man, intense days, I'll tell you. But—" He glanced down at his gun. "I can't imagine another day without her."

"Wow!" Luke grabbed Trent in a bear hug. "That's awesome, man. Did she like the ring?"

"Actually, I haven't gotten her one yet. I want it to be a Christmas present." Trent looked from Luke to Scott. "Do you think I should surprise her or have her go with me to pick it out?"

"Surprise her," Luke said emphatically.

"I dunno…" Scott shook his head. "Women can be weird about rings. I'd take her shopping. What if you pick out something she hates and then she's stuck wearing it the rest of her life?"

Trent and Luke took a moment to consider his advice.

Luke put his hand on Scott's shoulder. "This is why he's been my best friend since high school. He considers all the angles. Very observant. Better take her shopping. But to surprise her—you could put the empty box under the tree. Then tell her you're taking her to the jeweler the next day."

"Ah, good one," Trent agreed. "So, Luke, what are you getting Sarah for Christmas?"

"I was thinking about some new drill bits," Luke deadpanned.

"Right," Scott said. "She'll be thrilled."

Luke broke into laughter. "Nah. I got her a sapphire bracelet. To match her eyes." He smiled wistfully.

"Very romantic," Scott replied.

Trent grabbed his box of shells. "So what are you giving Isabelle? Want to make that a double date to the jeweler's?"

Scott's mouth went dry. "Uh, we don't exchange gifts."

"You what?" Trent and Luke said in unison.

"Man, no wonder…" Luke didn't finish his thought. He went over to his gear and fussed with his holster.

"Isabelle and I aren't like that," Scott began.

"You mean not romantic?" Trent asked.

"Uh, no. Not really." Scott aimed at the target again, pretending interest in the exercise. He felt more like the bull's-eye was drawn on the middle of his chest. "Isabelle and I are friends. You know?"

"Yeah?" Luke narrowed his eyes. "Is that because that's how she wants it or how you want it?"

"It's how it is."

Trent unloaded his gun into the target, then turned to Scott. "I thought you told me you two were sweethearts in high school?"

"We were just kids then." Scott turned away, avoiding Luke's steely gaze. He knew exactly what his best friend was thinking.

Scott had returned to Indian Lake four years ago to take care of his mother, who had needed a new heart valve. He'd had to leave his job at the *Chicago Tribune,* but he'd sensed a layoff was around the corner anyway; journalists had been losing their jobs across the nation, and it was only getting worse.

He'd been in town a few months when he'd run into Isabelle at one of Mrs. Beabots's Sunday dessert parties. Sarah Jensen had invited him, and since Sarah's mother had recently died, Scott thought he was doing the friendly thing by attending. Sarah's girlfriends were all there, including Isabelle.

In minutes they'd struck up a conversation. Scott had been surprised she didn't seem to hate him for not staying in touch as he'd promised.

Isabelle had told him she was now the bookkeeper and sometimes-hostess at the Tall Pines Lodges of Indian Lake. He remembered the green-eyed girl who'd painted sea nymphs and faeries for a high school play he'd codirected. Isabelle had designed the backdrops: stunningly beautiful moonlit forests that pulled the viewer into their magic. Scott had been mesmerized by her back then.

However, Scott's ambitions had been strong and he'd already been accepted to Northwestern which tempered his romantic feelings. Once Scott left for Chicago, Indian Lake and the girl back home had seemed like part of another life. He had immersed himself in creative writing and political science, spent nights huddled with new friends from California, New York and Beijing whose viewpoints stretched his thinking and blew apart what he thought he knew about the world.

Scott had believed then that the world was his oyster and he would only be satisfied with the pearl.

He hadn't told Isabelle any of this that Sunday evening at Mrs. Beabots's house. Like the investigative journalist he was, he'd asked her about her life instead.

Isabelle had been taking art classes for years, including a few at the Art Institute of Chicago. She couldn't stop talking about walking along the shores of Indian Lake and imagining water sprites looking up at her from the cool depths. She was compelled to paint them.

Scott had become mesmerized all over again.

That summer after returning home, Scott had

done everything to be near her. He paid Sarah Jensen double the going cost for a booth at the St. Mark's Summer Festival to make sure his booth for his coffee beans and books was next to Isabelle's art display.

As the months rolled on, Scott realized Isabelle had changed, as well. When it came to her art, she was fiercely ambitious. He'd recognized the same fire in her eyes that his own had held when he'd worked at the *Tribune*. Because his situation had altered so drastically, Scott had had to reinvent himself. He'd had to learn to be satisfied with lesser aspirations. Which was why he'd opened his bookstore and coffee shop.

Since those first months of his return, everyone in town had considered him and Isabelle to be a couple. But the truth was that Scott had no idea if Isabelle loved him. The one time he'd told her he loved her, she'd dismissed his declaration, telling him he couldn't possibly love her because she hadn't become her true self yet— hadn't accomplished enough. She intended to do a great many things with her talent and her life. She hadn't "come into her own."

Scott had scratched his head over that one, but he'd let it go. He'd made his intentions clear, and he hoped that one day Isabelle would see what was right in front of her. There had never been another woman for him, and to his knowledge Isabelle wasn't interested in another man. They were good friends. Best friends, really. Isabelle was Team Isabelle. Though not in a selfish way.

"Guys. What can I say? We're just not 'there' yet."

Luke shot a glance at Trent, who shrugged. "So, this gives you another year to save up for a really big rock."

Scott shoved his hands in his pockets. "I don't think a diamond would impress this woman."

"What would?" Luke asked.

"That's easy. Hanging her paintings in The Guggenheim."

Trent whistled and slapped Scott on the back. "Come on, I want you guys to help me with something before we leave."

"Yeah? What's that?" Scott asked as he put away his GLOCK and gathered his ammunition and protective glasses.

Trent stuck his arms through his black jacket and stuffed his gloves in his pockets. "I received a call from Richard Schmitz at CPD..."

"He's your counterpart in Chicago, right?" Scott asked. "I interviewed him for my articles."

Luke led the way out of the shooting range,

waving to the attendant as they left. "By the way, Scott. That article was fantastic. Great writing. I felt like I was right there in the middle of the action." Luke stopped short, and Scott nearly ran into him. "Wait! What am I saying?" Luke snickered. "I *was* in the middle of the action."

Scott didn't need reminding. Luke's daughter, Annie, had been talking to little Danny when Le Grande had appeared, grabbed Danny like a sack of flour and raced off with him.

Dozens of people had witnessed the kidnapping. Le Grande might dodge the drug dealing and selling charges, given his high-powered and expensive criminal attorney, but that kidnapping was another matter. Scott hoped Le Grande would be locked up for decades. "Trent. Tell us what's up."

"Le Grande has been busy behind bars. Like many powerful people in the drug trade, I'm afraid."

"That does tend to be the case," Scott replied. Apprehension seemed to snake across the frozen ground and grab him by the heels. It had only been three weeks since Trent had nailed Le Grande and arrested five of his gang members in Indian Lake. Trent had later told Scott the heroin alone was worth over a quarter million. The meth had a street value of half a million. Scott knew exactly what Trent was about to say. Deals like that didn't die. They morphed into something bigger and more sinister.

"Come on," Trent said as they walked quickly toward Luke's SUV. "I want to drive by the old WWII ammunitions plant that's just down the road from here."

"Why?" Scott asked, climbing into the back seat.

"Richard has reason to believe that members of Le Grande's gang are scouting Indian Lake, Gary and possibly up into Berrien Springs, Michigan, for a place to make methamphetamine."

"No way," Scott exhaled. "They'd come back here?"

"Why not? They know the terrain and a lot of the existing dealers."

Scott peered at Luke, who glanced at him in the rearview mirror. He shook his head. "I was hoping this was behind us."

Trent turned in the passenger seat to look at Scott. "You both are sworn to secrecy. Off the record, Scott. You got that?"

"This can't be good." Scott sighed, his eyes still locked on Trent. "Yeah. Sure."

"I've got a lead on a guy who is making the meth."

Scott sat up straighter. "And?"

"I've been on stakeouts, but the guy moves

around a lot. He's got his playbook down pat. He wheedles his way into friendships with disabled young people he finds in soup kitchens and churches. Lately, he's been recruiting construction workers, too."

Luke chimed in. "That's because it's winter and guys like me don't have a lot of work. And they hang out at pool halls, bars." He turned into an unplowed drive that led through a cluster of trees.

"That's right," Trent continued. "So our guy's name is Frankie Ellis. Or that's his alias this week. Anyway, he gets these kids to let him bunk with them, then he talks them into making meth. They become accomplices. And he's got them." Trent made a fist.

"And you think he's out here at the old ordinance plant?"

"I do."

Scott looked out the window. "I was hoping Indian Lake kids would be safer after you nabbed Le Grande."

"Me, too." Luke clutched the steering wheel.

"Afraid not," Trent said, shaking his head.

They'd reached the end of the drive and were approaching a row of long, narrow manufacturing buildings from World War II. The white paint on their exteriors was chipped, and some of the faded green shutters hung at odd angles.

A concrete drive circled a naked flagpole and a raised planter that at one time, Scott imagined, had been filled with red, white and blue flowers. Weeds and poison ivy, now strangled by winter's kill, decorated the front of a matching office building. To the far right were what appeared to be barracks and hangar-like buildings for transport vehicles.

During the war, the compound had been a source of pride and hope for Indian Lake residents. They had thought they were fighting back against the greatest evil of all time.

Luke drove into the complex and stopped at the heavy rusted chain across the entrance. Trent turned to Scott. "Take photos with your phone. I'm going to check it out. You both stay here."

"What?" Scott stared at him "What if Ellis is in there?"

"Both of you know how to handle yourselves in any situation. I wouldn't put you in danger. Scott, you're the best journalist around. You see things that I even miss. I'm relying on your eyes. And Luke, I could take lessons from you, man."

"We've got your back, Trent," Luke said.

"Yeah, we want to help. It's our town, too," Scott added. Scott watched with a clenched jaw as Trent jogged away, ducked under the chain and hustled up to one of the buildings.

"What if this meth dealer has friends? Like some of Le Grande's murderous gang?"

"I'm sure Trent thought of that."

"I hope so," Scott replied warily. "This is nuts."

Luke shook his head slightly. He had slipped his gun out of its holster and put it on the passenger seat.

Scott swallowed hard. "Okay." He picked up his phone and took a series of photos, using his zoom. "I need a telephoto lens for this. And the sun is going down."

Luke pointed out the window. "It's abandoned. See? No tire tracks on the snow. No footprints around, except Trent's. It's probably safe enough."

"Why do I get the feeling Chief Williams doesn't know anything about this?"

"Of course he knows. Trent wouldn't jeopardize his job. He said the chief trusts Trent's instincts when it comes to intel."

Luke sighed. "It's getting dark. He won't be able to see in there. And if he finds anything substantial, he'll need to get a warrant."

Scott was relieved to see Trent hustling back toward the SUV a few moments later. He climbed in and buckled up. "I can't see anything through the windows and even that broken one didn't help since I don't have a flashlight. I should get a warrant."

Luke laughed to himself and backed out of the drive. Scott's phone pinged with a text. "Problem there, buddy?" Luke asked.

"No. Just Isabelle. She wants me to bring some ice to the party. She said I'm late."

"Party?"

"Yeah. Her mother has a Christmas party every year on the twenty-third. It's tradition. Just family."

"Really? And she didn't have you working KP duty all afternoon?" Luke met Scott's eyes in the mirror, eyebrows raised.

"She asks for lots of other help, but not for the dinner. Except for the ice," Scott replied. Scott sensed where this conversation was going. His buddies thought they were supporting him with their inquiries and suggestions. But when they brought Isabelle up like this, it embarrassed him that he helped her out with so much, and yet, she wasn't as serious about him as he wanted her to be. As he felt about her.

He read the text again. It was terse and hurried.

Where are you? You were supposed to be here an hour ago. Bring ice.

Scott would have been on time if not for the unscheduled trip to the ammunitions plant. Maybe only slightly late. This was the third

Christmas that Scott had been invited to the Hawkses' family party. Her two sisters, Sadie and Violet, would be there, of course, since they both lived at home. Dylan, who was twenty-nine and only eleven months younger than Isabelle, would be home from the South Side of Chicago where he was a prosecuting attorney. Christopher, an EMP and first responder, lived north of town and Ross, a forensic CPA who commuted into downtown Chicago for work, would also be on hand.

Scott liked all of Isabelle's family but for some reason, she always seemed tense during this party. When he'd asked her about it in the past, she'd always said she was fine and that there was a lot of work to be done. But Scott had long wondered if her family made her nervous.

Or was it possible that *his* presence at Christmas upset her?

Luke and Trent were talking about their families and the threat of the rising drug problems. They both vowed to risk their lives to save their loved ones.

Scott slid his phone back into his pocket.

He knew, without a doubt, he would put his life on the line for Isabelle. But suddenly, he wondered if she had ever felt that strongly about him.

CHAPTER TWO

ISABELLE WIPED THE sweat from her forehead with her sleeve as she hoisted the stack of Christmas plates out of the cupboard in the storage room. After steadying herself, she placed the stack on the counter below and climbed down the ladder. When her mother had designed this storage area, Isabelle had praised her for it. She hadn't realized that she'd be just about the only family member using this room.

It was always this way on holidays. Isabelle's family talked for months about these big gatherings, the food they'd buy at the deli, the bakery, the butcher—nearly all premade since her mother, Connie, didn't have time or the desire to cook for everyone. Neither did Sadie or Violet. All three boys were excellent at ordering takeout. Isabelle was the only one in the family whose culinary skills were self-taught. She was no gourmet, but she could get by. But she drew the line at preparing a feast when no one else seemed willing to lift a finger.

The food wasn't the problem. Connie ordered

turkey, mashed potatoes and green bean casserole from the grocery store. Pumpkin pies came from the bakery. Sadie made stuffing out of a box on top of the stove. Gravy came from a jar and was heated in the microwave.

But as had been the case for nearly all their lives, everyone left the rest of the details up to Isabelle. Today, she'd arrived at her mother's house to find that not only had the table not been set, but the linens for it hadn't even been laundered.

Isabelle felt like she was ten years old again, when all the household responsibilities and childcare had fallen on her shoulders.

That was the year her father had dropped dead at the age of thirty-six from a heart attack. The doctors told her mother that he'd had an undetected congenital heart condition. Isabelle had helped her mother dress the younger kids for the funeral. She remembered half the town showing up at their little house off Main Street where there was barely enough room for all of them, let alone guests. Her mother's friends brought food enough to feed them for weeks.

Within a week, Connie had applied for a position as a receptionist at an architect's firm. A few months later she bought a used drafting table to tinker with blueprints in the evenings. A few months after that she signed up for night classes at Purdue University. By the time Isabelle was thirteen, Connie's talent and training had landed her a job as an apprentice architect. Nineteen years after the sudden death of her husband, Connie was now a partner in the firm and had helped finance portions of each of her children's postsecondary education.

Yet this had come at a cost. Isabelle had become the housekeeper, the nanny, the errand girl, the stand-in parent and all-around Cinderella to her younger siblings. Though Connie often expressed her gratitude for all that Isabelle had done during those years, she'd also told Isabelle that she'd provided her with invaluable preparation for adult life.

Isabelle wished she'd been a little less ready for adulthood, with more happy memories under her belt. Instead, she had spent her teen years worried about her mother working so many hours. Overwhelming herself with extra design classes instead of enjoying summer picnics at the beach. If Isabelle had missed out on a great deal of fun, Connie had had even less.

Isabelle pulled the red tablecloth out of the dryer and brought it up to the dining room. Earlier, she'd clipped an armload of fir, spruce, cedar and pine branches outside. Once she'd spread out the tablecloth, she arranged the pines in the center along with silver and gold beads, red votive candles and shiny red balls. She scattered a bag of cranberries along the length of the table then made the place settings.

From the den, she could hear her brothers shouting as their football team executed another touchdown. They clinked their beer bottles together and high-fived each other.

"It's beautiful, Isabelle," Connie said as she hauled a precooked glazed honey ham out of the stainless steel convection oven. It only needed to be warmed. Ironically, when Connie designed this house five years ago, after finding a secluded three acres surrounded by forest and fruit trees, she'd installed a massive, high-tech, cook's dream of a kitchen.

The house was one story, with red barn siding. Isabelle loved the glass walls that surrounded this section of the house, which contained the kitchen, living and dining areas; the vaulted wood ceilings and three-sixty-degree view made her feel like they were living outside. The only paintings were Isabelle's water nymphs: one above the fireplace on the south wall and one above the built-in redwood buffet on the north wall.

Connie knew her craft well.

"Thanks." Her gaze veered to the den. "You'd think just once somebody could help me. Volunteer at least."

"C'mon, let them be," Violet said, opening a can of jellied cranberry sauce. Violet was twenty-three and would be graduating in June from the University Police Academy in Bloomington. "They never get to all be together anymore. Football is a male bonding thing."

"I like football as much as anyone. What if I wanted to watch the game and not help with the food, set the table, do the laundry…"

"Oh, Isabelle." Sadie walked into the kitchen. She was wearing a University of Notre Dame sweatshirt, her dark hair in a ponytail. Sadie went straight to the stuffing that Violet was making and pinched a taste. "Yum."

Isabelle poured heavy cream into a bowl and turned on the mixer. "And where have you been all day? You could have been helping, as well."

Sadie's green eyes matched Isabelle's spark and brilliance. Isabelle always had a hard time staying mad at Sadie.

"I was with a client," she replied haughtily.

"What, how? You only just started law school," Isabelle countered.

Sadie tilted her chin defiantly. "I have an internship already. A prestigious Chicago firm. Actually, the job doesn't start until next semester, but I'll be working on real cases."

Isabelle looked at her mother. "Seriously?"

"Dylan arranged it. Apparently, he has a lot

of connections. He's so proud of Sadie getting into Notre Dame," Connie gushed. She put her arm around Sadie's shoulders and scrunched her to her chest. "We all are."

"This is great news!" Isabelle was thrilled for her younger sister. There was no question. Sadie was smart and quick and honest. She would do well as a lawyer. She threw her arms around Sadie and gave her long hug. "They must have you on a very fast track."

"*I* put me on a fast track. That's why I asked Dylan to help. If all goes well, I can test out of more classes and finish up law school sooner than the three years I'd planned."

Then Sadie leaned over and whispered, "I'll save Mom a bundle. Then I'll pay her back for everything." She winked.

"Sadie, you are the best," Isabelle said. Though her mother's job paid well and Connie had garnered a stellar reputation throughout the Midwest for her design and structures, paying tuition for her children had strained her bank account. Her brothers had already paid Connie back, and Isabelle had never borrowed from her, even when she'd taken art courses at universities across the region. Still, Isabelle was in awe of her mother's generosity, the way she always just "made it work."

And as much as Isabelle admonished her siblings for not helping with chores, she wanted the best for them. She wanted them to succeed. Though she sometimes wished her childhood had been different, she also believed she was doing what her father would have wanted her to do for her younger brothers and sisters. And once they were all fully fledged, which wouldn't be long now, she could finally focus on herself.

"So," Violet said, scooping the stuffing into a pretty aqua serving dish. "Is Scott coming to dinner?"

Isabelle looked at her watch. "Yes, he said he'd bring ice. Nearly an hour ago..."

"Uh, oh," Sadie teased. "You better watch it, Isabelle. Maybe he got a better offer." She laughed and stole a Christmas cookie out of the white bakery box.

Isabelle sucked in a breath. Scott with another woman? Impossible. Wasn't it? "No, he was at the shooting range with Trent and Luke."

"Wow." Violet was now placing parsley sprigs around the turkey.

"'Wow' what?"

"Trent Davis? He's the talk of the academy right now. Before break, half the people in my class asked me to get a selfie with him. He's a legend," Violet said, respect and awe thrumming through her voice. "Hey, maybe Scott could introduce me. I'd love to talk to him. Pick his brain. Absorb."

"I'll ask Scott, if you want me to," Isabelle offered.

"Absolutely!" Violet's eyes filled with anticipation.

The sound of tires crunching against cold gravel and the slam of a car door signaled Scott's arrival.

"That's him!" Violet squealed and raced past Isabelle. "I'll ask him myself."

"Sure," Isabelle said as the timer went off in the second oven. "The dinner rolls."

Connie handed her a pair of oven mitts and then breezed past her. "Scott! How lovely to see you. And you brought the ice."

Out of the corner of her eye, Isabelle saw her mother give Scott a big hug.

"Merry Christmas, Mrs. Hawks." Scott handed her a gold foil-wrapped box.

Isabelle suspected they were chocolate turtles made by the confectioner who had just opened in town. They were the best Isabelle had ever tasted.

She took the rolls out of the oven and placed them on top of the stove. She waved at Scott as she took off the mitts.

Sadie shouted, "Isabelle! The whipped cream! You forgot. It's probably butter by now."

Isabelle reached over to the mixer and turned it off, took off the towel and inspected the firm peaks. "It's fine. I'll add the sugar."

"Give it extra for me," Sadie said, taking two casseroles to the table.

"Oh, Sadie."

"Hey, Scott!" Dylan, Christopher and Ross got up from the game to greet him.

Isabelle moved the ham to the pineapple-shaped wood carving board. Dylan was less than a year younger than Isabelle, and when she was very young she'd liked telling kids at school they were twins. Now, Dylan was as immersed in his career as she was in her art. He never talked about his cases until they were over, but she knew his stance against the drug dealers that had infiltrated his district consumed him. He was passionate about delivering justice and keeping schools and streets safe.

Though Chris didn't live far from town, it was amazing how little he got out to the country to see his mother. He spent even less time in Indian Lake. Honestly, if it weren't for holidays and special occasions, Isabelle didn't think she would see him at all.

Ross was the most private of the bunch, even though he lived here. Everything about him was top secret. He didn't talk about work, and none of them knew if he had a girlfriend—or any friends, for that matter. Ross was observant, quiet and pensive. Isabelle often worried about him, though he assured her he was fine.

She went up to Scott and took the two bags of ice from him. "I was hoping you'd be here sooner," she said pointedly.

"I'm sorry. Trent had…well, I couldn't get away earlier."

"That's so cool!" Violet said. "You were with Trent Davis. What's he like?"

Isabelle took the ice to the kitchen. She filled the water glasses and put them on the table. *Of all the days for Scott to be late, he had to pick this one.*

Today was important to her. She'd been bursting with good news, and had wanted to tell Scott first. Not even her mother knew. She had planned to tell the whole family at dinner, but now that plan was flushed.

She was irritated with him, but also frustrated with everything about this holiday. She didn't know why today's party should bother her more than any other. She was always the one to put all the final pieces together at family gatherings. She surveyed the food waiting for her to put out on the table.

While everyone greeted Scott, teasing and joking about his lack of skills with a gun, Isabelle continued getting the dinner ready. She placed the turkey at one end of the table for Ross to carve, while the ham went to her mother's place at the other end. Connie would say the blessing and serve the ham.

With the rolls, vegetables and stuffing steaming hot and two bottles of wine on the table, Isabelle called everyone to supper.

Isabelle sat opposite Scott. They bowed their heads, said a prayer, toasted Christmas and began the meal.

Everyone in the family asked Scott questions about his article and the drug bust, and Violet peppered him with questions about Trent until Scott told her he was buying Cate Sullivan an engagement ring. Isabelle stayed silent as Scott stole glances at her.

"I want to talk to you after dinner," she said, when Violet was distracted by passing the stuffing to Dylan. "Alone."

"Sure," he replied and took a deep slug of wine.

SCOTT CARRIED TWO heavy wool serapes and followed Isabelle out to the patio where Ross had started a fire in the brass fire pit earlier. Isabelle had made hot buttered rum for everyone, another of their Christmas traditions.

Scott remembered last year when the whole

family sat around the fire beneath falling snow, sharing stories. Laughing. Living.

He glanced inside. Everyone had pitched in to handle the cleanup. "I'm surprised we got out of doing the dishes," he said. "As I remember, you and I are usually the last ones out here."

"I told them I wanted to talk to you privately."

"Oh," he said, placing the red-and-white serape around Isabelle's shoulders. She lifted her thick, caramel hair for him. Then settled back into the chair.

With the firelight dancing across her face and her green eyes glimmering like bits of emerald, she looked like one of the water sprites she painted. "You're beautiful tonight," he told her.

"Thank you," she said. "It's probably because I'm so excited."

"Excited?" He took a sip of his drink. "I thought you were mad at me."

"Why would you think that?"

"Because of that clipped text you sent me. And then you didn't even hug me when I came in. Frankly, I was a bit put off myself."

"To be fair, you were late. And when you got here you were mobbed by my family and I was busy putting the meal together. My mother gave you a hug," she added petulantly.

"Not the same thing."

"Fine."

"Fine." He glanced at her, then at the fire. Then back at her. He felt his insides untwist just looking at her.

She smiled at him. "I don't think I've ever actually been mad at you," she countered. "Anyway. I'm not now."

"Good." He couldn't take his eyes off her. He was wrong about the firelight. It was her own incandescence. She was glowing. "Tell me why you're so excited."

"I've had some good news. Fantastic news. I was hoping you'd be here earlier so I could tell you. I wanted you to be the first to know. I haven't said a word to my family."

Scott moved forward. She'd never acted like this before. She almost always discussed important stuff with her mother and sisters first. He wasn't quite sure how he should take this. He held his breath. "Go on."

"You, of all people, know how many queries I've sent to gallery owners, buyers and collectors, hoping I'd get my break."

"I do." In fact, Scott had spent countless hours working his journalism contacts to help Isabelle get placed. Each time a rejection came, he felt her pain.

He'd spent many a summer's night sitting on

a towel at Cove Beach with his arm around her shoulders while she sobbed. He'd been with her fireside at the Lodges as she cried into a glass of wine. One year, he'd brought her to the annual Halloween hay ride thinking to cheer her, but all she'd done was lay her head on his shoulder and talk about "what ifs." Several Christmases and Valentine's Days had been ruined by the arrival of another rejection.

He didn't know what kept her going. How she found the strength and courage to pit herself against the brick wall that the art world threw up. Time after time they all told her the same thing: her work was commercial, but not exceptional. Her attempts at Impressionism lacked the *"je ne sais quoi,"* that special something that would make curators or art dealers give her a chance.

"Well, I finally got some interest," she said now. "A gallery in Chicago. He said he loved my work."

And that's what Isabelle wanted. Recognition. She craved it. She was obsessed with it.

Now she had it.

He leaned over and took her hand. "I'm really happy for you, Isabelle. Truly." He kissed her palm.

Her smile was bursting with energy, and he leaned closer, so their lips almost brushed. All she had to do was tilt her head slightly, and they'd be kissing.

Instead, she took a deep breath and kept talking. "It's happening, Scott. My dream. I'm going to get my dream," she whispered so low he barely heard her, but he saw the tears slip down her cheeks. "I've waited so long."

"And worked very hard for this. You deserve it all. Now give me the details. Who is the owner? What are his credentials? Have you looked him up on the internet? Is this one of the galleries you approached?"

"Okay, Mr. Reporter. One question at a time. Yes, I did approach him. Malcolm Whitestone, that's the owner. Whitestone Gallery is in Evanston."

Scott was thoughtful for a moment. "I've heard of him, haven't I?"

"Possibly. Maybe when we were making lists of potential galleries a couple years ago. Anyway, he wants me to branch out. You know I've always thought my impressionistic water sprites were fine for the tourists here, but I can do better."

"I've always liked them," he mused, tracing the rim of his glass. "Some are so fantastical I want them to be real."

"That's sweet, but the critics want depth and bold ideas."

He studied her. She still amazed him. She kept digging inside herself for something that he didn't know if he would ever understand. She was never satisfied. She always kept reaching.

"So what's the next step?"

"He wants me to pick out more pieces and send them to him. This was just an initial introduction."

"So you don't have a show lined up," he said, a bit surprised she was this excited when it could all fall apart in a subsequent email.

Her jaw tightened and her face turned to stone. "It's a chance, Scott. Can't you see that?"

"I do see—"

"This is just like you. Always negative."

"Isabelle—"

Her voice rose as she continued. "I shouldn't have told you. I should have waited until I had everything wrapped up. A contract signed and in hand before I said anything. You've always doubted my art."

"That is not true!" His tone was harsher than he'd intended, but Isabelle's words were like a punch to the gut. "I've always supported you. I adore your mermaids and nymphs. Wasn't I the one who said we should go to Paris and see the impressionist and art nouveau paintings that inspired them?"

"See? That's exactly what I'm talking about. You think I'm only capable of my water sprites."

"I don't see anything wrong with them," he said. "They've brought you a second income, a loyal following and admiration from practically everyone who meets you. And I love them. Why isn't that enough?"

She shot to her feet. "Because it's not, Scott. It's just not."

Isabelle stormed into the house and slammed the door. He watched through the glass walls as she marched through the kitchen past the den and disappeared down the hall to the wing of bedrooms.

He looked down at his drink. "And a Merry Christmas to you, too, Scott."

Going after her would get him nowhere. He was floored. He'd always been there for her. He'd truly believed he was supporting her. But clearly Isabelle didn't agree.

He'd wanted to kiss her and she pulled away. Her rejection cut deep, and he wasn't sure how he would heal from it.

It was time for him to reassess things.

He dug in his pocket for his car keys and went inside to say goodbye to Isabelle's family.

CHAPTER THREE

THE DAY AFTER Christmas was always a good business day for Scott. Kids had Christmas money to spend on the books, games, puzzles and toys he stocked in his children's section. Parents were always in need of the hot coffee, cocoa and extra whipped cream that he served up while they browsed his extensive classic literature and bestseller sections.

Scott's espresso bar was not in the same league as Maddie Strong Barzonni's Cupcakes and Cappuccino, but then he'd never intended it to be. His shop was about the books with hot beverages served on the side for convenience and to get the customers to stay longer and buy more books.

After he'd moved back to Indian Lake and his mother had recovered from her surgery, she'd insisted on loaning him the money to open up his shop. Scott had hired Luke Bosworth, the best carpenter in town, to renovate the historic but demolition-ready building he'd bought for a song. Between having a mortgage and investing in his coffee equipment and inventory, Scott now felt tied to the shop, to Indian Lake.

Throughout his days at Northwestern and then at the *Chicago Tribune,* he'd dreamed of traveling the world in search of news stories. He'd wanted to meet intriguing people. Heads of state. Visionaries who molded the future. Scientists searching for cures to the most deadly diseases.

His life was different now. Those dreams had morphed into a quieter and yet still fulfilling life, which he now lived…for the most part. A great deal of his new visions for the future had Isabelle at the core.

"Scott!" A familiar voice boomed as the bell over the front door tingled.

Whisking away the cobwebs of his long-ago dreams, Scott smiled at Trent and Cate. He held out his hand to shake theirs. "Great to see you. How was your Christmas?"

"Super," Trent said with a wink.

"Magical," Cate added, putting an arm around Trent's waist. "We've been shopping today. Next door, actually," she said with a brilliant smile.

"Go on," Trent said. "Show him."

Cate extended her left hand. "You're the first to see it." Cate blushed.

Scott gazed at the pretty solitaire diamond. Then he peered more closely. "What is that? It's not exactly round."

"It's an antique ring," Trent said. "We bought it at the antique dealer."

"Mrs. Beabots told us about him," Cate said. "It's a rose cut. Doesn't it look just like a flower? The dealer said it dates back to 1898."

Scott lifted his eyes. "The art nouveau period. My favorite."

"I never guessed you to be so romantic, Scott," Cate said, still admiring her ring.

Scott straightened and put a plucky smile on his face. "Oh, I'm the most romantic guy in town."

"Hey, now..." Trent said.

Scott raised both his palms. "Sorry. You're right. Trent has me beat in the romance department—at least this Christmas. So, can I get you anything? Cocoa? Coffee?"

He didn't want them asking any embarrassing questions about Isabelle. Because the fact was, he hadn't heard from her since he left her mother's house. No call on Christmas Eve or Christmas Day. He'd kept the shop open until late Christmas Eve and sold quite a few books. Christmas Day he went to church with his mother, Theresa, and they drove into Chicago for their annual Christmas dinner at the Drake

Hotel. It was costly and worth every dime, she always said. She loved the harpist. He loved the food. Then they walked up and down Michigan Avenue, window shopping and looking at the lights, before driving home along Lake Shore Drive.

Each year Scott was thankful that his mother was still alive and that she wanted to keep up their Christmas tradition. He wondered if Isabelle would ever want to do things differently, but she'd never invited him for Christmas. As close as Scott and Isabelle were, they were still just friends and this was their family time, she'd always said. He didn't intrude.

"Not for me," Trent said. "But Cate wants to get some activity books for Danny. She didn't have as much time to shop before Christmas, as you can guess."

Scott's eyes widened. "I'm so sorry, Cate. I should have picked out some things for Danny and brought them over. After everything you've been through…"

Cate chuckled. "It's okay, Scott. Santa still paid him a visit. But he did mention some pop-up books you showed him, and I didn't have a chance to swing by earlier."

Scott snapped his fingers. "I know just the ones. I'll get them."

Scott went to the children's section which

was nearly wiped clean. His new shipments wouldn't be in until after he did inventory next week. Amazingly, he had one *Encyclopedia Prehistorica* pop-up left.

Scott rang up the sale and put the book in a shopping bag.

"We should talk about New Year's," Cate said. "Tell Isabelle to call me."

"Will do." Scott saluted Trent as they walked out.

Trent was just closing the door when he stopped and mouthed to Scott, "I'll call you later."

Scott knew from the look in Trent's eyes that his call had nothing to do with champagne or noisemakers. Trent had information.

With the shop empty, Scott went over to his desk where his laptop waited for his return. Scott had been working on an article for the *Indian Lake Herald*. For months, the mayor had been downstate lobbying for funds to improve the city streets. Scott had covered the progress each week.

Scott edited his article and then sat back in his chair, staring at the words.

Indian Lake's infrastructure needed work. Some streets were nearly impassible. It was an important issue for the town, but...

He saved the work and flipped off the computer. He dropped his head into his hands and raked his fingers through his hair. "How much lower can you set your bar?" he groaned.

Concrete and asphalt. That's all his talent was being used for. When he was in Chicago, he'd covered stories about political corruption. Police brutality. Topics he'd thought would make a difference if he brought them to light.

He drummed his fingers on the desk. His articles used to be well-researched and thought-provoking. Or else he wouldn't write them.

But that was long ago. Lately, he measured his importance by his relationships to his friends and family. Not in how many minds he could sway with his written words. He was a different Scott now.

Or was he?

The door whooshed open, breaking into his thoughts.

"Hello, Scott." Her voice floated toward him with the magnetic force it always had.

He spun around in his desk chair. "Isabelle."

She was stunning, dressed in a winter-white wool coat with a collar that rose up under her chin, two huge black buttons off to the side. Her hair, which fell in torrents nearly to her waist, gleamed in the winter's sun as it broke through the store window. Her dark-lashed green eyes looked, as always, like she'd just risen from the lake.

He stood, went to her and hugged her. She felt so good in his arms and yet he had the familiar, nagging sense that she could vanish at any moment like one of her faeries.

"I need you," she said.

He held his breath. *Not possible*. She was still upset with him, wasn't she? "Why?"

She lifted her shoulder strap that was attached to a tan leather briefcase. "I brought my iPad. Can you please help me? I have to find the right projects to send to Malcolm."

"Malcolm." He blinked. The gallery owner. That's what she needed him for. Made sense. How could he think she wanted anything else? She was bursting with enthusiasm and he caught its fire.

"Come. Sit down and let's look," he said. "Do you want some tea or cocoa? Anything you want."

She gazed at him with so much anticipation and hope, it made him ache. He remembered being this excited about his own career. Once. He wanted this for her. He did. No matter how much it might hurt her. If she got rejected, he would be here for her. Again. He would do that.

Scott pulled up another chair and they sat

nearly forehead to forehead as she scrolled through dozens of photos of her paintings.

"I had over two thousand pictures, Scott. Can you believe it? I spent nearly all of Christmas Day discarding the bad ones, and I came up with these. They're the best of the best. But I can only send three."

"Three. Out of two thousand?"

"Well, you can imagine all the duplicate shots. Trying to get the right light. That kind of thing. So," she said, not taking her eyes from the screen. "This one is my favorite mermaid."

The watercolor was painted in every shade of green an artist could devise. The mermaid had long dark hair, nearly to the end of her tail fin, which was spun with jewels, starfish and pearls. The expression on the mermaid's face was one of wonder and bliss as she broke through the surface of glistening, iridescent water. "I've never seen this one before."

"I know. I've never shown it. I love it."

"It's—astounding."

"Good. Then that's number one.

"This is another possibility," she said, showing him the painting of a faerie who walked among the stars toward a quarter moon where another faerie was sitting, beckoning to her. This one was all in blues. "It's a mother and daughter. I like to think it's my mom and me."

"Fantastic. I've never seen better," Scott said. "This is pick number two."

They perused another dozen photos before Scott stopped her. "I like this one. It's so…so real." A boy sat in a sailboat, gazing up at the moon as a faerie sprinkled stardust on him. It was fantasy, yes, but there was something so genuine in the boy's expression.

"You don't think it's too, well, childish?"

"Absolutely not. And it's a departure. There's such longing in his face. He's so unhappy."

Isabelle considered the boy. "He's you."

"What?"

"I painted him two years ago. He reminds me of you. Looking to the stars for something, but he doesn't know what. At least not yet."

Scott stared at her. She'd done it again. Stopped his heart. Mesmerized him. He took her hands. "I'm sorry we argue so much, Isabelle. I don't want us to be like that."

"Neither do I. It's my fault. I'm too ambitious for my own good." She squeezed his hands. "But I can't help it, Scott. I have so much I want to do with my life."

"Isabelle, I don't want to hold you back or do anything to discourage you."

She turned off her iPad. "I hate it when we argue. I need to be able to count on you, Scott.

But this is my golden opportunity. You do see that, right?"

"It's just that I don't want you to be hurt again…if it…if it doesn't work out."

She moved close and dropped her eyes to his lips. "It will work out. I can feel it. Have faith."

Then she pressed her lips lightly to his. It was a good thing he was sitting down because he was completely under her spell.

His cell phone buzzed and played the screechy, sci-fi sound that Scott thought was funny, but which was annoying to just about anyone in listening distance. Isabelle broke the kiss and passed him his phone. "You better answer this," she said. "It's Trent."

"I can talk to him later," Scott replied.

"No. I have to go anyway." She rose quickly as his phone rang again.

The doorbell tinkled. "Are you still open, Scott?" a woman's voice called.

"Sure am." He turned around. "Hi, Mrs. Knowland. How are you? You remember Isabelle?"

"Of course. Isabelle, how are you? And your mother? Did you have a nice Christmas?"

"My mother is fine and it was the best Christmas ever," Isabelle gushed.

Helen Knowland looked between them, a knowing smirk on her face.

Scott turned, wiped off Isabelle's lip gloss and rose. He held out his hand. "I'll call you later, Isabelle," he said.

"Great," Isabelle said and kissed his cheek. "Bye."

Isabelle gave Helen a little wave as she left.

"Lovely girl," Helen said, watching Isabelle's back for an inordinately long moment, no doubt formulating a new round of gossip, Scott thought. Finally, she looked down at Scott's lighted glass case. "Are those the South African coffee beans that Mr. Knowland bought me for Christmas? If so, I'll take those last three bags."

"Great." His phone rang again, and he smiled apologetically at Helen as he answered while ringing her through. "Trent. What's up?"

Scott handed the coffee to Helen, swiped her credit card and handed her the receipt and a pen while he listened to Trent telling him about a bust that had just gone down.

Helen took her coffee and left.

"I'm closing the shop right now," Scott said. "Be there in ten."

CHAPTER FOUR

SNUGGLED AMID TOWERING sugar maple trees, just a block off Main Street and three blocks from Maple Boulevard stood the only remaining apartment building in Indian Lake. Four stories high, built in the early 1920s with masses of heavy oak and walnut stairs, doors, coping, molding and trim, the building creaked, moaned and extolled its history and brittle bones to Isabelle's artistic soul. Isabelle had first seen the apartment when her mother had been commissioned to build an estate-sized home for a Chicago investment banker who wanted to retire to Indian Lake. The man and his wife had rented the north-facing top floor apartment of La Bellevue on a month-by-month basis during the construction of their home. With only two apartments per floor and eight units in the building, Connie Hawks had deemed the residence safe, suitable and affordable for Isabelle.

Isabelle had no idea how many times the building had changed hands, but in the ten years she'd lived in 4A, she'd not seen a single improvement. The plumbing, electricity and heating worked fine, and the landlord's hired maintenance company claimed they weren't responsible for anything else.

On the flip side, Isabelle had been free, if not encouraged, to paint and decorate in any way she pleased—at her own cost, of course.

Isabelle unlocked the heavy iron dead bolt with her antique key. There were no chains on her door, no keypads forcing her to remember codes. The walnut door was ten feet tall and weighed a ton. A weightlifter would have a hard time breaking it down, she thought, as she placed her keys on the half-moon entry table in her miniscule foyer. Because all the apartments had twelve-foot-high ceilings, the climb to the fourth floor was a workout. Intruders would have to be in excellent shape to want to break into La Bellevue—at least her unit.

Climbing the stairs, along with sculling on Indian Lake with Sarah Jensen Bosworth, Olivia Melton, Maddie Strong Barzonni and Liz Barzonni, the two sisters-in-law who would soon be welcoming Olivia to their family, and occasionally Cate Sullivan, meant Isabelle didn't have to worry about workouts. Besides, she didn't have time, she rationalized. A gym rat, she was not.

She hefted her heavy bag onto the scarred

antique dining room table she'd bought at an estate sale for twenty dollars. She'd intended to fix the uneven, wobbling pedestal, but never got around to it. She was always in a rush to get to her painting and put the vision in her head on canvas and make her dreams become real. Today was no exception.

The bag contained supplies for three new canvases; Isabelle preferred to stretch her own to save money. However, with the possibility of showing her work in a gallery, time was of the essence. She wondered if she could get Scott to help her.

She moved to the kitchen with her groceries: some yogurt, a bag of spring salad and a baguette. Her kitchen was barely eight feet by eight feet. She'd painted the walls in pewter, dove and pearl grays and had hand-painted angels and faeries in the corners of the cabinets as if they were peeking out at her. She hoped their inspiration would never fade.

Isabelle shoved the food into the seventies-era refrigerator, the newest feature in the entire apartment. The sink was a wide single bay porcelain monstrosity that still bore the year of its manufacture: 1919. It stood on black wrought iron legs.

Just as she hung her wool coat on the peg,

next to a shelf filled with model sailboats, her phone pinged with a text.

"Scott," she said aloud as she scrolled through his long message. The gist was that he was happy they had "made up."

Isabelle smiled, relieved he wasn't upset anymore. She punched out his number. He answered on the first ring. "What? No customers?"

"Not at the moment. Are you home?"

"I am. I just got here. I had to run some errands," she replied, her eyes darting to the dining table and the empty canvas. She forced her gaze away in order to concentrate on what Scott was saying.

She walked over to the living room window and looked across the bare treetops to the snow-covered county courthouse clock tower. December days were unbearably short, and though it was only four in the afternoon, the lights on the massive Christmas tree on the courthouse lawn came on as she watched. Spotlights showcased the red sandstone courthouse walls. Up and down Main Street, crystal lights twinkled in the pear trees along the sidewalks. It was the one time of year her town resembled the magical images that flitted across her mind day and night.

"I thought you might stop off at the art supply store." He chuckled.

"The trouble with us is that you know me too well. I have no mystery for you."

"Sure you do," he countered. "So. Tell me. Why are you buying more stuff right now when we just picked out what you're going to send to Malcolm?"

"I should start something serious."

"Tonight?"

"Well, I should…"

"Isabelle, I can tell when you're feeling guilty that you aren't working, and the lilt of your words when you're inspired. You're just nervous. Admit it."

Isabelle's shoulders slumped as his truth settled over her. "I am. Time passes so quickly when I'm working. There's no way I'll be able to sleep tonight, so I thought—"

"You called me so I could tell you stories."

"Oh, Scott. You don't have any stories." She laughed.

There was dead silence on the other end, and she felt the cold between them stretch from her apartment to Scott's shop.

She backtracked. "I didn't mean that the way it sounded. We just know each other so well that—"

He cut her off. "No, actually, you're right, Isabelle. I don't have any stories. Stories should be my life, and they aren't. Look, I have a customer. I need to go. Good luck tomorrow." He hung up.

Isabelle held the cell phone to her ear as the call disconnected. She hadn't heard the bell over the door ring or any other voice on Scott's end. He'd never faked a reason to get off the phone with her. If anything, she was the one who usually had to go first.

She had hurt his feelings.

They'd been doing that a lot lately, but she couldn't seem to figure out why they both were so on edge.

Earlier, Scott had told her that he admired her for raising her own bar. Challenging herself. Just how deep were his regrets about his past work as a journalist? All these years, she'd thought he was happy in Indian Lake running his coffee shop, selling books and writing for the local newspaper. Most men would be thrilled to have their own business, especially a successful one.

Edgar was more than fulfilled by running the Lodges, she mused. He often remarked how busy he was, and he'd never said he wanted to do anything else with his life.

But then, Isabelle hadn't exactly asked.

Isabelle sank into her 1940s club chair, a realization taking shape.

She'd worked for Edgar for ten years, yet she barely knew the man at all. She suddenly thought of dozens of questions she'd never asked Scott, despite their years of friendship.

Was she so immersed in her own needs and aspirations that she didn't take the time to learn what mattered to others?

Tears filled her eyes as she stared out the window at the falling snow.

"There's one word for you, Isabelle Hawks. Selfish."

She was so desperate to be recognized that she put her ambitions ahead of everyone in her life. She never made time to see her siblings or her mother on a consistent basis. She was either working at the Lodges or she was at the easel. And Scott. It was amazing the guy still spoke to her. Other than meeting him at her mother's for their Christmas dinner, she hadn't made time for him since before Thanksgiving.

If things went well with Malcolm tomorrow and if she was lucky enough to have even a single painting hang in his gallery, she would have no one with whom to share her joy. She needed to start giving more attention to the people she claimed to love.

She picked up her cell phone and punched in Scott's number.

"Hi. It's me. I'm ordering a pizza. When you close up would you like to come share it with me?" she asked.

"I…" He hesitated.

"Please?"

"I can't. Not tonight."

"Uh, okay. You've got plans. I understand."

"It's unexpected and unplanned, if you want to know," he said. "Are you okay?"

"Sure. Why?"

"You never ask me over for dinner….er, pizza."

"I'm just nervous about Malcolm, and…"

He broke in. "Isabelle. I'm covering a story. I really have to go."

"Oh, sorry. Sure. Later, then."

"Later." He hung up.

Disappointment rattled through Isabelle like an old locomotive. Seldom had Scott turned her down if she asked a favor. She needed to be with someone tonight to help quell her anxieties. Though they hadn't spent much time together lately, she could usually count on him to find just the right words to help when she felt low and small. Scott was good at things like that.

Tonight was different, though. Yes, she wanted comfort, but she also wanted to explain that she was beginning to see herself in a new light, unflattering as it was. She wanted to make up for hurting his feelings.

But now she'd have to wait. She supposed there would be time when she got back from Chicago. Scott would want to see her then. He always did. For so long, she'd relied on his loyalty and friendship.

Chicago. Isabelle put her cell phone on the small kitchen table and rushed into her bedroom, where she flung open the walnut door to her walk-in closet. Tomorrow could be the turning point of her life. She had to dress for it.

Twice, she ran through her wardrobe. Because she was the hostess at the Lodges, she had over a dozen black sheath dresses for every season and weather condition. Tomorrow would be a conservative black sheath day. With her white wool coat with the black buttons, she would present a picture of a serious artist to Malcolm.

She held up a jersey wool dress with long black sleeves and turned and looked at her reflection in the full-length mirror.

"Serious artist," she whispered. Once her work was in Whitestone Gallery, she wouldn't be a fledgling anymore. She would no longer be overlooked. Even if she was never famous, she would always be able to claim her day… her moment.

She stared at the woman in the reflection. Unafraid, nearly audacious. Isabelle felt a change happening inside her and around her. Her own green eyes gazed back at her. She imagined she saw them twinkle.

CHAPTER FIVE

NORTH OF DOWNTOWN CHICAGO, a half mile from Lake Michigan and centered in a block of shops, cafés and boutiques stood Whitestone Gallery. Its massive black awning, white Greek key design fringe and a bold white *W* stretched imperiously over the beveled glass door, which was executed in an art deco design that reminded Isabelle of the water spray in her nymph paintings. It was the first sign that perhaps she was meeting her destiny.

Isabelle gathered her paintings, which she had carefully wrapped in bubble wrap, out of the back of her SUV. Apparently, Chicago had not been the recipient of any of the lake-effect snow that had been dumped on Indian Lake last night. The sidewalk here was so pristine, it looked as if someone had used a blow dryer to remove any hint of dampness. Along the wall of glass that formed the front of the gallery was a window box holding perfectly shaped boxwoods. Two more English box planters on either side of the front door held round topiary trees. As she walked up the red carpet, also meticulously devoid of dirt, slush or leaves, she couldn't help but reach out and touch one of the plants.

She shifted the bubble-wrapped canvases under her left arm and pushed the polished brass door latch. A waft of fresh pine and cedar scent drifted through the air. Mellow classical piano music put her instantly at ease.

Framed and unframed paintings, from impressionist, cubist, abstract impressionist to contemporary, hung in strategic patterns against putty-colored walls.

A tall man emerged from behind the center partition. Thick, pearl white hair ringed his handsome face. He walked toward her, his hands outstretched. "You must be none other than Isabelle Hawks."

"I am," she replied with a smile, though inside she felt daunted and intimidated. If the skilled artwork on the walls hadn't caused her nerves to jump, the self-assured man who held the golden ticket to her future surely did. She extended her hand toward him then quickly retracted it. She'd forgotten to take off her driving gloves, and her index finger poked through a hole. With her other hand clutching her canvases, she had no choice but to pluck off the glove with her teeth. "Pleasure," she mumbled.

"Malcolm," he said with two raised brows and a hearty chuckle. "Here, let me help you. That's quite a load."

As he took the paintings, Isabelle snatched the glove out of her mouth and shoved it into her coat pocket.

"We'll go into my office," he said politely. Taking a step back, he held out his hand with a slight bow, indicating the way.

Isabelle thought the movement so exquisite she was reminded of a ballerina.

"Thank you." Isabelle rounded the show wall into an even larger display area. The wood plank floor was polished to such a mirror's gleam, she felt guilty walking on it. There were four smaller viewing rooms off the two main ones, and a back hallway held four offices.

"To the left," Malcolm said. "Mine is the largest office, and with the natural light from the window, I'll be able to see your paintings to their full potential."

"Lovely," Isabelle replied sweetly. Inside, she was a mess. Why on earth had she agreed to come here and show this erudite curator her absurdly inadequate water sprite and faerie watercolors and acrylics?

Isabelle. Isabelle, you idiot. You need to go right back home as fast as you can before what's left of your self-esteem is annihilated. Forever.

Even the office was imposing. It was as huge as the front showroom and the exterior wall was all glass. White art deco sofas filled the space, and she had no doubt they were re-covered originals from the 1930s. Two square chairs in black leather sat opposite a glass and steel coffee table. An enormous vase held at least five dozen white gladiolas.

Isabelle couldn't help wondering where the gladiolas had been flown in from. California? South America?

"I have a box cutter here in my desk," Malcolm said.

Her mouth fell open. He'd seen her work already? He hated them so much he was going to rip them to shreds?

He looked at her and gave his head a shake. "For the bubble wrap," he said, holding the box cutter up. "I'll save it for you. Little costs add up, don't they?"

"They do," she agreed, trying to ignore the sting of his condescension.

He pulled the wrap off and hoisted the painting up and put it on the desk so he could view it properly. His face was expressionless.

But wait. Was that a lift to the corner of his mouth? Admiration?

Isabelle's heart leapt in her chest. When he opened the second painting, the faerie walking among the stars, she heard an intake of breath. It was only a slight puff of air, but it gave her so much encouragement that her heart whacked itself against her breastbone. She was stunned. Was this happiness?

He whisked away the wrap on the third painting and smiled. "I like this boy in the boat." He looked at her, blue-gray eyes shining. "You have the heart of a French Impressionist, even though your style is art nouveau in so many respects. Yet the faces…the faces are ethereal, unlike any other artist I've seen. I wanted to view them up close to make sure what I thought I was seeing in the photos you sent me was real."

Isabelle wasn't sure she was hearing him correctly. He liked her work? This man whose gallery had been lauded for being on the cutting edge of what collectors wanted before they knew they wanted it?

She couldn't stand the suspense any longer. She had to know. "Is there anything there you like? I can always bring you something else, something more…"

He turned to face her. "They're perfect for what I want in the spring."

Isabelle was at a loss for words. As she stared

at him, trying to formulate something coherent, he crossed the room briskly and opened a white lacquered cabinet to reveal a refrigerator filled with wine, champagne, water bottles and…were those strawberries in that silver footed dish?

He handed her a bottle of French spring water. "Here. Drink this. You may need it for what I'm about to tell you."

Isabelle thanked him and drank deeply. She felt the blood rush back to her head and knees. She was almost back to normal. Until he spoke again.

"I want all three."

"You what?" Isabelle doubted she'd ever been as stunned. She didn't want to appear ridiculous or not deserving of the honor, but now that she'd gotten over the initial shock, she just couldn't hold back her excitement. "This is amazing. I can't thank you enough, Mr. Whitestone. I had hoped, obviously, but I never dreamed you would accept me…"

The heavy clomp of heels against the wood floor outside the office made her pause. Isabelle turned toward the doorway.

Backlit against the hall lights stood a tall man dressed in scuffed cowboy boots, faded jeans and a black, paint-splattered T-shirt. His shoulders were wide and nearly filled the doorway. Though it was just below freezing outside, he wore no hat or gloves, and Isabelle wondered where he'd put his coat. His sky-blue eyes lingered on her face and he sent her an audaciously appreciative smile.

He held out two takeout coffees, gesturing toward Malcolm. Isabelle couldn't help but notice how his biceps bulged as he raised his hand.

"I brought cappuccinos for two. I didn't know you were expecting company."

He never took his eyes off Isabelle, and she didn't mind one bit.

"Wes," Malcolm replied, propping Isabelle's painting on the floor next to his desk. "Come meet Isabelle."

Wes moved toward her stealthily, as if still sizing her up. He handed Malcolm his cappuccino. "No sweetener and an extra shot. Just how you like it, uncle."

Isabelle tore her gaze from the masculine vision in cowboy boots back to the man who was about to define her future. "Uncle?"

"Yes. This is Wes Adams. My sister's one and only. Thank God."

"Oh, Malcolm." Wes laughed and turned back to Isabelle. "He says things like that to keep me on my toes."

Malcolm rolled his eyes and sipped his drink.

"This is really good. Best I've had since Italy. Where is this from?"

"The new café down the street," Wes said. "I told you. Cupcakes and Cappuccino Café. It's different. I like it."

"Maddie's place," Isabelle gushed. Malcolm and Wes shot her quizzical expressions. "My friend from Indian Lake owns those cafés. She started the first one over a decade ago in our town. I forgot that she'd just opened up her third here in Evanston."

Wes's smile got broader, if that was possible. "I'm a fan already. And they stay open till midnight, which is when I need a triple caffeine fix. The cupcakes aren't bad, either."

"They're the best." Isabelle replied feeling a flutter of defensiveness. She was as protective of her friends as she was of her family.

"I'm sure they are," Malcolm said. "Neither of us is very into sugar. Nasty stuff. Bad for the brain." Malcolm grimaced and shook his head. "And since Wes is my most talented protégé—" he shot his nephew a purposeful stare "—I try to keep him in check."

"This is true. Sadly. I'd be freer in prison than under my uncle's watch." Wes chuckled and slapped Malcolm's shoulder good-naturedly. "I *am* grateful for all he's done for me."

"Which is a lot." Malcolm nodded sternly.

"And I won't apologize for my mercenary ways. I believe my investment will pay off in the long run."

Isabelle gaped at them. For the first time, she wondered if getting involved with Whitestone Gallery was a good idea.

Wes burst into laughter. "We're just kidding," he said. "From the horrified look on your face, I'm guessing we should dial it down. You know how it is with family sometimes."

"Oh." She let out a breath. "I understand now."

When had she become so uptight? She couldn't even take a simple joke for what it was. Maybe if she hadn't dreamed of this kind of interview since she was a kid, she might be more at ease. Without a mentor, without a supporter who knew the ropes of the art world, had connections with the critics and acquisitions houses, she didn't think she would ever be able to succeed. She attempted a smile at Malcolm and Wes. She needed this.

"I should explain, Isabelle. Wes fancies himself a contemporary artist and I have recently landed him a large commissioned painting."

"Enormous is more the word for it," Wes interjected. "One of the old residential buildings on Lake Shore Drive is being renovated, and I'm painting three murals for their lobby."

"Wow, congratulations," Isabelle said. She couldn't imagine being sought after enough to have her work hung in one of the Gold Coast historical buildings. The thought gave her goose bumps. When she smiled at Wes, she realized he was beaming at her. The moment seemed suspended, reminded her of what it felt like whenever she was painting. She wasn't exactly on the earth, yet she hadn't left it, either. She could feel the paintbrush in her hand, but the energy that flowed through her arm to the brush and onto the canvas came from somewhere else. She didn't know where. But she knew instantly that Wes understood. He went to those places, too.

And he recognized the artist in her.

Isabelle thought she'd melt on the spot, which would cause a great deal of trauma to perfectionist Malcolm.

Wes finally tore his eyes from her and glanced down at the paintings. "You did these?"

She blinked. Her paintings. Yes. That's what she was here for. To sell her paintings. To impress Malcolm. Not flirt with Wes. Not conjure romantic daydreams about an artist, no matter how perfect he seemed to be.

"Yes." she gulped back a huge block of fear. "I did."

Wes's gaze snapped to Malcolm. "This is

what you were talking about last night? For the art nouveau showing in the spring?"

"Precisely." Malcolm finished off his cappuccino and put the paper cup in the wastebasket, being careful not to splash any errant drops on the floor. "Isabelle's work intrigues me."

"Because it's rudimentary," Wes quipped. "I don't mean to insult," he said to Isabelle. "I just know how fastidious my uncle is when he's selecting pieces for the gallery. Trust me, if Gustav Klimt were to sail in here with the *Woman in Gold*, Malcolm wouldn't be impressed."

"Oh, stop. Of course I would." Malcolm folded his arms over his chest. "I want something startling."

Isabelle looked at her acrylic of the blue faeries. "And are they startling?"

Malcolm went to stand by Isabelle as they studied the painting. "It's their expressions, their demeanor. Their apparel is luscious. I'm fascinated by your use of figurative, abstract and decorative combinations. There's an overlay of silver, here, is there not?"

"An underlay," Isabelle said, not taking her eyes from the faerie's face. "Then an overlay. You're right."

"Gives it depth. I like that. I'm interested to see what you can do with oils," Malcolm said, twisting his face to her.

"Oils?"

"You have worked with them?"

"Yes. Of course, but…" She wrung her hands. "They're intimidating."

"Ah," Wes interjected. "That's because they demand the utmost from your talent and vision."

"They do." She smiled at him. When his eyes, filled with admiration, met hers, she felt validated in a way she'd never experienced before. These men were professionals with exacting tastes. They saw potential in her. Isabelle could not have been more honored.

"Would you be willing to explore your vision in oils rather than only watercolor and acrylic, Isabelle?" Malcolm asked.

"I would."

"Good answer." Wes stepped toward her. "I'm off. I wish you luck, Isabelle. Clearly, my uncle is charmed." He extended his hand.

As she slipped her hand into his chapped palm, he whispered, "But not as charmed as I am." Without another word, he walked out of the office. Isabelle listened for his boot heels on the wood floor.

After a few moments the sound faded. Then silence. She turned to Malcolm. She wondered if he could see the hot flush in her cheeks and rising up her neck. "Wes is…"

"Talented," Malcolm said curtly, still watching the door. "Impressively talented and he knows it. I apologize if you found him rude."

"It's all right, I'm hardly the caliber of artist—"

"Stop. Don't denigrate yourself, Isabelle." He lifted his chin and fixed her with an imperious gaze. "You should know that I pride myself on finding raw talent. I enjoy being the maestro sometimes. I've been wrong on occasion, but usually when the student wasn't as committed as me. Do you understand?"

"I'm beginning to."

"I like these three paintings, but when I went over the others in the file you sent, I was not as enamored. I feel you can do better. I want you to think about it, Isabelle. Think about what you truly want for yourself and your future."

He went over to the pile of bubble wrap and began rewrapping her paintings.

"You don't want me to leave them?"

"Not yet. I like them a great deal, but I'd planned for my spring show to be contemporary art. I want to strategize. Look over my client list and evaluate their needs."

"I see," she replied, swallowing her disappointment.

"I'll call you," he said, handing her the paintings and gesturing toward the door.

"It was a pleasure meeting you, Malcolm.

And I want you to know I've already given consideration to your advice. I *will* start working with oils. Perhaps I'll have something for you soon."

Malcolm's eyebrow cocked and a smile spread across his face. "Entice me, Isabelle."

"I intend to."

Isabelle left the gallery, memorizing each wall and corner, imagining her pieces, new creations that came from the saplings of desire she felt growing inside her.

From the second she'd opened the door at Whitestone Gallery, she'd felt the promise of change and challenge whirling around her, pulling her toward her future. Malcolm and Wes spoke of master artists, icons she'd revered since she was in middle school and stumbled upon her first art history book in the Indian Lake library. She'd been drawn to art nouveau— Toulouse Lautrec and Aubrey Beardsley as well as Klimt and Mucha. She'd adored Erte and his movement into art deco, but it was the short span between 1890 and 1905 that fascinated her, as if she'd been a part of it somehow. Perhaps she'd underestimated the universal appeal of her faeries and nymphs along with her talent. The only place her paintings had hung was in the gift shop at the Lodges.

Malcolm had said he was fascinated with

the faeries' expressions. Odd. She'd never put much thought into their expressions. She knew from art school that other painters labored over faces, the nuances of the eyes, of the lips, hoping to capture the next *Mona Lisa* smile. She did not. Often, Isabelle simply closed her eyes and waited for her heart to guide her hand. Her faeries were the faces she saw in her dreams. She knew them well.

Malcolm hadn't commissioned her projects or presented her with a contract. Yet her elation was undeniable. Only Scott had ever made her feel this hopeful.

All these years, it had been Scott who had shored up her crumbling emotions when she'd been rejected—again.

For the first time, she realized he'd been the one pushing her to try again. Paint again. Submit again.

Scott...

He was the first person she wanted to tell about her visit with Malcolm.

CHAPTER SIX

NEW YEAR'S EVE was the last night the Lodges was open for the season. Edgar Clayton preferred to close the cabins and facilities for the winter, though he'd confessed to liking the solemn yet dazzling interlude between autumn and spring more than any other time of year. Edgar was a pensive soul, Isabelle had decided. Never married, he devoted himself to making the Lodges a memorable experience for his guests.

She had to admit she admired Edgar's sentimental side, which was why she would not abandon him this New Year's Eve. Once again, she'd agreed to organize the decorations, the flowers and the menu for an extravagant party…at least to the extent that his somewhat limited budget would allow.

Aqua, silver and indigo helium balloons with long, metallic ribbons that nearly skimmed the heads of the tallest guests covered the ceilings of the main dining room and the enclosed patio. Isabelle always used a lake or water theme for her New Year's decorations and this year was no exception. She'd filled the center of each table with silver netting studded with glitter. Aqua tapers and votive candles nested among silver and aqua glass balls and branches that resembled coral. Soft cedar and bells of Ireland created the illusion of seaweed, and the overall effect was that of a mystic lake.

The silver-banded wine and champagne glasses and the matching bone china had belonged to Edgar's mother. Each time Isabelle helped the serving crew place the dinnerware, she wished she'd met the older woman, but she'd died years ago.

Odd, she thought, that she yearned for guidance from Edgar's mother but not her own.

Connie didn't feel the joy of creating "tablescapes" or planning parties the way Isabelle did. When Isabelle was a child, she'd told herself that her mother simply wasn't creative and artistic the way Isabelle was. However, Connie was a gifted architect. She had phenomenal vision and was capable of creating entire cities in her head, then rendering them on graph paper and in the intricate and time-consuming balsa wood and paper model layouts she perched on bookshelves in her den.

Still, Connie had shunned all domestic duties once Isabelle's father died. Those duties had gone to Isabelle and she still resented them. She had felt too much like a servant to the needs of her brothers and sisters. She didn't blame them for her fate; it was the way it was. The heart-breaking truth was that Connie had become emotionally disconnected from her children once she became the sole provider. As much as Isabelle understood that, now that she was an adult, it didn't mend the fissure in her heart. A dull ache, perpetual and reliable, thrummed inside Isabelle, underscoring her decisions, actions and needs. Connie had sacrificed her love and care for her children and had burdened Isabelle with responsibilities that were too great for a ten-year-old to bear.

Isabelle admired her mother's career, but deplored the mundane, day-to-day rut of domesticity. Children held an artist back and Isabelle decided it would be best for her career if she never had babies. Isabelle had seen what having a family and an absorbing career could cost. And the price was too high.

"Isabelle." Scott wrapped his arm around her waist. He'd walked up from behind, surprising her.

"You look amazing," he said as she turned toward him, his hands still on her waist.

She shrugged, sending ripples through her iridescent silver crepe de chine gown. "I thought I'd blend in. Match the décor."

Scott's lips quirked into a rascally grin. "You couldn't blend in any more than fireworks in a midnight sky." He pulled her closer. They were nose to nose. "You're a knockout."

"I could say the same about you," she said, glancing down at his blindingly white tuxedo shirt, black silk bow tie. He wore his immaculately cut tuxedo every New Year's Eve.

Scott in a tuxedo was nothing short of a woman's dream. His wide shoulders were enhanced by the jacket, though she noticed that this year, his biceps seemed to be straining against the sleeves. But all that was eclipsed by his ease and manner when he wore his tux.

That first New Year's Eve when Scott had moved back to Indian Lake, she'd commented on the fact that he owned a tux. He told her then he'd bought it his first year at the *Tribune* and had intended to wear it when he won prizes for his journalism.

She lingered on the gold flecks that sparkled in his eyes. Did he think about those days anymore?

"I aim to please," he said, holding her gaze.

Isabelle didn't know what was happening, but she could swear Scott wanted to kiss her. Not one of his friendly pecks on the cheek, but a real kiss. Suddenly she felt uneasy. Why was she noticing how handsome Scott was? He was just Scott. He would dance with her at midnight and she'd finish her chores like they always did on New Year's Eve. Wouldn't they? She looked around nervously and gave him a wide, friendly smile.

"Scott, I have to get back to work. I was just checking the champagne glasses."

His eyes never left her lips. He lifted his hand to her neck and touched her tenderly. "Right. The glasses."

His thumb traced the line of her jaw. She was melting and she never melted. Everything about this night was orchestrated for romance, including a torchy love ballad being played by the Milo Orchestra in the background.

"Glasses," she repeated, trying to recover her composure and remember her job. What had she been doing before she'd slipped into this dreamy state?

"Isabelle."

She'd never paid much attention to his voice before, but now, when he said her name, her stomach fluttered. Why was she reacting to him as if she had a crush on him? She didn't need a mirror to know her cheeks were flushed.

All she could feel was his hand on her waist.

The sound of Scott saying her name echoed in her head.

She swallowed hard. She had to snap out of this. It was this kind of romance that lured women into domesticity.

She had to force herself to focus. "Yes, the glasses. Uh, for the midnight toast."

He brushed his lips against her cheek. "And I'll find you for my kiss to ring in the New Year."

Isabelle hadn't realized she'd shut her eyes, immersing herself in the moment with Scott.

She felt a whoosh of air, the temperature dropped and she blinked, returning to the present. Scott had left her to join Luke and Sarah at their table.

Luke had risen from his chair to slap Scott on the back. Trent Davis sat nearby, looking more like a *GQ* model than the Indian Lake police detective that he was. He stood to shake Scott's hand, then Scott bent down and kissed Cate Sullivan's cheek before going around the table to hug Sarah. The glimmering, moonglow lighting Isabelle enhanced Scott's good looks. Or was she seeing Scott in a new light tonight?

Isabelle had a dozen chores to finish before midnight. There were party favors, hats, noisemakers and streamers to distribute. The servers were busily placing clean champagne glasses at everyone's place. The soloist who would sing "Auld Lang Syne" had not yet arrived. Edgar always gave the countdown, but as she wended through the dining room, making sure guests were happy, she didn't see him anywhere.

At midnight, her duties would be over. The kitchen crew and extra bus boys she'd hired would handle the cleanup. Then she would have Scott all to herself and Isabelle planned to dance with him until the band's contract was up at one in the morning. Admittedly, she felt terrible about the way she'd treated Scott over these past weeks—months, really. Immersed in her ongoing quest to get her work noticed, she'd lost sight of what a good friend he was. He'd always been fun to flirt with and she'd forgotten how much his smile lifted her spirits. Overlooking Scott had become a habit, and she was ashamed of it. She owed him thanks for so much.

This old year was ticking away and Isabelle wanted her regrets where Scott was concerned to die with it. In the new year, she would be more conscientious toward him. She was grateful that he'd been patient with her selfishness. She intended to scrape her egocentric attitudes off her palette. Scott deserved better from her.

The folds of her silver gown eddied around

her silver, open-toed, peau de soie heels as she breezed up to his table. She greeted Sarah and Cate again with a little wave. Scott was in deep discussion with Trent.

She placed her hand on his shoulder.

He reached up to touch it, but he didn't take his focus from Trent, who was now whispering.

"Scott?" Isabelle said.

He turned his face to her.

Why was his expression so disturbed? Lines of worry settled around his eyes. She knew that look and she didn't like it. "Is everything okay? It's not your mother again, is it?"

"No." He cleared his throat. "No. Mom is fine. What's up?"

She leaned closer and smiled. "I just wanted to say that at midnight, Scott, you're all mine."

He kissed her palm and smiled. "Ditto."

SCOTT WAITED UNTIL Isabelle was out of sight and earshot before he said to Trent, "Why tonight?"

"Captain Williams has given my team the nod. We want to catch Ellis in the act. Remember the ordinance plant?"

"Yeah, sure."

"He's set up a lab out there. We found it yesterday. I didn't tell you because we were waiting on confirmation about an apartment where we thought he was living. I just got the word."

"Should I wait till the morning? I don't want to get in the way," Scott said, though he was already bursting with anticipation of another on-the-scenes story.

"I trust you to hang back until I give you the signal. You can stay in your car, take video and photos. And stay low. Then you come in. And trust me, the chief knows you're involved."

Scott nodded. He knew it was his job to be objective when covering a story. At the same time, he admired men and women in uniform who made sacrifices, risked their lives to protect others. They made the world a better place to live. And what had Scott done? He'd reported it. Written a few sentences about some brave men who should have been commemorated in bronze.

Suddenly, he felt ashamed and sharply disappointed in his life lately.

Only he could make the kind of changes he needed to put himself back together and find that feeling of worthiness again.

Scott remembered the prickles of commitment and even flames of ambition spur him when he'd written the article about the bust. He'd lost track of time. He'd investigated, interviewed and researched for every snippet of fact.

"So are you game?" Trent asked.

"I am," Scott said. He wanted to help. To make a difference in the frightening rise of drug dealing in his town. "So, when is this going down?" Scott asked.

"Right after midnight."

"Okay." Scott rubbed his chin thinking of beautiful Isabelle and the fact that they'd both caught the magic of New Year's. "Isabelle's not going to like this. And what about you and Cate?"

"Luke and Sarah will take Cate home. Danny's staying over at their house tonight. Danny's always up for a sleepover with Timmy and Annie. I don't know if it's their golden retriever or playing in the tent in Timmy's room that he likes most."

Scott chuckled. "It couldn't be that cute little red-haired Annie, could it? I mean, I know Danny is only six…"

"Just turned seven."

Scott spread his hands. "Well then, there you are!"

Their smiles faded as their thoughts went back to the seriousness of their decision.

"I promised Isabelle I'd dance with her at midnight."

"Sorry," Trent replied, looking over at Cate, who was pointing to the dance floor. "I'm being summoned. It's up to you if you want to come,

Scott. But I'm leaving at twelve." Trent rose from his chair and started to walk away. "I forgot to tell you…this is top secret. You can't tell Isabelle about any of this."

Scott sighed.

Trent slapped his shoulder. "Tough changing the world, isn't it?"

"Seriously," Scott replied as he watched Edgar walk toward the stage with a microphone in his hand. It was nearing midnight. The witching hour. The New Year.

Isabelle walked toward him through the groups of couples making their way to the dance floor for the final countdown. Her face was filled with expectation and more happiness than he'd seen in her green eyes in a long time. Her smile was enough to kill most grown men.

He held out his hand. "Wanna dance, beautiful?"

"I do," she said, taking his hand and then yanking him toward the floor. The orchestra was just finishing up a romantic ballad. Edgar was thanking everyone, rattling off the Lodges' reopening dates.

Scott inhaled the scent of lavender and rose that Isabelle wore, and rested his cheek against her soft one. She felt perfect in his arms. Tonight she looked like a goddess, silver and sparkling like a moonbeam off the lake.

"I have plans for us," she whispered wistfully.

He opened his mouth and then snapped it shut. For months they'd been at odds. They'd had little that reminded them of why they were together at all. He knew she wanted to be with him tonight. Maybe share a brandy by the giant fire in the Lodges' bar. Or her favorite, a moonlit walk in the snow by the lake. Half an hour ago, Scott would have given anything to do either of those things with Isabelle, but he'd committed to leaving with Trent. He needed this story.

"Ten!" Edgar shouted into the microphone.

"Isabelle, I can't."

She stared at him. "Can't what?"

He could feel his insides ripping in half. He wanted to be with Isabelle, but a rare opportunity had presented itself. Scott was taking a chance on this assignment with Trent, but he knew if he didn't try, he'd never know if he could live out his journalism dreams. He was hoping Isabelle would understand. He'd always supported her art; surely she'd return the kindness.

"Nine!" Edgar shouted. The crowd was now counting with him. Excitement sparked through the room.

"I have…another commitment."

"Eight!"

"Tonight? Is it your mother?"

"Not my mom."

"Seven!"

"Scott, it's New Year's Eve," she replied, her eyes filling with confusion. Then, her eyes misted as if she was truly disappointed that he was leaving. With a shock, he thought: *She loves me*.

"Six!"

"I know. It can't be helped."

"Five!"

Isabelle stopped dancing. She dropped her arms. "What is it? Someone else?"

She loves me not.

"What?" he asked incredulously.

"Four!"

"There's only one reason you would leave me here on New Year's Eve in the middle of all of our friends…"

"Isabelle, there's never been anyone but you. You know that! You have to know that," he urged. *She loves me*.

"Three!"

He stared at her. *She loves me not*. "If there was someone else, would that even matter to you? You've never come close to committing to me."

"Two!"

Isabelle's eyes watered, but she didn't answer him.

Scott took a step back from her. She backed up a step. Tiny movements, yet that distance between them felt as wide as the universe. This was Isabelle. His Isabelle. Or so he'd thought.

"One!"

"Happy New Year, Isabelle."

Scott moved past her and stalked toward the door. Never had he thought his New Year's Eve would turn out like this. As the clock struck midnight, Scott had turned onto a new path in his life. He was finished with being underappreciated and inconsequential. Isabelle only paid attention to him when it suited her and she didn't have anything better to do. Of course she wouldn't commit to him. He was nothing but detritus to her. No more. His anger toppled the pedestal he'd put her on.

He would regret not kissing Isabelle soundly that night, but the last chime of the New Year's clock was Scott's signal to make some big changes in his life.

And he was ready.

CHAPTER SEVEN

SCOTT SAT IN his truck outside the two-story house, dictating notes into his iPhone. The front porch boards were rotted and looked as if they'd collapse with the weight from the next snowfall. One window had a black plastic garbage bag taped over the half-broken pane.

Trent and other cops in unmarked ILPD cars had surrounded the house and blocked off the street. There were no lights or sirens cutting through the night, though in the distance, Scott could still hear the fireworks explosions over Indian Lake.

"Probably at the Lodges," he mumbled. Scott was glad he'd downloaded an app for shooting in very low light. He took another photo of Trent and the cops advancing on the house in a semicircle as two other cops raced around the back. They wore black parkas with ILPD emblazoned in bright yellow letters on the back.

Trent had his gun pulled and at the ready as he banged on the front door and announced, "Police!"

Scott zoomed in to record the scene. Of course there was no answer.

Trent tried the door, which was locked. He kicked the flimsy door down.

Scott heard a woman scream. He guessed it was the woman Ellis had duped into letting him stay with her. She screamed again.

Scott heard shouting from behind the house. He couldn't take it. He got out of the truck and inched closer to the house, still recording. Two cops, one he recognized as Sal Paluzzi, were walking a scrawny man, handcuffed now, toward the front of the house.

The man was cursing and spitting at the cops, trying to wrench himself out their grasp. He kicked Sal, but Sal kept his cool. Scott kept recording.

Just then, Scott's phone rang. The caller ID said it was Trent.

"What's up?" Scott asked.

"It's safe enough now. I think you should come inside."

Scott sped toward the front door as Sal and the other cop put Ellis in a squad car. He heard Sal reading Ellis his Miranda rights.

Scott dodged the rotted steps and hopped up onto the porch, which wasn't all that stable. He pulled back the screenless screen door and entered the dimly lit living room.

Sprawled on a dirty couch was a thin woman who looked to be about forty years old. Her light brown hair hung in clumps over her face. She wore a pair of men's sweat pants and a sweatshirt with the lettering cracked and flaking off. Her head lolled on the arm of the couch.

"Who's that?" Scott asked Trent.

"The landlady, apparently. And if we're lucky, she'll be our witness."

Scott took another step closer, scrutinizing the woman. Her nails were cracked and stained yellow from nicotine, he guessed, glancing at the ashtray full of cigarette butts on the flowered metal TV tray at the head of the couch. The only other furniture in the room was a floor lamp in the far corner.

"Are you arresting her?" Scott asked Trent.

"Right now, we're taking her in for questioning."

"Questioning?" Scott frowned. The woman seemed oblivious to their presence. "Any idea what she's on?"

"The guys found heroin and a syringe in the bathroom."

Just then Bob Paxton, a member of Trent's team who had also been a Green Beret like Trent, came in from the hallway. "Detective? I think you need to see this."

"What is it?"

"A wrinkle." Bob headed back down the hall.

"Should I stay here?" Scott asked.

"Bob's already scouted the house. There's no danger."

Scott nodded and followed the officers out of the room.

Bob stopped in front of a closed door. "I thought this was storage because it was locked. Didn't take much to pick it."

"More drugs?" Scott asked.

"Not exactly," Bob replied, opening the door.

The room was small and smelled musty, with only the light from an old television illuminating the faces of a little girl, about five or six years old, and the toddler in her arms.

The girl stared at them fearfully. Her lips quivered, but she remained silent. She took a step backward and hoisted the baby closer to the crook of her neck. The baby grabbed a handful of her cotton shirt and started fussing.

She made a cooing sound into the baby's ear and whispered something Scott couldn't make out, but it was clear she knew exactly how to react to the baby and the baby to her.

It was as if this little girl was the mother.

What's your name?" Trent asked her.

She pressed her lips together, remaining silent. Her big blue eyes darted to Scott and then quickly back to Trent.

Scott knew Trent to be compassionate and endearing to kids. He had certainly won the heart of Cate's little boy, Danny, who wasn't much older than this girl.

"Is this your little sister?" Trent asked the girl.

She lifted her chin defiantly, then shook her head.

"Your brother then?" Trent asked.

She stared at Trent, hugging the baby tighter. Scott noticed that her hands were clean and the baby looked well cared for. His heart ached for these children.

"He's your brother, then," Scott said, crouching down to her level.

She turned to him, and her gaze pierced him to his core. She looked to be in desperate need of a hug. A hundred hugs. He wanted to give them to her.

"What's his name?" Scott prodded. Bob had left the room and Trent was slowly backing away.

"Michael," she replied in a sweet voice.

The light from the TV flickered across her face, and he saw that her hair was gathered in a rubber band. He felt his heart thrum with compassion. "And what's your name?"

"Bella."

"I like that. It suits you. Did you know that it means *beautiful*?"

"No. My mom named me. She didn't name Michael. I named him."

"You did? That's very interesting," Scott replied gingerly, reaching out to touch Michael's little back. "He's a good baby brother, isn't he?"

"Yes. He's mine." She put her hand on his head and held him tighter. Michael turned his face enough for Scott to see he had a pacifier in his mouth.

No wonder the baby was quiet. His eyes were closing slowly as sleep crept over him.

"I can see that," Scott said.

Bella cocked her head and stared at him. He felt oddly like a specimen on display.

She frowned and she started to say something and then stopped herself.

"What is it, Bella?"

"Are you an angel?"

"An angel? No. I'm not. Why would you ask that?" Scott was taken aback.

Still holding Michael, she turned around and went to the rickety table where the television sat and picked up a DVD case. She handed it to Scott.

It was *The Bishop's Wife,* an old film starring Cary Grant. He glanced at the television. It was the movie she'd been watching while her mother zoned out on heroin in the living room.

"You look like him," she said.

He glanced down at his tux. "You think so?"

"Uh-huh."

"Well, this is just a movie," Scott said. He turned the case over and saw a price sticker from St. Mark's resale shop. It had cost fifty cents.

"The angel comes to earth to help the people. Even the little girl," Bella insisted.

"You're right. And angels do exactly that, Bella. They help people. But I'm not an angel."

Bella's gaze shifted to Trent, who was watching them from the doorway. "Ellis said if I ever told anyone about him, the police would come and take my brother from me. Is that true?"

Trent hesitated long enough for Bella to draw her own conclusions. She backed up against the wall. "You can't take him away from me! He's mine!" she screamed.

Michael jolted awake and started crying, a piercing wail that seemed louder than the approaching police sirens.

"We're not taking him from you," Trent assured her. "Your mother has gone with some other police officers to the police station. There's a lady coming from Department of Child Services who is going to take you to a safe house. It's warm there and she's a very good cook. I know. I've tasted her chicken and noodles."

Bella remained silent but took in every word.

She looked at Scott. "Will you come with us?"

"I, er…" Scott glanced at Trent who nodded. "Sure," Scott said. "I'll help you pack your things, too."

"We don't have much," she replied, swaying back and forth to quiet Michael. Then she laid him on one of the two sleeping bags that Scott guessed were their beds.

An open box of diapers and a pile of faded baby clothes, bibs and pilled blankets sat nearby.

"Where did you get these things?"

"The churches give them to me," she replied matter-of-factly.

"The diapers, too?"

She nodded. "There's a lady who owns a store three streets over. I go to her back door and she gives them to me."

"Who's that?"

"Miss Nancy. She gives me food and a little money, but I don't tell my mom. It's a secret."

Scott thought he'd be the next one to cry. Nancy St. Marie owned Celebrations To Go, a gift shop. He didn't know her personally, though he'd met her from time to time around town. People talked about her generosity, but this kindness made him feel inadequate and unworthy.

It was a simple thing, wasn't it? Giving a kid some diapers and a few bucks. And what had he done lately—or ever—that was even close to that?

One tiny act of charity. That's all it took to make a difference in this little girl's life. Right now she needed someone to tell her that everything was going to be all right. He wasn't a miracle worker, but he could help her tonight.

It had to be a frightening thing to be uprooted like this. Though from what he could see, she and Michael were living in an unsafe situation. Her mother kept drugs in the house and got high with her kids in the other room. Depending on what happened at the police station tonight, she could end up in prison.

It was New Year's Eve. The start of a new year for everyone and possibly a new life for Bella and Michael. No matter what happened, their lives would be altered.

Bella stood, shoved a few of the baby items into a plastic bag and turned to Scott. "Can you carry this?"

"Yes," he said. "Do you have a coat?"

"Just a sweatshirt." She picked up a too-small hoodie and pulled it on. Then she pulled a girl's parka out from under one of the sleeping bags and put it on Michael. Scott guessed it was a hand-me-down, and that their mother hadn't replaced many of the clothes Bella had outgrown. His heart broke a little more.

Bella scooped Michael into her arms, and Scott was amazed at her strength.

"I can carry him for you, too," Scott offered.

"Nobody takes care of Michael but me. Not even my mom."

"She doesn't?"

"No. She said she doesn't want him. She told me I'm the mother now. That's why he's mine."

"I see," Scott said, aching for these kids and the burden Bella carried.

Trent went to the corner of the room and grabbed more clothes and the DVD. He put them in another plastic bag. "We'll go in my car," he said. Then he whispered to Scott. "I don't have child seats. Maybe you should sit in back and hold the baby. If she'll let you."

Bella looked up at Scott, and for the first time that night, she smiled. "I'm ready."

She slipped her little hand into his. Her skin was surprisingly warm, he thought, since the apartment was chilly.

But then, temperature wasn't supposed to affect angels. Even little ones.

CHAPTER EIGHT

IT WAS TWO O'CLOCK in the morning when Isabelle was awakened by the knocking on her door.

"What in the world?"

Few people in Isabelle's life called on her unannounced. In fact, even her mother called or texted before a visit. Isabelle shoved her arms through a worn terry cloth robe and put her feet into the new slippers Dylan had given her for Christmas. He'd thought the ridiculous reindeer design was funny, but they were lined with sheepskin and too comfortable for words.

Brushing her hair from her face, she went to the door. "Who is it?" She peered through the peephole. Scott stood there in his tuxedo. She unlocked the door.

"Are you out of your—"

"Isabelle, I'm sorry."

His bow tie was hanging around his neck, his top shirt button unbuttoned, and he held a bouquet of wilted flowers. But his face radiated an energy she'd never seen.

"It's after two, Scott. You never stay up late. And you never just show up at my front door even in daylight. What's going on?"

"These are for you." He thrust the sad bouquet at her. "It's all they had at the mini-mart."

She took the flowers. "And you've never given me flowers. Fresh or wilted." She ushered him in and closed the door.

"I didn't want another hour to go by without apologizing to you."

"You left me on the dance floor at midnight. On New Year's Eve. New Year's Eve, Scott. Friends don't do that to friends."

"I know. And you should be mad."

"I should. I mean, I was," she replied, studying the pink rose that was ready to drop a round of petals. "Come into the kitchen while I try to revive these," she said, walking away.

She took out a small wood cutting board and whacked off the stems with a butcher's knife then filled a vase with ice water and plunked the flowers in. "They'll perk up in an hour or so, and I'll arrange them." She turned to Scott, who was leaning against the doorjamb, arms folded across his chest. He was staring at her intently.

"What?"

"I want to tell you what happened tonight," he began.

"I know what happened tonight. You chose your story over me."

Scott froze. She hadn't meant for her words to come out like that, but for some odd reason, his abandonment had hurt. Which was ridiculous, because Scott hadn't acted any differently than she did most of the time. She was always choosing her art over spending time with him.

"Okay," she said. "That wasn't fair. I'm sorry."

"Accepted. Can we start over?"

"Yes. Let's sit in the living room. I do want to hear about your story."

Isabelle curled her legs beneath her robe, the antlers of the reindeer poking out from under the folds, and reached behind her to turn on a lamp.

The soft glow settled over the rugged planes of Scott's face, enhancing the dark shadow of scruff that he would shave off in the morning before seeing his first customer. Despite the late hour, and whatever he'd been up to since midnight, he still looked handsome.

"I'm all ears." She smiled.

"My story isn't only about the arrest that Trent made tonight, though I will cover it for the newspaper. He took a methamphetamine producer and dealer into custody, along with the woman he lived with, who will be charged with possession, if nothing else. Drugs are doing awful things to this town."

"I couldn't agree more. But you're saying there's something else?"

Scott nodded. "There were two little kids, in the apartment, Isabelle. A girl—five years old, she finally told us, though she doesn't know her actual birthday—but she does remember her brother's birth and the date. That's how we know he's eighteen months old."

"Oh, my God." Isabelle straightened against the back of the sofa. "You saw them?"

"Not only did I see them, I talked with the little girl, Bella, for quite some time." He looked down at his hands and smiled. "She thought I was an angel."

Isabelle felt a strange jab of guilt. Scott *was* an angel, to his mother and to many of their friends. And especially to her. He helped her stretch canvases. He often picked up art supplies for her and brought them to the Lodges when she had to work long hours. He brought her coffee on chilly mornings after she went sculling with Sarah and their friends. He did a thousand and one things for her, and though she thanked him, she'd never considered his devotion, his selflessness. Yet a five-year-old stranger recognized Scott's kindness on sight.

"You are," she murmured.

"Not like that. She'd been watching an old Christmas movie with Cary Grant, who was a literal angel."

"I love that movie." Isabelle brushed a bit of dust off his jacket sleeve. "Guess it was your tux."

He shrugged. "Must have been. Anyway, this little girl has been taking care of her baby brother practically since he was born. The mother is a heroin addict. Maybe meth, too. Bella has taken it on her shoulders to find food and diapers for Michael. She goes to St. Mark's and gets donations—and there are others in town helping her out."

As Scott continued, Isabelle found herself immersed in the past. She knew what Bella must feel like, being responsible for a younger sibling at such a young age. But Isabelle had been ten when her father died, and she'd been blessed with a hardworking, loving mother, despite Connie's shortcomings. Bella was only five.

"This little girl, Isabelle, she's different from any kid I ever met. It's like she's a hundred years old but in a child's body."

"Mmm." Isabelle knew exactly what he meant. People had said that about her, too.

"She asked me to go with her to the police

station, and I did. She held my hand while Trent talked to Zoey Phillips."

"Who's that?" Isabelle asked.

"She's the head over at Department of Child Services. She told us that she'll find a temporary foster home for Bella and Michael. If their mother is convicted, they'll be put up for adoption. The tough part is that Bella goes into a panic at the mention of being separated from her brother." Scott rubbed his forehead and then swiped his face with both hands. "Isabelle, the thought of those two innocent kids being lost in the system makes my skin crawl."

"What do you mean, 'lost'?"

"Some kids get lucky, but others get shuffled from foster home to foster home until they age out. They never have a real home. Never know what it's like to be safe. Trent says sometimes the conditions are really bad. I'll get more details tomorrow when I go see them and have a chance to talk to Zoey."

Isabelle sucked in a breath as his words hit home. "You're seeing them again? For your story, you mean?"

"No." He flicked a piece of lint off his pant leg.

"I don't understand." Isabelle felt as if she were still waiting for the clock to chime in the new year. Those unbearably long pauses between seconds that stretched into the unknown future. Something was clearly happening but she hadn't been debriefed.

Scott leaned toward her, gazing at her with a force of longing and desire she couldn't remember seeing before. "Isabelle, I came here tonight…" He placed his hand on hers. "To ask you something."

A sense of foreboding settled over her. "Scott, I don't think…"

"Hear me out. We've always been best friends. You're the first person I think about when I wake up. We spend so much time together. We know each other inside and out. I want us to move forward with our lives." He squeezed her hand earnestly.

"We are moving forward," she said reflexively.

"I mean together. I've thought a lot about where my life is going, and I realize now that writing articles for the local paper is not going to make a difference in this world. I saw that tonight, in that apartment. But I can change the future for these kids. I can take something horrible and make it happy. It's my hope that you'd do that with me."

All Isabelle could do was stare at him. "You

just got through saying we were best friends, but you don't know me at all. You of all people know that I just won the chance of my lifetime. A shot at a gallery show! The one thing I've worked for since high school." Her voice cracked. "It might be selfish, but it's my chance, Scott. The one I dreamed about while I was raising my siblings." Her palms were sweating and her heart rammed against her chest like a caged animal. She shot to her feet. "You are not asking me this right now."

"Oh, but I am," he replied quietly.

"I don't believe this," she said, raking her hand through her hair and turning from him.

"You don't want to be together?"

"I don't want children," she said in a rush.

"You never told me that before."

"Not in so many words." How could he have missed this obvious fact about her? She'd often confided how heavily the responsibility for her brothers and sisters had fallen on her. How she valued her independence above all.

"Why?"

"I've told you, Scott. My whole childhood was cooking, cleaning, doing my siblings' laundry while they played on the swing set or went to football practice or piano lessons. I was sweeping and changing diapers. I walked Violet in the middle of the night when she had bronchitis, so my mother could sleep and go to work."

Isabelle's voice rose and tears streamed down her cheeks. She could feel resentment in every teardrop. She hated that she felt that way, but she did. "I rarely had time to draw. I desperately wanted to be in the art club in high school. You remember. But most of the time I had to drive one of the other kids to their lessons or the library or whatever when they were supposed to meet. There was never any time for me." Her cheeks were blazing hot.

"I knew you resented the responsibilities…"

"Resented?" She snorted. "All I dreamed about was drawing and painting. No one ever asked me what I wanted. What kind of lessons I wanted."

Her tears were coming in torrents and as she dropped her face to her hands, Scott enfolded her in his arms. "I'm so sorry, Isabelle. I didn't realize how deep this went. There's so much emotion in your paintings… I should have understood."

She sniffed and pulled back. She placed her palms on his chest and felt his thundering heart.

She was hurting him, but she didn't know what course to take other than escape. "Don't you see, Scott? This is my chance to be free.

My art has always meant freedom to me. I can explore the entire universe if I make this sale. With the Lodges closed for the winter, I have time to paint what Malcolm wants. I can do this. It will be my grand adventure."

"Your new life," he said huskily.

"Yes."

He smoothed her hair back from her face and traced the edge of her cheek with his thumb. "You go for it, Isabelle. Be the best you can be."

"I intend to."

Then he kissed her with so much longing and passion, she felt weak.

He pulled her closer, and she melted into him, catching the faint scent of the spicy cologne he always wore.

"Isabelle," he whispered, as he released her. "I have to go."

She lowered her head. "I understand. Bye, Scott," she said, her voice quaking.

He gave her his usual two finger salute. Then he walked out of the door.

Isabelle struggled to smile as her mind frantically scrambled for logic. She had visions of them sitting in a Chicago restaurant overlooking Lake Michigan toasting her success with champagne. Not once in all the sketches of her future had she penciled in children or erased Scott out of the drawing.

And she wasn't about to do it now.

Eventually, Scott would understand. It was important that he give her this time. This opportunity. That's what she needed right now.

Time.

CHAPTER NINE

SCOTT DIDN'T KNOW what to expect as he drove through a heavy snowfall to the address of the child services center that Trent had given him.

He'd told Zoey that he wanted to take the kids for an outing. She'd explained that she wanted to have a discussion with him first. Then she'd asked if he had child safety seats for the car. He told her he'd have them by the time he arrived.

He'd stopped off at the Indian Lake grocery, which was thankfully open for four hours on New Year's Day. With the help of a woman in the baby aisle, he'd bought diapers, diaper rash cream, a pacifier, a couple sleepers with feet in them, shirts and a pair of "jeans" for Michael.

Next door at the Tractor Supply, open all day, he'd found excellent quality child safety seats for the car, a proper crib for Michael and a high chair. There were aisles of warm children's parkas and he bought one for Bella in pink and one for Michael in blue with the Cubs emblem on it, which was on sale.

He would have bought shoes and boots but he wanted to make certain of their sizes. The next time he went shopping, he intended to bring them with him. If the director of DCS would allow.

Scott rubbed his eyes and turned up the windshield wipers. The snow was coming down fast, but his bleary vision was due to the fact that he hadn't slept all night. After he'd left Isabelle's apartment and come back to his shop, his mind and emotions had been on overload.

He'd grabbed an armful of books and puzzles from his shelves, hoping Bella liked books. He hadn't seen a single toy in the sparse room the night before.

Everything he'd witnessed about Bella and Michael's situation made his heart reach out to them, yet listening to Isabelle divulge her own history and deep-seated fears to him last night had deepened his compassion for Bella.

Isabelle had her reasons for everything she was doing. Good ones. She was determined to move on with her art, wherever it would lead her. It was going to take him a long time to imagine a life without Isabelle in it.

He supposed he was in shock.

He'd gone to her apartment essentially to propose, but she'd cut him off at the pass. Come to think of it, he'd never told her that he loved her. She'd never said she loved him back.

That would have been a good place to start.

He and Isabelle had come to a fork in the road last night and gone in two different directions. Scott hadn't seen it coming. He realized now that he'd done them both a disservice over the years. He'd indulged himself in some dangerous passive behavior that had given Isabelle the impression that he shared her feelings about not wanting a family.

He'd never pressed her. He'd never expressed much about his feelings. In fact, it had only been recently, that he'd started thinking about what he truly wanted out of life—other than Isabelle.

It wasn't until he'd seen little Bella and Michael that he knew: he wanted kids.

And he wanted these kids.

At least, he wanted to help them. And overnight, he'd come to the realization that he could do more for Bella and Michael as a foster parent than by writing about them for the *Indian Lake Herald*. For Scott, the idea of being a foster parent was about as far-fetched as his illusions about winning a Pulitzer. Foster parenting was something "other" people did. *Dedicated and trained parental guides* was the description given on the DCS website.

Scott would muster "dedicated" and the training was a matter of time and effort.

He pulled his truck into the circular drive at the newly built DCS building. The slate-gray-and-white trimmed building was surrounded by a thick grove of snow-covered trees.

He gathered his purchases and tromped up the unshoveled walk to the entrance. He wiped his feet on the mat and went to the reception desk.

"Hello. Scott Abbott. I'm here to see Zoey Phillips."

"Oh, yes. Mr. Abbott," the blonde, sixtyish woman replied as she eyed his parcels. "Won't you have a seat? She's on the phone, but I'll let her know you're here."

Scott sat and glanced around the room, noticing dozens of parenting pamphlets, magazines and journals. Before he had time to pick up a magazine, Zoey came down the hallway.

"Mr. Abbott. How nice to see you," she said, holding out her hand.

Scott shifted the bags to his left arm and smiled. "Call me Scott, please. I was a bit surprised to get your text—I didn't think you'd be open on New Year's Day."

Zoey led the way to her private office, a small room just off the reception area. There was only space for a small metal desk, her chair and two chairs opposite her. Her files sat in piles against the far wall, but there was a huge window at her back that looked out into the forest.

Scott put his bags on the chair next to him as they both sat.

Zoey was a pretty blonde woman, whom he guessed to be around the same age as him and Isabelle. *Isabelle.* His mind started to wander.

He studied the wall on his right where she'd hung a dozen framed certificates and licenses attesting to her expertise in child protection. "These are from downstate," he said.

"Indianapolis mostly," she replied, glancing up. "That's where I met Sarah Jensen. Er, Bosworth."

He smiled. "Luke's my best friend. How do you know Sarah?"

"We were at IU together. We met at a party her senior year. I was just a freshman then, but she was so kind and generous I never forgot her. We stayed in touch. Then when I broke up with my fiancé a few months ago, I emailed her and she suggested I look into the opening up here." She spread her palms in front of her. "And that is the story of my life." She grinned.

"I doubt that." He couldn't stop himself from grinning back.

But just as quickly, Zoey grew more somber. "Listen, I wanted to talk to you because Bella was quite distressed about leaving you last night. This interested me a great deal since the two of you had only met. Isn't that right?"

"Yes. I was only there at the bust as a reporter. Believe me, I wasn't prepared for what happened."

She folded her hands on the desk. "That's what I wanted to hear from you. What, precisely, did happen?"

Scott looked down at his hand, the one Bella had held. How did he say to a professional social worker that a complete stranger had stolen his heart? How did he tell Zoey that he wanted to help Bella and Michael segue into their new life? How could he explain the protective emotions he felt? "As you know, the police have proof that Bella's mother was indeed dealing drugs."

"I do. Detective Davis tells me they also believe she was an accomplice in making the meth with her boyfriend."

"I didn't know that." Scott frowned. "So, there's no question she'll go to prison."

"None. She confessed to the charges, hoping her sentence will be lessened."

"And will it?"

"That's up to the judge, but it will go in her favor."

"How long do you think she'll be in for?" Scott asked.

"I don't know. Ten, fifteen years. That much is certain."

"Fifteen..." He rubbed his eyes. "That's nearly all of Bella's childhood. And Michael's, too."

"I know."

"What happens to them?"

"Right now, we are in a...situation. Because of the holiday, our foster parents have taken on extra kids from the group home. We all want the children to have as happy an experience over the holidays as possible. It's been an extra burden for our foster families, but at Christmas, everyone is very gracious. Kids should have Christmas, I believe. So, we've all worked very hard to place them."

Scott lowered his head. "And Bella and Michael came late to the party."

She nodded. "There are no foster homes for them right now."

His head jerked up. "Where are they, then?"

"I stayed here with them last night," Zoey replied. "I couldn't leave them alone, and there was no place..."

"Nowhere at all?" Scott knew his voice held shock but he couldn't help it.

"Scott, there are over twelve thousand children in foster care in the state of Indiana alone. And the numbers rise every day. I have checked all my foster families, sources and I have no place for them right now. We're so overloaded and you wouldn't believe how sad some of the stories are."

"I'm beginning to," he replied morosely. "Where will they stay tonight?"

She leaned forward. "That's what I wanted to discuss. We need your help over the next few days."

"I want to help Bella and Michael in any way I can."

"I was hoping you'd say that. Actually, I didn't know what I'd do if you didn't. Could you take care of them? I mean, not just for an outing, but for possibly the next week?"

"Of course I would. I'd be thrilled. But isn't there a great deal of protocol and paperwork?"

"There is, but this is somewhat of an emergency," Zoey said. "However, I've done some preliminary checks on you—obviously, hoping you would agree." She smiled.

"It's okay," he assured her.

"So that you know, I called Sarah and spoke to her about you. She gave me a very high recommendation about you, your character. She gave me several other people to call. Mrs. Beabots. Gina Barzonni. Sam Crenshaw. In addition to Detective Davis's recommendation, I couldn't ask for a more qualified foster parent."

"Except that I'm single."

She cocked an eyebrow. "That isn't as great a deterrent as it once was," she replied. "Not with so many children in need."

"I understand."

"I'm required to run a complete background check. So, if you'll fill out these papers," she said, handing him several documents. "Please understand, Scott, this is not standard procedure…"

Scott picked up a pen and started writing. "It's fine."

Zoey exhaled. "And this would be just a few days…until our personnel comes back from holiday. We'll find a foster home for them—"

"How long?" he interrupted and stopped writing.

"How long what?"

"How long will they stay in that house until they're moved again?"

Shrugging, she replied, "Six months. Maybe not that long—depending."

"On what?"

"If they get adopted. Placing Michael would be easy. He's only a year and half and we have requests for babies all the time. Bella is a different story."

"I'll take them." He choked back a fiery ball in his throat. The thought that Bella and Michael might be split apart seared through his mind. He couldn't let that happen.

"Thank you, Scott. This is such a big help."

"Zoey, I'm not just talking about the next few days. I'd like to become a foster parent for Bella and Michael. I know how much work this will be, but I don't want them being shuffled around like checkers. I want them to learn what a real home is like. My home."

"Scott, I wasn't intending to ask you to…"

"I know that. I'm making this decision. Look, I realize I'm single, that I've never been a parent before, but something happened the minute I saw Bella and Michael. They've already changed my life. I'll do anything to make this happen. Tell me, is it possible to be a single foster father?"

"Yes. It is. There are licensing requirements—you have to pay for your own proof of financial stability and you'll have to complete ten hours of parental training. You pay for the course up front, but the state will reimburse you."

"That's not a problem."

"There are home study courses through this county but since we are the governing agency, I can help you with that. Here is a checklist of our requirements. We'll need your medical records. You'll need to complete a CPR and First Aid course. We have parent support groups and we plan special events for the children that you might find fun and helpful."

"That sounds great. Zoey, Bella told the police during some of their questioning that she didn't know her exact birthday. Is there a way of finding that out?"

"The police will question the mother and see if there are any records. If she can remember the hospital and the city, we can generally track down what we need."

"That would be good. If she's five, next year she'll be ready for kindergarten."

Zoey smiled broadly. "You've really thought this through."

He put his hand over his heart. "I can't walk away from them." He already loved them like they were his own.

Zoey heaved a deep breath. "You are an exceptional man, Scott Abbott."

"I don't know about that. All I know is that I want to help."

Zoey stood up. "Well, all right then. Oh, before I take you to them, did you get those safety seats for the car?"

"Got a great deal at the Tractor Supply. They're installed and ready to go."

She nodded. "I'll gather the rest of the paperwork. I need to inspect your home, Scott. If I came by your place on Wednesday, would that be all right?"

"Sure." He paused. "Zoey, I'll make certain I do everything required to take care of the children. If not, I'll fix it. I don't care what it takes."

Scott had finished filling out the documents by the time Zoey returned with a folder of papers, pamphlets and schedules of parent meetings.

"I can pick up the rest of your forms on Wednesday," Zoey said, handing him the folder. "Come with me and I'll take you to the kids and you can get them ready to go home with you."

Scott rose and shook her hand. "Thanks for your help, Zoey."

"This is what I'm here for," she replied as she led him down the hall.

She tapped on the last door on the right and opened it, then stepped aside so that Scott could enter.

Bella stood on a step stool beside a changing table. She was talking to Michael as she changed his diaper. She'd just taped the clean diaper as Scott walked into the room.

"Bella?"

She turned to look at him and he realized

he'd underestimated the impact of her wide-eyed gaze on him.

She burst into a brilliant smile. "Scott! You're here!"

"I am."

"Did you come for us?" She kept her right hand on Michael's belly so that he wouldn't roll off the table.

"I did."

"I knew you would." She beamed.

"Really? How did you know?"

"It was like in the movie. I prayed for you to come back and you did."

CHAPTER TEN

ISABELLE SQUEEZED OUT a dab of indigo blue oil paint onto her palette, slipped her palette knife into the blob of white paint and began mixing. Sliding the knife through the indigo and adding bits of white, she struggled to create an intense Mediterranean blue for a faerie's eye. With art nouveau butterfly wings and a butterfly-inspired skirt that filled the foreground, this painting was more about the stained glass design than the faerie herself. But the color was not coming together.

No matter how much she tried to stay on track, her thoughts drifted back to Scott.

"Ugh!" She whacked the palette knife against her board. What had happened with them? Were they even friends anymore?

She glanced at her phone. No calls. No texts. It had been nearly two weeks since New Year's Eve. Yes, she'd been lost in her painting. The new year meant he was doing inventory, but considering she'd turned down his proposal, his silence caused an ache inside her she'd never felt before.

She grabbed her cleaning cloth and swiped the knife against it. She picked up another tube of paint and didn't look at it, still thinking of Scott.

Really, he owed her an apology. He should have called her days ago. Actually, she'd expected him to call because he always was the first to apologize when they argued.

This had been their biggest disagreement yet. She tried not to dwell on the possibility that she had caused permanent damage between them. She'd said things that she'd never intended to say to anyone.

Was she hard-hearted and selfish? Just thinking about what she'd said made her cringe. She'd never thought of herself as cold…

But she was on the cusp of something momentous in her career. If she abandoned it now, she would never know what she could have achieved. She'd always regret it.

On the one hand, she believed she owed it to herself to pursue her art. She cared about Scott, but she couldn't give him the kind of commitment he'd asked of her. On the other hand, she was very good at raising kids. She had five younger brothers and sisters to attest to that. She could probably give lessons. Scott had no idea what he was getting into. He didn't have siblings. He'd never cared for a baby. He was living in a dream world. As much as she was determined to follow her own path, she felt guilty leaving Scott alone in that situation.

She mixed the paint.

She needed to calm down and stop over-thinking things. That had always been her problem.

Now that the Lodges was closed for the winter, she had too many hours on her hands to do precisely that...overthink.

It was a good thing she was consumed with her painting and getting this work done for Malcolm.

Taking a dab of paint, she lifted her brush to the faerie's face.

Last winter she'd filled some of her empty hours by hanging out with Scott in his coffee shop. He'd taught her how to use the espresso machine and steam milk. She quickly learned to draw pictures in the foam just like Maddie Strong Barzonni over at Cupcakes and Cappuccino. Maddie's expensive brass and copper Italian cappuccino machine could not be equaled, and Scott didn't try. His customers came as much for the books as they did for his coffee. Last year he'd experimented with selling handmade chocolate truffles and turtles from a woman in town who was hoping to build clientele and then open her own shop.

Isabelle had had fun working in Scott's store. The winter days had passed a bit faster. She'd still had time to paint while earning extra money and spending time with Scott.

Isabelle finished the faerie's eyes and stepped back.

Her hand flew to her mouth. "What the..."

Somehow, her anger at Scott and her musings of their happier times had flowed into her work. Forget a blue-eyed faerie; she'd painted Scott's deep brown eyes with golden flecks and long, black lashes. She'd often teased him that his lashes were the envy of all her girlfriends.

Her eyes misted over as anger gave way to concern. A fog of apprehension enveloped her. But this was something different. And she didn't like it. She'd lost her focus. Her heart and mind were consumed with Scott. What was he thinking? What was he doing? He'd never gone this long without calling her. Seeing her.

And she couldn't remember more than five, maybe seven days at a stretch without making contact with him.

This had never happened to her before. She'd always been able to put the real world aside and walk into her artistic world.

Now she couldn't seem to leave reality behind. She dipped her brush in linseed oil and carefully wrapped a piece of linen cloth around it. Then she hit Scott's name on her cell.

The call went to voicemail.

"Scott, it's me. I think we should talk—again. I know I was harsh, but it's been twelve days and I haven't heard from you. Call me. Please?" Isabelle shucked off her paint-splattered shirt— an old one her brother Christopher had given her years ago. She threw it across the back of one of her garage sale walnut dining chairs.

"If the mountain will not come to Muhammad, then Muhammad must go to the mountain."

She'd head right over to the coffee shop and confront him. She couldn't possibly go another hour letting him think the worst of her.

She felt awkward and ashamed about revealing her feelings to him. Isabelle had always been private. She didn't even share much with her girlfriends, though Sarah, Maddie, Olivia and Liz often confided in each other and her. Olivia's Valentine's Day wedding was fast approaching, and that subject appeared to enthrall everyone. The more Olivia talked about writing vows and picking wedding songs, the more Isabelle clammed up. When they all sat around the deli at lunch talking about their lives, their concerns, Isabelle kept quiet. She laughed when they joked around and commiserated when someone was sad or upset. But she didn't share.

Sharing might cause too much introspection. She felt she'd done a good job with her life, living on her own, not asking anyone for help. Except for Scott. She didn't like to think too much about what that meant.

If she got too close, too intimate, shared too much, she might get lost in him. And after all she'd sacrificed for her siblings, she couldn't afford to lose herself to someone else again. She was proud of her brothers and sisters, and of herself, for how she'd raised them. But she had to focus on herself now.

Isabelle, the adult, didn't like to reflect on Isabelle, the child, who saw things that didn't exist but believed in them with all her might. Her father had indulged her when she came home from an afternoon at the lake and told him that she'd seen water nymphs among the cattails and lily pads. He was fascinated with what she saw and had encouraged her to draw the faeries. Once, she'd taken him to the spot where she'd seen a water sprite, but that day the little people hadn't come out to play with her. She'd described their antics to her father and he'd told her that he loved her all the more for her gift of "seeing."

Connie had derided him for encouraging Isabelle's fantasies, claiming that Isabelle's faerie visits were a child's imagination. Nothing more. Nothing real. But her father had stood by her.

After he died, Isabelle had never seen a faerie again. She realized her mother was right. The faeries weren't real. But then she'd painted one and it sold for over a hundred dollars, and Isabelle had come to see them as guides to her future. Each time she painted one, she was inspired to paint another.

She studied her butterfly-skirted faerie, peering into its brown eyes, and felt a sense of loss.

She had to see where her art would take her. She couldn't give up that opportunity for a man. Especially one who was about to start a family. But she wasn't willing to give up on her friendship with Scott.

At least not yet.

CHAPTER ELEVEN

ISABELLE ARRIVED AT SCOTT'S store to find it closed. The little paper clock suggested he'd be returning at three.

"Five minutes." She harrumphed and walked over to the right side of the shop where a second door led upstairs to Scott's apartment.

It was unlocked. That was unusual, but he occasionally left it open when he was renovating, which was an ongoing process since the apartment needed a lot of work. Maybe he was finally putting in the gas fireplace he'd always talked about. The apartment had high ceilings and was difficult to heat.

She climbed the familiar wood stairs, remembering last year's Super Bowl party. He'd invited everyone over on the spur of the moment, and because he didn't have enough seating, she'd gone with him to a local furniture store to pick out two matching sofas. She'd taken it upon herself to pick out end tables and lamps. Scott had admitted that his bachelor apartment needed professional help.

Upon reaching his apartment door, she knocked.

No answer. She knocked again. "Scott?"

She heard voices inside but she didn't recognize them. Footsteps rumbled across the bare wood floors. Scott flung the door open. He held a toddler in his arms.

He froze when he saw her. "Isabelle? What are you doing here?"

Stunned by the sight of Scott with a baby, she took a step back.

"Why are you holding a baby?" she asked.

Scott smiled and turned the baby around. "Isabelle, this is Michael." He picked up the baby's hand and waved it at Isabelle. "See? He says hi."

"Scott, I…"

Just then a little girl came running out of the bedroom. She was thin with a tumble of blond hair that reminded Isabelle of herself when she was a child. Her eyes were enormous deep blue pools with thick black lashes that made Isabelle want to paint her portrait. There was something mesmerizing about this child, but Isabelle shucked off the thought because she didn't paint children.

The little girl wore a flowered shirt, red corduroy pants and brand new red sneakers. She pulled at a price tag on the pants.

Isabelle held her breath. *What in the world?*

"Mr. Scott, I can't get this off," the little girl said, looking up at Scott. Scott leaned down and yanked on the price tag.

"There you go," he said.

Isabelle's eyes widened as she looked from Scott to the baby and then to the little girl, who moved closer to Scott and put her hand around his thigh.

"Mr. Scott?" The girl flinched as Isabelle continued looking at her. She reminded Isabelle of a baby bird, sweet, young and just trying its wings.

Isabelle put her hand on the doorjamb because she felt as if the ground had shifted and she'd lost her balance. "Scott? What's going on?"

Scott's smile looked as if it had bloomed from the sun. She'd never see so much happiness. "I'm their foster parent, Isabelle."

"Oh."

Bella's wary eyes never left Isabelle's face. "Who's this?"

"It's okay, Bella. This is my friend, Isabelle."

"Has she come to take us away?" Bella asked fearfully.

No child or adult had ever considered Isabelle with so much terror. She felt like an interloper, but her heart went out to Bella. "Don't be afraid. I'm just a friend."

Isabelle locked eyes with Scott. "This is them? The ones you told me about?"

"Yes." He replied, his voice tight. She could tell he was ready for an argument. Battle.

For some reason, tears stung her eyes. She had a thousand questions. Their relationship had changed irrevocably, and she realized with a jolt that that had been her decision. Scott had told her what he wanted and she'd turned her back on him. She'd rejected him and the promise of a family.

She wanted her art career and her friendship with Scott. But obviously, she couldn't have it all. Scott wanted something entirely different.

And this was it.

Bella and Michael studied her warily, without a glimmer of trust. Isabelle couldn't begin to imagine what these children must be feeling. They'd been taken from their home and their whole world had been altered. Now they lived a new life. Already, Bella had bonded with Scott judging by the way she cleaved to him. He was her protector and she trusted him.

What kind of life had this child endured that every time she met someone new, she was afraid her life would be ripped apart again?

No wonder Scott had come to their rescue.

He'd always had a strong heroic streak. It was one of the qualities she admired most about him. Though usually, he was coming to *her* rescue.

That thought had never crossed her mind before. Truth was funny like that. Had she been taking advantage of Scott's kindness?

Isabelle dropped to her knees and held out her hand to Bella. "I'd like to be your friend, too, Bella."

Bella didn't make a move. Instead, she tightened her grip on Scott's leg.

"Isabelle, maybe we better give Bella some time, huh?"

Isabelle rose slowly. "Sure."

"So, what did you want?" Scott asked, picking up Michael's pacifier, which had fallen into the crook of his arm.

"I, er, I called you and you didn't call me back. About the other night. New Year's Eve, I mean. I didn't want you to think…" She looked at Bella and then Michael. "But clearly—"

"I made some decisions, Isabelle."

"I see that."

"Look, my mom is going to be here in a few minutes to watch the kids so I can open back up for the afternoon crowd. You know, I get a rush for a couple hours after school lets out."

"Yeah. I remember."

"Was there anything else, Isabelle?"

"Well… I was wondering if you could drive me into Chicago next week. To the gallery. I have a really big painting, and your truck… It would help me out a lot."

"I'm not sure. I'll have to see. I've got the kids now, so I don't think I can take a day off like that."

"Sure. I understand," she replied, taking a step back.

"Let me see what I can do."

"No, it's okay. You have a lot on your plate now."

"I do." He grinned joyously at Michael, who put his little hand on Scott's cheek and smiled back.

Isabelle was still in shock. She wasn't sure she'd ever seen Scott this happy. She simply didn't understand. Kids weighed a person down. They were demanding and their needs had to come first with just about everything. But then again, Scott was new to the game. He hadn't been a parent for two weeks yet. When the years dragged on and the responsibilities increased, he'd find out how it was.

"I'd better go," she said.

"Yeah. Nice seeing you." He glanced down at Bella. "Say goodbye to Miss Isabelle, Bella."

"Bye," Bella whispered.

"Goodbye, Bella. It was my pleasure to meet you."

Bella's smile appeared to be a struggle.

"Say goodbye to Michael," Bella said. "Just because he's not grown up like me, doesn't mean he doesn't understand."

Isabelle blinked. For the first time in years, she remembered how snippets of wisdom used to fall out of the mouths of her brothers and sisters when she least expected it. She'd been astounded that the little person she'd rocked and burped, bathed and bandaged could utter something so immeasurably profound. She'd buried those words and those memories under canvases or *in* her canvases. She didn't know which.

"You're absolutely right, Bella," she said, smiling. It was a good feeling. "Goodbye, Michael. That's such a nice name."

"Do you think so?" Bella asked.

"Yes. I do."

"Thanks. I named him."

"Oh, so you like it, too."

"Yes," Bella said with a nod. "At St. Mark's they said it was the name of the greatest angel soldier."

Her breath caught in her throat. "That's right. Well, goodbye, then."

"Goodbye, Isabelle," Scott said, but his smiled was directed at Bella.

Isabelle couldn't take her eyes off Scott. She'd never pictured him holding a baby or having a young child cling to his leg.

He quietly closed the door.

She gripped the handrail as she went down the stairs; her feet were unsteady and her hands were shaking. When she reached the bottom she grabbed the door handle and took a deep breath to steady her nerves.

Scott has a family.

He was a foster parent to two children he'd met on New Year's Eve.

It was unfathomable. The Scott she thought she knew had been an illusion. Or maybe she'd never really known the man at all.

Isabelle had always thought that she and Scott had been on the same page. She realized now that her ambitions, her desire to make a name for herself had dominated nearly every aspect of their relationship.

Scott had goals of his own and he had decided to pursue them.

It was no different than what she was doing. Isabelle believed in her art, her talent, in the opportunities she could make for herself in Chicago. She believed she could make her own dreams come true.

But if the future was so magnificent and wondrous, then why was her heart so heavy?

She thrust the door open and squinted into the street.

The sun was as brutal and blinding as her awareness that she'd lost Scott forever.

CHAPTER TWELVE

SCOTT DROVE THROUGH the I-Pass lane on the Chicago Skyway. The GPS directed him to Stony Island Drive. Then he'd take the Outer Drive up to Evanston. He wanted to drive by the lake since it was a rare sunny winter's day in Chicago, which was usually slate gray and dreary this time of year. But even if it had been gloomy, nothing could have dampened Scott's spirits. He was bone tired from being up all night with Michael, who was teething and had a runny nose, but he'd never been happier. The kids had changed his life for the better and this was the first time he'd been alone with Isabelle for weeks. He was on top of the world.

"I can't thank you enough for doing this for me, Scott," Isabelle said from the passenger seat.

"It's okay."

"But I really mean it. There's no way I could have gotten these paintings to the gallery without your help."

"Yeah, that new one is huge," he replied, giving her a sidelong glance. She was as nervous as a cat in a roomful of rocking chairs. He supposed that was to be expected. If this meeting today didn't go well, her dreams would turn to ash. But Scott suspected there was more going on in Isabelle's head than career anxiety. She couldn't possibly be thinking about him. Or could she?

When she turned to face him, her smile was stretched too thin. She wasn't feeling it. He knew her too well. "Scott, you haven't told me what Theresa thinks of all this...of your, er, new family."

"Mom? She loves them already." He grinned.

"Really?"

"Yeah, Isabelle. Really."

She shook her head.

"What?"

"I guess—I mean, I'm having a hard time wrapping my head around this. You made this decision so quickly."

He gripped the steering wheel and shot her a steely glance. "What was I supposed to do, Isabelle? They had no place to sleep! There wasn't a single foster bed available. Zoey Phillips stayed overnight with them in the DCS facility before she called me. They have no one."

"But now they have you."

"They do. Thank God."

"Thanks to you, you mean," she replied softly.

"Are you passing judgment on me, Isabelle?"

"No. No, it's just so out of character for you. You always think things through. Plot out your next move. You spend weeks poring over the new children's book releases before you place an order. If it weren't for me, you wouldn't have any decent furniture in your apartment, if you remember."

"I remember."

"And if we go to one of our friends' parties you call me to ask what you should wear. I've seen you deliberate more over which sweater to wear with which pants than I do. But you decided to become a parent overnight. How do you explain that?"

"I've been thinking about it for a long time."

"But we haven't talked about it," she shot back.

"You're right, Isabelle. I stopped bringing up kids with you. If I even mention how cute a little girl is at a restaurant or the kids playing at the beach, you stiffen up."

"I do not."

"You do."

She paused and considered this. "I do that?"

"Yup." He turned onto the Outer Drive. They drove past McCormick Place, the Field Museum and Adler Planetarium. "Man, this city is fantastic. Even in the dead of winter. Look at the lake."

Isabelle gazed out the window. "The sunlight on the lake water. It's like thousands of—"

"Faeries dancing," he said aloud, remembering that Isabelle had often made that remark about the sun on Indian Lake.

"Yes." She smiled. "You remembered."

"I remember a lot," he replied, clenching his teeth. He remembered New Year's Eve and her revelation that she didn't want a family. She didn't want the same things he did. She didn't want him. That was what he remembered most.

Yet here he was, driving her into the city. Throwing himself into the fire again. Too bad having insta-kids hadn't put out the flames in his heart that still burned for Isabelle.

"Look, Isabelle, I think I should tell you that when we get back to Indian Lake, I'll be getting rid of the truck. So I won't be your delivery service anymore."

Isabelle whirled around. "Scott. I have never thought of you as my delivery service. But if that's how I came across, I'm so, so sorry. I needed your help, but I also wanted to spend the day with you. We haven't had a chance to talk since the children came to live with you—"

"They are demanding." He smiled. "Just as you said they'd be."

"I have to be honest, Scott. I need you with me today. This is crunch time for me and if it goes badly, I want you with me. For…"

"A shoulder to cry on?" he asked, wondering if that was all he'd ever been to her. Maybe that was it. He was "Team Isabelle" and though he did want her to be happy, what he mostly wanted was for her to be happy with *him*.

"Is that awful of me? No. Don't answer that. It is. It's self-centered. I know."

He put his hand over hers. "It's okay, Isabelle. I'm your number one fan. Always have been."

She sighed deeply. "I'm glad I can count on you."

They came to a stoplight and Scott checked the GPS for the next directions.

"By the way, why are you selling the truck?"

"Trading it in. I got a deal on a minivan. My mother found it, actually."

"Theresa is that excited?"

"Yeah, she said she thought it would never happen. Grandchildren." He stole a glance at her and saw her crestfallen look as his words hit. His mother had wanted what all moms her age dreamed of, he supposed. She'd often hinted that she thought Scott should either push for a commitment from Isabelle or move on.

Maybe it was from Theresa that the germ of his decision to take Bella and Michael had grown. "Anyway, she's even getting beds for them at her house, a high chair for Michael for when they come to stay... That stuff all costs a fortune. I'll need a bank loan for everything I've bought and still need to buy for them."

"Oh, Scott."

"I'm kidding. It's not that bad."

Isabelle was quiet for a moment. "I wonder how my mother feels about grandkids."

"Maybe you should ask her sometime." The rest of the drive was mostly silent. When they got to Evanston, Scott parked in the back alley of the gallery and helped Isabelle unload her paintings. Though he hadn't seen the rest of the building yet, the art-filled hallway filled him with awe.

"I like this place," he whispered to Isabelle as they waited for the warehouse attendant to announce them to Malcolm Whitestone.

Scott wandered farther inside, studying bronze sculptures in plexiglass cubes.

"This is amazing." He pointed at a sculpture that looked like twisted glass and bronze ram's horns.

"It's from Russia." A man emerged from a pool of light at the end of the hall. "One of my favorites. I'll die when I actually sell it."

He extended his hand. Scott shook it. "Malcolm Whitestone. And you are?"

"Scott Abbott. Friend of Isabelle Hawks."

"Ah," Malcolm replied with a cocked eyebrow.

"Where do you want me to put Isabelle's paintings?" Scott asked.

"For the time being they'll remain in the back warehouse room. And where is Isabelle?"

"Right here," she said, closing her purse and hoisting the strap onto her shoulder. "Hi, Malcolm. I see you've met Scott." She shook Malcolm's hand.

"I have. And I must say, I admire your taste in men. Very handsome." He looked at Scott again with a discerning scrutiny that made Scott feel as if he were one of the pieces of art. "Hang around, Scott. You make the gallery look good."

Scott bit his tongue so he wouldn't laugh. "Okay."

"Just kidding. Isabelle knows her way around, but how about a tour?"

"I'd love it," Scott replied, slipping his arm through Isabelle's as they followed Malcolm past the offices.

The four private rooms displayed sculpture, watercolors, oils and acrylics. Each had been curated according to theme, Malcolm explained.

"Many of these works must be new acquisitions," Isabelle said. "I don't recall them from my last visit."

"They are. We had quite a good Christmas, I'm happy to say," Malcolm replied proudly. "Frankly, this last room is a bit sparse. I'm gathering our art nouveau works in here. We'll keep it closed off until the show. I understand you have a new piece for me, Isabelle?"

"I do."

Scott noticed there was no excitement in her tone. No gleam in her eye like she always had when she proudly displayed her newest work at the Lodges. She was still anxious and unsure. He put his arm around her waist and hoped she felt his support.

"It's remarkable," Scott said with a wide smile.

Malcolm faced her. "Then I can't wait to see it. Go bring it to me, then, Isabelle. If I like it, we'll find a place for it here immediately."

"Sure." Isabelle hustled back down the hall.

Malcolm clasped his hands behind his back and rocked on his heels. "She shows promise."

"I've always thought that," Scott said, still watching her retreating down the hall.

"And how long have you known her?"

"Since high school. Although we didn't… there wasn't anything serious." He swallowed back a strange lump. Regret? He continued. "I went to Northwestern. Journalism. Then I went to work here in Chicago for the *Trib*."

"Ah!" Malcolm's eyes lit up. "Great publication. Keen on the arts here in Chicago. Their critics are coming to the spring show."

"Is that right?"

"They're tough to please. The *LA Times* is difficult, but these guys here are merciless."

"Merciless," Scott repeated as Isabelle came toward them, her unwrapped painting at her side and her face filled with trepidation.

Malcolm took the painting. "Let's bring it into the light where I can see it properly."

He went to an empty space close to an original Alphonse Mucha poster and propped Isabelle's butterfly-wing faerie up against the wall.

Scott's stomach turned. *Malcolm is comparing Isabelle's work to masterpieces!* How could any newcomer survive competition like that? The gown on her faerie was as good as Gustav Klimt in Scott's opinion, but he was no art critic.

No wonder Isabelle was wary. He'd have a tough time keeping his sanity in a place like this.

He glanced at her. She looked the epitome of

cool and poise. This was what she'd dreamed. She was up to it.

A few weeks ago, BK (before the kids), he would have counseled her about the challenges she would be facing. But she'd chosen this. Not him. It wasn't his place anymore.

Scott took a step closer to the painting. As he peered at it, he realized the faerie was a man. His wings were massive and his near-naked chest and arms resembled the depictions he'd seen of archangels fighting evil. The faerie's tunic was belted with a gold sash. Though the skirt matched the butterfly-like wings, there was no question the faerie was male.

And then he saw its face. Isabelle had painted *his* eyes. The cut of the jaw wasn't as sharp as Scott's and his nose was more prominent. But Scott's own gold-flecked brown eyes stared out at him.

Scott stared at Isabelle in astonishment.

It's me. She's been painting me ever since our "separation." Scott didn't know what else to call the distance that had grown between them.

But she didn't return his gaze.

She was looking over his shoulder.

Scott turned and saw a blond man dressed in tight jeans, cowboy boots and a leather jacket, whose eyes were glued on Isabelle.

"Scott," Malcolm said, "I'd like you to meet my nephew—Wes Adams."

"Great to meet you, Wes," Scott said, offering his hand.

Wes nodded vaguely in Scott's direction before locking eyes with Isabelle once more.

"Isabelle and Wes have already met," Malcolm explained.

Scott dropped his hand to his side. "I can see that."

CHAPTER THIRTEEN

ISABELLE HAD HEARD of it, being caught between the rock and the hard place. She'd never experienced it.

Wes was giving her that laser stare she remembered, as if no one else existed, and for him, maybe they didn't. Scott, surprisingly, did not appear hurt or betrayed, but the curiosity that played across his face was quickly replaced with placidity. She'd seen that face before, when he was interviewing the Indian Lake mayor. It was the expression he used when he was trying to remain objective. See things from a journalistic distance.

At this moment she was just as interested in Scott as she was in Wes's powerful, sensual gaze.

She couldn't quite wrap her head around the fact that Scott had moved on from her. He wanted a different life and he'd grabbed it. Already, she could tell he was immeasurably happy. Whatever her feelings for Scott were, she would have to temper them. He was showing her he didn't need her, and she couldn't afford to fall for a man with such different goals.

Standing in the center of the gallery, she wondered if this was going to be *her* new life. Was Wes drawing her toward her future?

Her eyes tracked from Wes to Scott and then to Malcolm. She couldn't let herself forget the real reason she was here.

"Malcolm didn't tell us you were expected, Wes," she said so sweetly she swore she tasted honey on her lips.

"Fortunately, my uncle did tell me of your appointment," Wes said. "I didn't want to miss you." He strode up to Isabelle, grabbed her by the shoulders and kissed her cheek. "Not even my canvas could keep me away."

He smelled of linseed oil, paint and something spicy that made Isabelle close her eyes. "I'm flattered," she managed to say. She wriggled out of his grasp. "I suppose you'd like to see my first stab at an oil piece."

"Most definitely." His smile was compelling and she felt her earlobes burn and her cheeks flame.

She had to get this situation under control before it combusted. "It's right over here." She stepped back a good two feet and gestured toward the painting. She wanted him to know she was all about the business at hand. "What do you think?"

Whether he suddenly understood her discomfort or was genuinely interested in her work, Wes shot over to the painting. It was as if he'd transformed into another person, as he focused on her work. His eyebrows knitted together, then his features softened. He clasped his hands behind his back in exactly the same manner as Malcolm did, and leaned down with his nose nearly to the canvas as he peered at the intricacies of her work.

Malcolm walked around Scott and stood next to Wes. "Interesting how she made the colors in the wings look transparent."

"Excellent use of light," Wes commented, not taking his eyes from the canvas.

Isabelle's heart thundered in her chest as both men critiqued every line, shade, tone and mood. She didn't realize she was twisting her hands over each other until Scott took one of them, stopping the motion.

She looked up at him, grateful, but he didn't smile. He was still placid. Observing. Yet supporting her.

She had to give him that. He was a rock when she needed a rock. She felt humbled by his graciousness.

"I don't know, uncle." Wes stood back. "It'll

be interesting to see what she can produce by the show. Perhaps with more guidance..."

"I see what you're getting at," Malcolm interrupted, nodding.

Scott whispered to Isabelle, "Do they even remember you're here?"

"I don't think they care. Every word they're saying is true. What they don't know is that I threw out four other tries before coming up with this version. The thing is, I do need guidance—desperately. When I think how bad my first shot at an oil was, I shudder."

"Really? That bad?"

"It wasn't good. And this still isn't good enough."

Malcolm turned back to Isabelle. "I'm going to keep it."

Isabelle was astounded. Her mouth fell open. "Why?" Had she just said that? She'd just been told by a major gallery owner that he liked her painting enough to display and she was questioning his expertise. Yep. She'd lost her mind.

"Because I think I'll sell it, Isabelle. That is the point, you know." Malcolm's tone dripped with condescension.

"I'm sorry." She backpedaled. "It's only that, well, I know I can do so much better."

"Really?" Wes asked. "How so?"

"Now that I've been working with oils, I'd like to interject silver overlays in the next one."

"Try it as an underlay," Wes suggested. "Then gold as an overlay. Try to imitate Klimt because that's where your talent is lending itself."

"Seriously? You see that?" She was elated, yet her excitement was shot through with threads of doubt. Was he really comparing her style to that of an icon?

"I do." His smile was brilliant. Dangerous. Her ears rang. Her heart was singing. She felt as if she could lift right off the earth.

Scott shuffled his feet next to her.

Isabelle felt her future expand before her. Every opportunity was at her fingertips. For so many years she'd been held back by finances and circumstances, her inability to break through to the next level of her own talent. She could do this. She would do this. This time when her heart pounded, it was with joy.

"Then that's what I'll try," she assured both Malcolm and Wes.

Malcolm smiled triumphantly. "That's what I wanted to hear. I do want this one, Isabelle. How many more can you produce in four weeks?"

Isabelle had never been asked such a question. She'd never painted on demand before.

Sure, she'd done this one painting, but she'd killed herself to perfect it in the past month. Only one painting and it had taken her five tries to get there.

The expectant faces around the room, even Scott's, made her nervous and edgy. What if she promised too much? What if she didn't fulfill that promise? Would her showing be rejected? Would her golden chance be obliterated when she'd only just gotten started?

Think, Isabelle.

They waited.

Wes shifted his weight to his right leg. He was getting impatient.

"Three. I can do three."

"In four weeks?" Malcolm asked.

"Yes," she replied confidently. She could do it. She would never sleep. She'd drink smoothies. And lots of Scott's espresso. Somehow she managed to keep a poised smile on her face.

Wes threw his arms up in the air, lunged toward her and hugged her. "Amazing!"

Scott cleared his throat. Loudly.

Wes kissed her cheek again. Isabelle wished he wouldn't do that. Why did he act like Scott was invisible?

Not that she and Scott were a couple. She wasn't even sure how strong their friendship was anymore. Still, his behavior made her uneasy. She didn't mind Wes being himself, but she didn't want to hurt Scott, either.

For the second time, she wriggled out of Wes's embrace.

She turned to Malcolm. "What about the other paintings? I brought them back for you to look at one more time."

Malcolm nodded. "Yes. Let's do that. Wes?"

"Sure." Wes marched ahead of them toward the back room where she and Scott had left her canvases.

Isabelle looked at Scott. "Are you coming?"

"No," he replied with a tilt of his chin toward Wes. "You go ahead. I'm going to look around. I haven't seen the front of the gallery yet."

"Ok—ay." She tried to tamp down her disappointment at his lack of interest in watching the viewing. She was so used to assuming that her needs, her wants, were important to Scott. She knew now that had never been the truth. She'd been self-centered. And she had hurt him.

Wes was holding a canvas up to the light. It was the one of the boy in the sailboat among the stars. "This is the same guy as the butterfly?"

"Uh, yes," she replied, realizing she'd painted Scott twice. She hadn't grasped that until now.

"Scott, right?" Wes asked while Malcolm set aside another of her paintings.

"Yes."

Wes met her gaze as he handed the painting to Malcolm. "This one will sell first," he announced.

Malcolm smiled. "Agreed."

Wes placed his hand on Isabelle's elbow. "My uncle and I have spent a great deal of time discussing you and your talent."

Isabelle swallowed the lump of anticipation that kept rising up in her throat. No matter how many times she beat it back down, it threatened to choke her. Fear of losing out and of never getting her chance had stopped her too many times before. She intended to grab this opportunity, no matter what the cost. "And have you come to any conclusions?"

"Yes." Wes's blue eyes were magnetic, drawing her away from her old life and into her new one. "My uncle will take all your paintings and show them. The public will always decide, you know. If they sell…"

Her skin broke out in goose bumps from her scalp to her toes. *If they sell.*

No. Not "if," she told herself, but "when." When they sold at the spring show, she would have made a name for herself in the art world. She would no longer be a "tourist painter" who could only hope for a weekend sale once or twice a month. Critics would write articles about her. People would value her opinion. She would be somebody. Not just Isabelle Hawks from Indian Lake. She'd be an artist showing in the Whitestone Gallery in Chicago, Illinois.

"Thank you." It was all she could manage. Her mind was full of possibilities.

Isabelle regained her composure and shook Malcolm's hand. "I can't thank you enough for this opportunity, Malcolm. It's a dream come true for me."

"My pleasure," he said. "But understand this. If the paintings don't sell, there's nothing I can do about that and our association will end."

Wes slapped Malcolm on the back. "That's not quite true, Malcolm. If they don't sell, I have a feeling Isabelle will discover a new method and skim off the next layer of her talent. She'll evolve. Improve. That's what I believe."

Isabelle sucked in a breath. She'd never heard such impressive predictions about her future. What did Wes see that she didn't? How did he know she'd have the courage to reinvent herself?

She was fascinated by his insight even more than his handsome looks. All his inappropriate affectionate gestures aside, he seemed to know her in a way she was only discovering. And that intrigued her all the more.

He held out his hand. "Isabelle, good luck over the next month. We'll see you then."

"Thank you, Wes." She withdrew her hand slowly from his.

From the hallway she heard footsteps. When she turned away from Wes, she saw Scott standing in the doorway.

"Ready to go?" he asked.

"Yes," she replied, realizing his expression hadn't altered a bit. His eyes were distant, objective, and he looked at her as if he didn't know her. A chill scurried down her back. She felt as if she'd truly lost her best friend.

CHAPTER FOURTEEN

ISABELLE DROVE DOWN Main Street after spending nearly an hour at the art supply store. Fortunately, they'd had every item on her list. She pulled to a stop at the traffic light east of Scott's bookshop. Parked in front of Scott's store was a large Ryder truck. She blinked and then squinted at it. "A moving van?"

Isabelle flipped her turn signal and swung into the empty space in front of the van. As she approached the door to Scott's apartment, it burst open. Scott emerged, holding the end of one of the sofas she'd chosen, followed a second later by Luke Bosworth carrying the opposite end. They marched the sofa over to truck's loading ramp.

"Scott, hi!" She waved. "Luke. What's going on?"

"Moving," Scott groaned as they placed the couch inside the truck.

Luke was wearing a T-shirt; apparently the February cold didn't faze him. Scott wasn't much better. His woven Henley shirt had long sleeves, at least, but it was quite thin.

"You're moving? Where?"

"I bought a house." Scott beamed with pride.

"A house." Isabelle didn't know what else to say, but she felt vastly unimportant. When had she become the last person Scott confided in?

Anger surged through her, only to be replaced with guilt. She was getting what she wanted. Her gallery showing was less than a month away. Everything in her life was just as she'd planned. She nearly had it all. Why did seeing Scott make her doubt that?

Luke came over and kissed her cheek. "How ya doin'?"

"Fine, Luke. And how's Sarah?"

"Always great. You should call her. She says she never hears from you. Especially with Olivia's wedding coming up and all."

"Right. The wedding. Valentine's day."

Scott tromped down the truck ramp. "Yeah. You know. You're the bridesmaid. I'm the groomsman? That one."

"I haven't forgotten. I've just been so busy."

"I know," Scott said, glancing down at the shoveled and salted sidewalk. He placed his hand on her arm. "But hey, listen. Now that you're here, could you lend us a hand?"

"Oh…" She glanced at her car full of art supplies. "Okay, sure." Tingles of embarrassment shot down her spine. She should have offered to help as soon as she saw them. Whenever Isabelle had purchased anything bulky or unmanageable for her apartment, Scott had been there to help. He'd carried Christmas trees, chairs, art supplies and even a new mattress a couple years ago. Scott was always giving of his time and energy for others—and until recently, Isabelle especially.

Now he was caring for two children who probably needed him more than she ever had.

"My mom's upstairs with the kids. She could use some help packing up. Trent and Austin are coming to help with the rest of the furniture. Do you mind?"

This was getting worse by the minute, she thought. He'd told all his buddies about his move and she didn't know the first detail.

"I'd be glad to," she said.

"Great!"

Isabelle went up the stairs to the apartment. The door was open. "Theresa?" she called.

"In the kitchen. Is that you, Isabelle?"

"It is." Isabelle put her purse on the floor near the window then gave Scott's mother a hug.

Theresa was tall like Scott and though she was in her early sixties, she looked a decade younger. She had the same strong facial structure as Scott and enormous, deep brown eyes. Theresa was striking. Isabelle hadn't realized how much she missed seeing her.

"Oh, honey, you look thin. Are you eating right?"

Isabelle chuckled. "I never could keep much from you, could I? I've been working harder than I ever have and both sleep and food have been low on the priority list."

"Hmm," Theresa murmured. "Scott told me you finally landed the showing you wanted."

"I did," Isabelle replied. "Where are the kids?"

"In the bedroom. I'm hoping Michael will nap. Bella's reading a new book Scott gave her."

"That's good." She looked at the stacks of boxes around the apartment. Luke and Scott started downstairs with the second sofa. The wooden blinds that she and Scott had chosen at the lumberyard store had been taken down from the windows. The silk flower arrangement she'd made for him last summer was nowhere to be seen. For years, she'd bought him antique books on his birthday or at Christmas. Some were first editions, and he'd proudly kept them on the bookshelf next to the fireplace. The bookshelf that was now bare.

Isabelle felt as if she were standing in the

middle of a divorce from a marriage she'd never known. Emotions rioted inside her and her stomach knotted. All she could do was stare.

"I've already emptied the refrigerator but I kept some sodas and bottles of water in the sink under ice." Theresa's voice startled her out of her thoughts. "Would you like something to drink, Isabelle?"

"Drink? No." She studied the bare walls where her paintings used to hang.

"You're a little pale. Maybe some water with electrolytes," Theresa said and went to the sink. She handed a bottle to Isabelle.

Tears pricked Isabelle's eyes as she considered the water. "Maybe I do need this."

Scott came back up the stairs with Luke behind him. Despite the cold, both men were sweating. She held out the bottle to him. "Here. You need this more than I do."

"Thanks." He smiled as his fingers brushed hers. Oddly, she didn't want to let go of the bottle. He tilted his head. "Everything okay?"

"Sure."

He took a long slug.

Luke went to the sink. "No lite beer, huh?" he teased Theresa as he popped the top on a root beer.

Isabelle put her hand on Scott's arm. "When did you buy a house?"

"I closed this morning. Cate found it for me. It's really nice. Or will be when I fix it up. I got such a good deal. Cate said it was because it was February. Nobody buys real estate around here in the dead of winter."

"I'm just surprised. The apartment is so convenient, your shop being right downstairs…"

"That was the problem. The stairs. Michael fell down half a flight a few weeks ago. It was my fault. I'd gone down to get the newspaper and left the upstairs door open. He came running out crying. I think he thought I had left him, and boom! Down he went. I felt horrible. Thank God he didn't hurt himself. He's still got a small lump on his forehead, but the doctor said he's fine."

"Scott, that's awful! I would have been terrified."

"I was. I got on the phone to Trent that night and he put Cate on the line. She'd found me a house by midnight. She said she knew just how I felt." He leaned closer. "Apparently Danny fell like that once when he was a toddler. Kids are resilient, but if Michael had fallen down the full flight, we might not have been so lucky."

"No. Absolutely. I agree with you. Poor Michael."

"After that, Mom has come over every day, but she can't put her life on hold because I've got kids all of a sudden. You know?"

"Right. But who's going to watch them when you're at the store?"

"Me."

"Huh?" She blinked.

"I've got it all worked out." He tapped his temple. "I'm going to expand the bookshop and stock several lines of educational toys. I'm putting in a play area and I'm going to have a storybook hour every afternoon. I'll have events and things for the kids on the weekends. I'm adding healthy treats and drinks for kids to the menu. I have a new advertising campaign figured out. And, I'm going to hire someone."

"Seriously? Can the shop afford employees?"

"I've got that worked out, as well. I've rented this apartment to cover my mortgage, and with the new inventory and focus for the shop, my sales should rise."

Isabelle was dumbfounded. He was on fire with ideas and plans. He radiated happiness.

"This is wonderful, Scott."

He took another slug of water. "I know. It's a lot, isn't it? I think I blew my mom away. But she loves the kids."

"That's great."

"Yeah." He searched her face in a way that made her heart stop.

Isabelle kissed his cheek. She needed to feel

close to him again. She didn't like this chasm between them—the one she'd dug herself.

Right now she didn't understand anything about either of them. Why did she feel the urge to throw her arms around him and hold him for the next several decades? Especially when the life he was pursuing—was already living—was one she'd renounced for herself.

All she knew was that she had a foot in two worlds and neither of them made her happy.

"Scott, I…"

Just then, Bella came down the hall holding Michael.

"Daddy. Michael woke up. I changed him, but he's hungry…" Bella halted and stared at Isabelle.

"Hello, Bella," Isabelle said.

"Hi." Bella tried to hold Michael but he wiggled out of her arms. He toddled straight over to Scott, who picked him up.

Scott covered his cheeks with kisses. "Hey there, munchkin."

Isabelle kept looking at Bella who didn't move from the spot.

"Bella? Are you packed?" Theresa asked, wiping her hands on a towel. Theresa looked at Isabelle. "I bought her two rolling suitcases. They have Disney princesses on them, right, honey?"

"Uh-huh," Bella said.

"Which princesses?" Isabelle asked.

Bella hesitated. "The one with hair like me. And the black-haired one."

"Cinderella and Snow White?"

Bella only stared.

Theresa put her hands on Isabelle's shoulders. "Those are the ones. Isabelle, if you would help Bella pack her and Michael's things, I can finish up the kitchen."

"We have to have the truck back by nine tonight," Scott said. "Or I get charged another day. That's why Austin and Trent are coming over. More hands make fast work." He grinned at Isabelle, a smile just for her.

Curiously, she felt a flutter in her stomach. Or maybe it was her heart. "I'd be happy to help you, Bella. Why don't you show me your room?"

"Okay," she whispered, and led Isabelle down the hall.

Isabelle followed her into the room where she found a brand new wood crib and a single bed with flowery pink sheets and a pink-checked comforter. "This is a nice room," Isabelle said.

Scott had bought a child's chest of drawers, a Cinderella lamp with pink lampshade and a changing table on the far wall for Michael.

The suitcases were next to the bed. Isabelle

picked them up and unzipped them. "Why don't you get me your clothes and I'll pack them for you?" Isabelle asked.

Bella didn't move. She only stared at Isabelle.

Sensing that the little girl was either frightened of her or didn't trust her, Isabelle knelt on the floor next to Bella. "What is it?"

"Are you a mother?"

"No, I'm not. Why?"

"My mother is in jail. She's not coming back."

"I can understand if that makes you sad."

"I'm not sad."

Stunned, Isabelle lifted her hand to touch Bella's cheek, but then thought better of it. "Do you miss her?"

"No."

"You don't?"

"I like it better here without her. Mothers are always sick. And the kids have to take care of them."

Isabelle wondered what Bella had seen or knew about her mother's drug addiction. It wasn't Isabelle's place to interfere or pass judgment. But she did want to get to know this little girl better. "I'm sure your mother loves you and misses you."

"No she doesn't. She told me she never loved me. I asked her."

Isabelle's hand flew to her mouth. She wanted to scream. "She said that?"

"Uh-huh. She didn't want Michael and she didn't want me. She said we got in the way."

This time, Isabelle reached out to touch Bella's hand. "Bella, sometimes people say things they don't mean. Your mother was—is—sick. Maybe now she can get some help. She'll get better."

"I don't care. I don't ever want to see her. I want to stay with Dad."

The magnitude of Scott's quick decision hit Isabelle. Bella didn't think of him as a foster parent or temporary guardian. He was her world.

And how could one take that kind of security and hope away from a child? She knew Scott well enough to be sure he wouldn't turn his back on Bella or Michael. He was a generous man. A man of his word.

When he'd taken Bella and Michael home, he'd signed on for a lifetime. "He's a good dad, isn't he?"

"Yes. He tells us that we're special to him."

"Well, you are special to him. All children are special."

"Really?"

"Yes, Bella, they should be. You know, I have five younger brothers and sisters. They're grown up now, but when they were little, they were special to me. They still are." The words came out of her mouth before she could think them through. Her mother had told her once that when that happened, it was her heart speaking. Isabelle held her breath, wondering if she'd actually meant what she said. Her siblings' faces floated through her mind. She'd always thought they were a burden. But were they?

"I'm glad you're not a mother," Bella said, putting her other hand on top of Isabelle's. The edges of her mouth turned up, but only slightly. Not enough to show love, but just enough to reveal promise.

"Why's that?"

"Because maybe you won't go away," Bella replied with a catch in her voice that told Isabelle she was clutching at hope. Isabelle wasn't about to destroy it.

"I'm not going anywhere, Bella. Scott and I have been friends for a long, long time. You'll see. All our friends here are very close. We take care of each other. That's the way it is with us."

Bella shook her head. "I've only been here a short time. We came from—another town. There was another before that. I can't remember."

"You moved a lot?"

"Yes. But I don't like walking along the highway much."

Isabelle realized they must have hitchhiked across the state. She could only imagine what this child had been through.

Isabelle spoke softly and hoped to reassure her. "Everything is going to be okay, now."

"That's what Dad said."

Isabelle wondered what promises Scott had made to Bella. Was he thinking to petition the court for legal guardianship? And how long would something like that last? What about the legal rights of the mother? When she got out of jail, surely she'd want her kids back. Where would that leave Bella and Michael—not to mention Scott?

Isabelle patted the bed with the suitcase. "I think we should get your things packed. You have a new home to go to. That's very exciting."

Bella stared at the suitcase. "I don't like moving."

"I understand. But you know what? This time it will be different. Scott is there for you. And you have a new grandma—"

"And you, Miss Isabelle? Will you be there, too?"

"Well, no. I have my own apartment and I live by myself. But I'll come visit."

Bella shook her head, blond hair ruffling around her stricken face. "I'm sorry."

"Sorry? Why?"

"I'm sorry you don't have anyone. I'm an orphan." She leveled her eyes on Isabelle. "I saw it in a movie. Orphans don't have anyone."

"But I told you. I have a big family. Lots of people."

"Oh." Bella touched Isabelle's cheek and peered deeply into her eyes. "I couldn't tell."

ISABELLE SPENT THE REST of the afternoon helping Theresa pack the kitchen, clean it and load boxes onto the truck. She helped buckle Michael into his car seat in the back of Scott's new minivan and she promised Bella she would follow them to their new house.

Bella wanted to show Isabelle her bedroom, which she would have all to herself. Isabelle got the impression the little girl was anxious about sleeping alone. She'd always slept with her brother, often in the same room as their mother, as well.

Scott's Craftsman-style bungalow was across the street and a few houses down from Cate and Trent's place. The paint was faded and peeling in places. The windows were dirty, but Isabelle spotted a lovely beveled glass front door. The concrete front steps had recently been patched along what looked like a crack.

"I see you've done some work already," Isabelle said.

"I did quite a few things. Zoey Phillips sent an inspection guy out here from DCS to go over the place."

"And?"

"There are a few more repairs, but I showed them the work orders and once the jobs are finished, they'll run a final check."

Though the sun was starting to fade in the west, Isabelle could see a few shingles were missing. The gutters were full of leaves and needed paint. The hardy evergreens around the front porch softened the sense of neglect. All in all it still looked like it needed a lot of work.

"Good thing it was a bargain," Isabelle mumbled, shaking her head. "I'm worried it's going to be a lot of work. Plus you have the bookshop, the kids, your column…"

Scott came up from behind her, holding Michael in one arm. Bella kept in step with him, never veering more than a few inches from his side.

His expression had lost some of its previous enthusiasm. "Told you it needed some work."

"It needs a wrecking ball."

"I thought of that, too." He laughed. "But we'll be fine. As time goes on, I may renovate. I mean, beyond the necessary fixes."

She gaped at him. "You? Seriously?"

"Why not?" he replied, taking Bella's hand.

"I want the best for my family." He walked up the porch steps.

His family?

She hustled after him.

While Scott unlocked the front door, Luke, Austin and Trent started unloading the truck.

"I came over earlier and turned up the heat, made sure the lights and plumbing were working, I've moved a few things," Scott said as he led Isabelle inside.

Now Isabelle could see why Scott had chosen the house. The living and dining rooms were large; the wood floors were solid, though they needed refinishing. There were three bedrooms, a large main bath and a master bath at the back. The kitchen wasn't large enough to eat in, but if Scott renovated it, he could install a banquette cove. There were no appliances, only a marvelous white porcelain sink that was original to the house along with the glass-door cabinets that ringed the room.

Propped on the counter was a framed certificate for First Aid and CPR along with two workbooks from the DCS. Scott had been doing his foster parent homework.

The sound of Michael's laughter drew her attention to the children. Turning, she saw Bella with her arms outstretched, head thrown back, whirling around in the middle of the living room, laughing and spinning until she was so dizzy she couldn't stand up. She plopped down in the middle of the floor.

"Where do you want these boxes?" Trent asked, coming through the front door.

"Against the wall in the dining room," Scott said, then told Isabelle, "I better help. Can you watch the kids?"

"Uh…"

"Thanks!" Scott bounded outside.

Bella took off running down the hallway to the bedrooms. "Miss Isabelle, do we get to pick our own rooms?"

Michael shot around Isabelle's legs and followed his sister. He pointed to the first room as if claiming it. The pacifier in his mouth twitched and jiggled, and his eyes twinkled. "Da!" He shot into the room.

"Looks like you get the other room," Isabelle said.

Bella frowned. "I wanted that one. It has a tree outside the window."

"I think Michael should have it," Isabelle said as she peered into the opposite room. "This room has southern light. That's a good thing."

"Why?"

"Because all winter long you can watch the sun climb higher in the sky, and it will warm your room right up. Southern sun has more yellow to it in the winter."

"How do you know?"

"I'm an artist," Isabelle explained as Bella considered this.

"Oh."

Michael toddled up and yanked on Isabelle's coat.

"He wants you to pick him up," Bella said.

Isabelle bent down and scooped Michael up in her arms. He put his hand on her cheek and took his pacifier out of his mouth with his other hand. His blue eyes focused on hers in such a way that for a moment Isabelle thought he was trying to communicate with her telepathically. His gaze was intense and eerily unnerving. Isabelle didn't remember any of her siblings looking at her like this. He didn't move his little hand, but rather increased the pressure of his fingers as if holding her face still for him.

Short of Malcolm assessing her paintings, she'd never experienced such scrutiny.

"Is he talking yet?" Isabelle asked, both out of curiosity and to break his deep stare.

"He talks," Bella said. "He learns something new every day."

Michael leaned closer and pressed his mouth on her cheek.

"He likes you." Bella offered a smile.

Isabelle smiled back at the baby. "I like you, too, Michael."

"Love," he said.

Isabelle felt something warm and liquid in the center of her chest. She thought it was her heart melting.

CHAPTER FIFTEEN

ISABELLE'S NERVES WERE wound tighter than piano strings as she walked into Whitestone Gallery with the new oil painting Malcolm had requested.

She'd spent far too many hours helping Scott unpack and not enough time tweaking the painting. By the time the rental truck had been unloaded, Sarah had arrived at Scott's new house with Annie, Timmy and their neighbor Mrs. Beabots, who had brought fresh baked bread, salad and of course her sugar pies. Cate had come over with Danny and a crockpot full of beef and noodles.

They'd sat around on chairs, sofas and the floor, eating from paper plates. Isabelle had noticed that Bella was hesitant around the other children, though they included her in their "kids' circle" on two rolled-up rugs. Theresa had set up Michael's high chair and Scott fed him noodles with a plastic spoon like he'd been feeding toddlers all his life.

Isabelle was still astonished at how casually

all her friends had adjusted to Scott's new family. They'd simply opened their arms to Bella and Michael and had drawn them in.

That was it.

Case closed.

Isabelle knew that was the way it should be with friends. Total acceptance. But she couldn't help her own misgivings and the biting fact that selfishly she missed Scott's attention. She missed even more than that. When she was with him, she felt a bit more positive and hopeful about everything.

There was no one behind the reception desk.

"Hello? Malcolm?"

No answer.

Then she spotted the sign saying the receptionist would return in ten minutes. She shrugged and carried her painting over to an empty pedestal near the door where it would not be in anyone's way.

She sighed. Time really had gotten away from her. It would be easy to blame Scott, his move, the kids, but the truth was, she'd chosen to help him.

Now she was behind schedule, and her painting wasn't where it needed to be.

There was no way she'd get three paintings finished for Malcolm by the spring show's opening on the first of March.

Mercifully, Malcolm had offered to critique her work in progress. The only problem was that he'd only been able to squeeze her in today, Valentine's Day. Olivia's wedding to Rafe Barzonni was at five thirty at St. Mark's Church.

She hated that she'd been so immersed in her painting that she hadn't been available for Olivia. Thankfully, all her girlfriends understood what was at stake for her. They had always cheered her on and told her how much they believed in her.

Her eyes slid to the snow outside. If these bothersome fat flakes didn't let up, they would impede her return to Indian Lake in time for the wedding.

Isabelle had always prided herself on her preparedness. It would have been impossible to raise five siblings and help her mother without being organized and armed with several backup plans at all times.

Isabelle was almost smug about the fact that she'd packed her bridesmaid's dress, shoes, jewelry and makeup in the car.

She glanced toward her parking space and gasped at the winter wonderland developing outside the window. "Oh, come on. The weather app said thirty percent chance of flurries," she groused.

"Those things are never accurate."

Isabelle whirled around. "Wes!"

She'd said his name with far too much en-thusiasm, she realized too late. He was dressed head-to-toe in black, from his wool coat to his black boots. His blue eyes flashed at her and his golden hair gleamed as if burnished with a fresh coat of gold filigree.

How was it possible for a man to radiate this much magnetism? Her heart slammed against her ribs.

I'm acting like a teenager. I need to chill.

"Uh, hi, Wes. How are you?"

"I'm great," he said, walking toward her with a fluidity that reminded her of a jungle cat. On the prowl.

"I see that." Had she just said that? Aloud? Her cheeks were on fire. She must be really at-tractive about now. Burnt to a crisp just look-ing at him. She wished he wouldn't give her that look. A person could turn to ash under that kind of scrutiny. Drop dead. Melt.

Then he put his hand on her shoulder, leaned down and kissed her cheek. It wasn't a light buzz or a peck. He let his lips linger there a moment, and she thought they'd leave a brand on her skin.

Why was she reacting as if she were being kissed by a movie star? A celebrity? It was just Wes.

Then again, he *was* a celebrity in the art world. She'd read an interview with him in the *Chicago Tribune* last Sunday. He was articulate about his work, informed, and the rapport he'd created with the interviewer was relaxed and accommodating. She fully expected the journalist to be here the day of the spring opening.

Wes pulled away, leaving the scent of spice, lemon and paint behind.

She teetered in her shoes.

"I'm, um, here to see your uncle," she choked out.

"I know. He's been delayed. He sent me."

She smiled at him.

He smiled back.

She knew she was being obvious.

So much for being professional. He must think I can't control myself around him. And he'd be right. But what is going on, anyway? Why am I paying more attention to the artist than I am to the art?

He took her arm, cupping her elbow in his strong hand. He held her steady, but his touch was light. Was that how he painted? And what exactly did he paint? She was dying to see his newest work, but she was too shy to ask. He needed to offer to show her first.

"Malcolm trusts me," he said with a twinkle in his eye.

She pressed her fingertips to her temple. Why was Wes having this effect on her? Maybe it was her precarious balance on this precipice between the life she had in Indian Lake and the art world opening up before her.

Wes seemed to be part of this dream she had for herself, which she'd worked so hard to achieve. An established artist, looking at her as if she had value.

"Malcolm trusts you to…" she prompted him.

"To advise you about your work. Yes. Where is it?"

"There by the door." She pointed.

He dropped her arm and whooshed past her as if he were saving the painting from a fire. He grabbed it and hoisted it onto an easel then withdrew a box cutter from the receptionist's desk. He held it up.

"She keeps a drawer full of these."

After making fast work of unswaddling the canvas, Wes stood back and studied the painting. "You're strength is your devotion to detail, and I don't say that lightly, Isabelle. There's something sacred in each water droplet. Each star. I noticed it in your watercolors. With watercolor your strokes are graceful and fluid, yet the renderings are meticulous. You have an extraordinary gift."

The improbability of his words caused her throat to close. She was speechless. And humbled. "Thank...you."

"I mean it," he said enthusiastically, turning that megawatt smile on to her. "I see what my uncle sees, as well. We also see that perhaps you feel confined by watercolors. That's why he's encouraging you to try oils. It's a new skill set, as any new medium would be. Are you comfortable with it?"

She sighed deeply. "Not yet. I feel like I've been thrown into the deep end of the pool and I'm paddling but getting nowhere."

He put both hands on her shoulders. "That's just as it should be. If you didn't feel this way, you'd be terrible at it. You're a fighter, Isabelle. That's what I like about you. Admire..." He seemed about to say more, but stopped himself.

All she wanted to do was throw her arms around him and hug him. Even if the gallery show went badly, she'd had this moment, this accolade from a bona fide, celebrated contemporary artist. That kind of thing didn't happen to Isabelle Hawks.

"I can't wait till my uncle sees this one. It's good, Isabelle."

"Good," she repeated. Though she couldn't believe it, Wes liked her work. It was only a single painting, this lake scene with tiny water sprites hiding under and among the water lilies, at sundown on a late summer evening. Fireflies vied with the faeries as dragonflies swooped across the water, their iridescent wings mirrored in the placid surface. Ribbons of lavender, pink, tangerine, lilac and aqua spun across the sky and looped around the blazing golden sun as it lowered into the horizon. It was the scene she saw evening after evening as she worked the books for Edgar at the Lodges. A thousand scenes like it nestled in her head, dormant, waiting their turn to be brought to life on canvas. Isabelle was their keeper. Their guardian.

"I wouldn't change a thing, Isabelle." Wes's deep, husky voice cut through her thoughts.

"You wouldn't?"

"No. You should leave it. I'll tell my uncle it's a must for the show."

"Oh, Wes!" Impulsively, she grabbed his hand. "That's just…so great of you. So sweet."

"It's not sweet at all. I expect it will bring a good price and my uncle will make a few bucks on you, sweetheart."

She cocked her head and shot him a sideways glance. "You're trying to be mercenary and it's not working."

He grinned sheepishly. "My uncle is always trying to get me to think like a businessman. How'd I do?"

She scrunched her nose. "Not so good."

He shrugged and laughed. "Oh, well. I tried."

He looked over her shoulder. "Uh, Isabelle, I was going to ask you to have lunch with me, but that storm out there…"

She turned, following his gaze out the window.

"I can't even see your car," he said.

"Oh my gosh!" Another inch of snow had accumulated while they'd been talking. "This isn't happening. I have to get back to Indian Lake. I'm the bridesmaid in my girlfriend's wedding this evening."

He looked at his watch. "What time?"

"Five thirty."

"It's twenty after one right now. If it's like this from here to Indiana, you might not make it…even if they don't close the interstate."

"Close? They wouldn't!"

"Give me your keys." He held out his hand.

"Why?"

"Because there's no way I'm letting you drive back to Indiana by yourself in a storm like this."

"But…"

He shook his head. "No arguments." He wiggled his fingers, signaling her to hand over the keys.

Isabelle dug around in her purse and gave him the keys.

Wes. In Indian Lake. All her friends, her family, her mother, Mrs. Beabots—they'd all be at the wedding.

Most important, Scott would be walking her down the aisle.

Lately, despite her determination to express her artistic talent and her desire to plunge forward in her career, she'd been daydreaming more and more frequently about seeing Scott at the wedding. She didn't know if the kids would be with him or not. She'd hoped to have a chance to talk to him.

She wondered if Scott had been looking forward to seeing her.

Right now, as thrilled as she was about her accomplishments, all she wanted was to make it through this snowstorm and see Scott.

CHAPTER SIXTEEN

WES HAD MANEUVERED them out of Evanston, though the snow had already begun to snarl local traffic.

"Here," he said, taking his iPhone out of his coat pocket. He tapped an app with his thumb. "Check this out to see which southbound route is moving."

All the traffic icons seemed to be blinking red. "Surface streets are blocked. The Dan Ryan is nearly at a standstill. Lakeshore Drive is moving well past Grant Park."

"Excellent. The good news is that while we're in the city, the moving cars will actually help with visibility."

Isabelle looked through the windshield, which, between each swipe of the wipers, became covered in fresh snow. Through the lacy snow pattern she could see the red taillights of the car in front of them.

They drove down Sheridan Drive and eased onto Lake Shore. Isabelle couldn't even see Lake Michigan, one of her favorite sights in

Chicago. She'd always been drawn to water. Lakes, especially, held a mystery for her that she could not explain, but endeavored to explore through her art. "Too bad I can't see the lake. I love it."

"Me, too," he said as the light changed and they moved past Grant Park where the traffic picked up speed. "Actually, it's boats that I really love."

"For real? I adore boats."

"I know."

"How do you know?"

"The painting of the boy sailing to the stars."

Scott. Forever Scott. And now he's sailing away from me.

Isabelle's mind skidded to a halt. Had she just thought that? Of course Scott was moving on; he'd made his choices.

Now she had to do the same.

"Do you sail or motor?" Wes asked.

"Uh, neither, actually. I row. Well, I scull with my girlfriends. But I love all boats."

"And if you had your choice?"

She sighed wistfully. "There's nothing so majestic as a sailboat. I've got shelves of history books on sailing, from schooners to clipper ships to catamarans. I scull every weekend with my girlfriends. Uh, in the summer," she quipped.

"Well," he grinned. "Aren't you a surprise."

"Yeah? Why's that?"

"I've been sailing Lake Michigan since, oh, I dunno—since I was six. Seven." His smile vanished and he gripped the steering wheel tighter. "My uncle taught me to sail. It was actually his yacht that I learned in."

Something must have happened to Wes back then. She didn't know him well enough to probe, but if she didn't ask, she might never get to know the real Wes. And she did want to know him. Especially now. He might feature heavily in her future.

"And Malcolm is your father's brother?"

They were moving a bit faster now. Wes straightened in his seat, steered with his right hand and grasped the seat belt with his left hand as if it was constricting him. "Mother's brother. I never knew my father."

She hadn't expected that. "Oh. I'm sorry." She looked down at her hands, regretting her venture down this path. Maybe this was too soon.

Wes, the charismatic artist, the effusive and assertive Chicago celebrity, withdrew like a turtle into his shell. Isabelle watched his transformation with both curiosity and compassion. He'd clearly been hurt back then.

Instantly, she thought of Bella and all the

tragedy she'd seen in her young life. Wes and Bella. Each helped by another human being.

"I didn't mean to pry," she apologized.

"Funny, isn't it?" He blew out through his nostrils. "You asked a conversational question, really, and for anyone else, a simple answer would be expected."

"But you're not just anyone else."

"Apparently not. My mother was an artist, as well. Runs in the family. Talent like ours isn't understood by the—" he swooped his hand across the space between them "—general public."

The misunderstandings that had plagued her all her life seemed to float over her, bringing up uncomfortable memories. "I know the feeling."

"I'm sure you do."

They settled into silence as he turned up the speed on the wipers and they mounted the overpass off Stony Island Drive that would take them to the Chicago Skyway and to the Indiana Toll Road, where they expected the traffic to be lighter and less hazardous than I-94.

The windows were plastered with snow and only the front and rear wipers kept any view of the outside world open to them. Isabelle felt as if she were cocooned inside a mountaintop cabin, warmed by the car's heater as if it were a blazing fireplace and they had nothing to do but…share fragments of themselves with each other.

"She was a hippie, my mother," Wes said. "An aging hippie by the time I arrived, but she'd spent all of the seventies and early eighties in San Francisco painting, living off friends and searching for—something. She decided that 'something' wasn't me once I was school age. When she could still cart me around in a sling over her chest and later in a back carrier and even later in a stroller she'd found at Goodwill, all was fine. I didn't get in her way."

Isabelle stifled a gasp with her hand. Bella's mother had said nearly the same thing. One mother used drugs to escape the world, the other disappeared into her art. Was that what Isabelle had been doing all these years?

She had always believed she had a duty to explore her gift, that she had a responsibility to her own talent. But what happened to that responsibility when others came along? When an artist became a parent? It was why she'd decided long ago that she couldn't have kids of her own.

Wes continued. "Malcolm came to visit one summer while we were living in a shelter. He'd suspected that my mother was on drugs, but she wasn't. She was addicted to her art. Each time she sold a painting she used the money to buy more paint. Another canvas. Not food for me. Not cold medicine when I needed it."

"Oh, Wes." She felt the horror of recognition. "She was me. I mean, I am her. I do that. All my spending money winds up in my next painting."

Lifting his right shoulder, he laughed. "Me, too. Cut from the same cloth."

"You do that?"

"Yeah. Always have. Un-artists, that's what I call lay people, who don't understand us. We would die for our talent. We push ourselves beyond human endurance. We stay up all night and day when we know we should sleep. We don't eat. That fast food burger is a tube of azure blue oil. Instead of saving money, we risk it on that next vision that screams for freedom and exposure and life on our canvas."

"Wes, do you think we're fools?"

His blue eyes flashed in her direction. "We're not like other people, Isabelle. We create something out of nothing. We see worlds that most people can't even dream of." He touched her cheek with his right hand. "You see worlds that I know are there, but I can't see them. You do, though. And that's magic."

Chills scurried down her spine. What he said struck a chord in her. She'd always thought her art was trying to talk to her. Say something. But she didn't know what, exactly.

His hand was warm and strong, and his touch was gentle. She wanted to cover his hand with hers, but she was afraid it was too soon—and too much.

There was no question that something inexplicable and momentous was happening between them. She had to admit she was attracted to him. But she hadn't expected this heartbreaking soul who had clearly overcome any bitterness he might have had and used his past to make his present triumphant.

"Your mom—is she still alive?" Isabelle asked, wanting to redirect the conversation, which was moving in a dangerous direction.

"Yes. She lives in Carmel now. She still paints. Fortunately, Malcolm and I have a friend who owns a gallery where she works, so she has an income and can afford her apartment."

"Do you talk to her?"

"From time to time. Not very much. She feels guilty for foisting me on Malcolm, but I don't blame her. I got in her way. Malcolm was always successful and had money, so he gave me the education I wanted. Took me to Europe nearly every summer."

"That's fantastic. I've always wanted to see Barcelona and Paris. For the light."

"You should," he said firmly. "It's really true that the light in Paris is pink. And it's not from pollution, as so many pundits would tell you. It's been that way for eons."

"And the sailing? When do you sail?"

"Ha! Every chance we get," he said. "Malcolm has always dreamed of harboring the boat in Miami during the winter so we could sail the Atlantic in February."

"Instead, you're getting ready for another showing."

"Yes." He grinned. "And hoping all our paintings sell out."

She matched his smile. "I'd like that, too!"

AFTER SPENDING AN extra two hours on the road, they crept through the blizzard into Indian Lake off the Toll Road and found that the roads in town, though plowed, were snow-covered.

They had agreed Wes would take the South Shore train back to Chicago. As they drove over the railroad overpass coming into the main part of town, Isabelle saw the lighted clock tower on the red sandstone county courthouse building that had been originally built in the 1880s, but she didn't need a reminder of the time. She'd been nervously watching the dashboard clock for the entire trip, afraid they wouldn't make the wedding.

"I've got twenty minutes to get to the church," Isabelle said anxiously.

"How far is it from here?" Wes asked.

"Four blocks."

"So, you'll make it," he assured her.

Isabelle picked up her phone and realized she'd turned it off when she'd entered the gallery. Once it was on, a dozen text messages came through from Scott, Olivia and even her mother. They were all wondering where she was. She'd meant to call one of them from the road, but she'd been so enthralled by Wes, it had completely slipped her mind.

She tapped out replies to Olivia and her mother, letting them know she was moments from the church. She would make the wedding.

Scott's text would be more difficult to respond to. He was worried. And mad.

Why haven't you answered my calls?
Where are you?
Call me. Now.

"Isabelle?" Wes asked. "Do me a favor and check the train schedule? I thought I'd be here for the four forty-five."

"Yeah, we missed that one," she said and

went online. "The next one isn't until six forty-five. Why don't you come inside the church? You've been so kind to drive me home."

"Are you sure?"

"Absolutely."

"Thanks."

He drove up to the church and entered the parking lot. "Are you sure this is okay? A stranger coming to their wedding? I don't want to impose, but…"

"They won't mind. They're wonderful friends. You can sit with my family," she said, gathering her dress, shoes and purse from the back seat. "I have to hurry."

"Let me help," he said, getting out and taking the long garment bag from her. "Be careful of the snow. I don't want you to fall." He took her arm.

They made their way as best they could over the snow and up the church steps.

Isabelle flung open the doors and all thoughts of snowstorms vanished. Inside the church it was spring.

Olivia's mother, Julia, a caterer and wedding planner had lined the center aisle with artificial trees in full blossom. Draped with crystal lights, they glittered and twinkled. Massive bouquets of pink and white flowers with pink bows and streamers adorned every pew. The church was filled with all her friends.

The organist was playing the theme from *Romeo and Juliet* as the groomsmen seated people.

On the bride's side, Isabelle saw her mother and her brothers and sisters. Behind them, Mrs. Beabots sat with Luke Bosworth and his children, Annie and Timmy.

Since Sarah was the matron of honor, she would be in the dressing room, where Isabelle was supposed to be.

Quickly, she turned to Wes. "I see my mother and family." She took his arm. "You can sit with them."

"It's okay. I can stand back here."

"Uh." She hesitated. In two seconds, Scott and the other groomsmen would be back here and she'd have to explain everything. She didn't have time for that. "This is where the wedding party has to stand for the trip down the aisle. It would be best if you sat in the church."

"Okay," he said. "Where do you want me to put your dress?"

"I'll take it." She laid everything down on a table filled with yearly calendars and old Advent prayer books. "Come on."

Isabelle led the way to where her family was sitting. Christopher was sitting closest to the aisle. Isabelle tapped him on the shoulder. "Chris. This is my friend, Wes. He needs to sit with you during the ceremony and then I have to take him to the train station for the six forty-five South Shore."

Christopher's handsome face blazed with curiosity and then blame. "Where have you been? Mom is going nuts."

"I'll let Wes explain. I gotta get dressed."

"Sis!" Christopher started to object.

She jabbed him with her finger. "Be nice." She turned to Wes. "I'll see you after."

"Sure." He grinned with impish delight.

Isabelle rushed up the aisle, scooped her dress and belongings into her arms and charged into the bride's dressing room. "I'm here!"

Olivia's face erupted in relief and joy. "Thank goodness! We all tried calling you."

They were all there, her friends from childhood and adulthood. Her world. Sarah Jensen Bosworth, Maddie Strong Barzonni, Liz Barzonni, Katia McCreary, Sophie Carter and Cate Sullivan. Their eyes were filled with concern and questions. Lots of questions.

"I have to hurry."

"Right! We only have ten minutes!" Olivia said.

Isabelle shimmied into her dress, a pink, tea-length crepe de chine and chiffon gown.

Sarah held out her shoes, while Liz zipped up the dress.

"Honestly, Isabelle, this is too much drama. Even for you. Where were you?" Katia McCreary asked, flipping a long lock of auburn hair over her shoulder while she pinned rhinestones into Isabelle's hair to match the rest of the bridesmaids.

"In Chicago. Then we got caught in this awful snowstorm."

"We?" all the women chorused.

"Uh-huh. Wes and I." Isabelle dug through her makeup kit for lip gloss and blush.

"Who's Wes?" they chorused again.

Isabelle looked up. Wes was the man she'd been bonding with for the past four hours. The man who had captured her spirit.

"He's just the nephew of the gallery owner who's showing my work next month."

Sarah stood, grabbed the blush brush and swept it across Isabelle's cheeks. "Just?"

"He, er, insisted on driving me back to Indian Lake. The storm was so bad. I was afraid they'd close the interstate."

"It's not state of emergency yet, but they're talking about it," Olivia said. "I just hope we can all get to Gina's for the reception before they close everything down. If we're going to be stranded, I hope it's out there. She has room for all of us."

Liz shot Olivia a conspiratorial glance. "There's a hundred people out there. You'd have to give up your wedding bed."

Olivia's eyes widened. "Okay. I'll pray they don't call state of emergency until morning."

Liz put her hand on her hip. "That's when you're supposed to be driving to O'Hare." Olivia and Rafe had planned a honeymoon in Italy.

Olivia picked up Isabelle's nosegay and handed it to her. "Well, I'm glad this Wes, who-ever he is, got you here safely and on time."

Isabelle's smile was thin. "He did."

Just then the door opened and Olivia's mother entered. She rushed over to Isabelle. "I'm so glad you made it. We were all so worried."

"I'm so sorry. I forgot my phone was off."

"Yeah, she was distracted," Liz quipped pointedly.

Julia put her arm around Olivia and smiled at her with so much love it caused Isabelle to wince. If she were ever to have a wedding day, she wondered if her mother would look at her like that.

She thought of Wes's disconnected relation-ship with his mother. Though Isabelle and Connie weren't as close as Olivia and Julia, they were not as distant as Wes and his mother.

With one last swipe of her lip gloss, Isabelle was ready. Together, the bridesmaids hurried to the back of the church, where they would meet the groomsmen to walk down the aisle. Julia would accompany Olivia, who hadn't seen her father since she was a little girl.

Isabelle steeled herself as she approached Scott. Before he had a chance to berate or accuse her, she whispered, "I was in Chicago and Wes graciously offered to drive me home through this terrible storm."

Scott, ever the gentleman, offered his arm, which she took.

"Then I should thank him."

Isabelle felt a stab of guilt. She'd found Wes attractive, interesting and, yes, lovable. It was probably written all over her face. And Scott still looked at her with nothing but appreciation and care.

She held his gaze as she had a hundred times—a thousand times—before, getting lost in those deep brown pools, recognizing every fleck of gold. When he put his hand over hers and caressed her thumb as the organ music swelled, she felt safe.

Scott. Her friend. Her harbor in the night. She'd painted him years ago as the boy in the boat sailing to the stars. That's how she'd seen him then. Free. Exploring vast universes, making an immense mark on the world.

Had she painted Scott or herself?

"How are the kids?" she asked.

"Fine. They're here with my mother. Bella is excited. She's never been to a wedding."

She realized she'd painted Scott accurately. He was changing the world. One life at a time.

"Here we go," he said. "Are you ready?"

"Yes," she replied as she positioned the nosegay at her waist.

They started down the aisle and everyone in the church stood for the procession.

Weddings always made Isabelle anxious. She attended them only when absolutely necessary, though she was happy for Olivia because Olivia truly loved Rafe. And that was okay. Over the past few years her girlfriends were falling in love and getting married. It was the natural course of life for most people, she knew.

But not for me.

All eyes were on her and Scott. Friends beamed at them. She spotted Edgar, and he winked at her.

Odd. He was standing with Charmaine Chalmers—Sarah's boss—and she was looking up at him with a radiant smile. Isabelle had often wondered if there was something between them, but Edgar had never alluded to any particular woman in his life.

At the end of the next pew, Bella sat next to Theresa, who held Michael in her lap. The little boy waved.

Bella wore a silver-blue dress with full skirt and deep blue waist sash. In her blond hair was a pale blue satin ribbon. Isabelle was struck with the thought that Bella had wanted to look like Cinderella.

Isabelle smiled at her and whispered, "Pretty dress."

Bella lit up with pleasure, and Isabelle was surprised at how much the reaction warmed her.

Next, she saw her mother, who watched her but didn't smile. Isabelle's eyes traveled down the pew, and she met the curious gazes of her brothers and sisters. Then she saw Wes.

He stood out from the crowd, his smile as brilliant as a supernova. Isabelle felt a blush rising up her neck and face.

As they reached the altar, Scott murmured, "See you later, gorgeous," before letting go of her arm.

Isabelle took her place across the church from him. She locked eyes with Wes.

Then it hit her.

I'm falling in love with two men. At the same time.

CHAPTER SEVENTEEN

SCOTT WATCHED WES with growing concern. The guy didn't take his eyes off Isabelle during the entire ceremony. When Scott had made his decision to move on with his life and away from Isabelle, he hadn't anticipated how much it would impact him if she fell for someone else. And it was evident she was responding to Wes, judging by her happy smile and the shimmer in her eyes when she looked at him.

Scott's heart pinched painfully. How much more proof did he need that he might lose Isabelle for good?

There was no question in his mind that becoming a foster parent to Bella and Michael was the right thing for him. He'd never been happier or more fulfilled. Every day was an adventure with the kids. Seeing the world through their eyes gave him joy.

Yet all the while, he realized, he'd thought, naively, that Isabelle would come around. She would realize that he loved her and that they were meant to be together.

And he'd made a mistake.

In all their years together, Scott had never fought for Isabelle. He'd been patient. He'd never pushed. He'd wanted her to have her dream.

And now she had it.

As he watched the photographer pose the wedding party for photographs after the ceremony, determination shot through him. He would fight for her.

Isabelle's brother Christopher offered to drive Wes to the train station while Isabelle smiled for pictures.

No chance for Wes to give her a goodbye kiss or more longing gazes, Scott thought. Maybe fate was turning in Scott's favor.

His mother had already taken the kids to the reception at the Barzonni farm, so when the pictures were done, Isabelle offered to drive Scott.

The whole way across town, he listened to her extol Wes's critique of her oil painting. Though he was happy that her work was garnering serious attention, he didn't like the prickly feeling that jealousy planted under his skin.

It was unfamiliar; Isabelle had never so much as flirted with another guy in front of Scott. There had only been him. He should take refuge in that fact, but he didn't.

Wes was exactly the type of guy Isabelle could fall for. They were both artists. That alone was a good foundation for a relationship. "At least the storm is letting up," Isabelle said, breaking into his thoughts.

"And the snowplows are out in full force. You should have no trouble getting home tonight."

"None of us will," she added as they pulled into the Barzonni farm.

As Gina did for every party, winter or summer, the trees around the house and pool were lit with strings of clear twinkling lights. In the middle of winter-dark farmland, the property looked like a galaxy of its own.

"How beautiful," Isabelle said as she parked.

Scott got out and came around to the driver's side as she swung her legs out the door. He reached down and picked up the folds of her skirt. "You don't want to get snow on that dress," he said.

When he took her hand, he felt like her prince. The night was starry, the air was cold and he could hear music drifting from the house.

Scott put his arm around her shoulder. "That little stole isn't enough to keep you warm."

"I know. Bad planning on my part. I was in such a rush to leave for my appointment with Malcolm, I forgot my dress coat."

They hustled into the house where the party was in full swing.

Theresa walked up to Scott and handed him a bawling Michael, while Isabelle was swept away by her girlfriends.

"I've tried everything, Scott," Theresa said, her voice full of frustration. He understood the feeling. He'd wanted some private time with Isabelle and he'd hoped Michael would fall asleep early tonight.

"Maybe he's hungry," Scott said, shifting Michael from one arm to the other, though nothing eased the child's wailing. Scott massaged his little back; Scott himself had always liked a back rub when he was upset.

Isabelle used to do that.

It was an absentminded thing she did. Second nature. If he'd been crouched over his computer too long on a story, she'd rub the tension away, while describing her newest painting to him. She barely seemed to register that her hands were on him. But he knew.

"He just ate. I changed him, but my guess is that all this excitement and upheaval is catching up with him."

Scott studied Michael, who was quieting down now that he had his hand on Scott's cheek. "You okay, buddy?"

Michael shook his head. "No." Then he buried his head in Scott's shoulder, sniffed and let out a huge sigh.

"Hmm." Theresa shot Scott a deliberate look. "Maybe all he wanted was you."

"Possibly. Bella used to be the only one who could quiet him."

"There's something about a father's strong arms that make a child feel safe, Scott. You give that to him."

His mother's words were comforting amid the storm of new experiences, worries and concerns he had to admit he'd been unprepared to face.

"But I do think you're right, Mom. He's been through a lot these past weeks. You can bet he's not used to a party like this."

"Who is?" she teased and then her eyes grew wide as she tugged on Scott's sleeve. "Wait till you see the food! Crab, scallops, beef Wellington. And three bartenders. I've never been to a party like this."

"It's a wedding, Mom, and it's my guess that after Gina's husband died last year, she probably feels like making things happy for Rafe."

"And then some," Theresa added.

"Mom? Where's Bella?"

"Over there with Annie, Timmy and Danny." She'd been pretty shy with other kids, but since they'd moved into the house, Bella had been seeing Danny nearly every day when he came home from school.

Scott smiled. "That's good. It seems like they're helping her come out of her shell."

Mrs. Beabots came up to them holding a flute of pink champagne. "Scott. It's so nice to see you. Theresa, don't you look lovely." She fixed her eyes on Michael. "And how is Michael this fine evening?"

"Cranky," Scott quipped. "I don't think he's a party animal. Bella, however..." He gestured toward the far corner where Bella was giggling with Annie. They were sharing a cupcake. "...is apparently learning how to steal desserts before dinner is served."

"You've certainly got your hands full, don't you, Scott?" Mrs. Beabots peered at him with that unswerving, laser gaze of hers. "Though I have to say, fatherhood appears to agree with you." She turned to Theresa. "You have such a handsome son."

"Thank you."

"I think it's the tux," Scott said. "I've found ladies like tuxes. Even five-year-old ones."

JUST AS DINNER was being served, Michael finally fell asleep and Gina showed Scott to her bedroom where there was a crib and playpen she'd bought for her new grandson, Zeke. He was already curled up on the mattress.

"I'll put Michael in the playpen. I don't want him to wake up Zeke," Scott said.

"Frankly, they'd probably both be fine in the crib. Once Zeke falls asleep, he's out and barely moves till the sun comes up. Gabe and Liz will stay out here tonight so as not to disturb him." She winked at Scott. "Aren't they just adorable? Little ones? I so loved having a large family."

Scott covered Michael with a baby blanket. "You have no regrets?"

"None," she replied. "I wouldn't have wanted any more—four boys…" She rolled her eyes. "They were a handful. Two handfuls. But now, with Rafe and Olivia getting married, well, I'm so happy they're staying here on the farm and making this their life."

"I heard they're building their own house."

"They are! You should ask Rafe to show you the plans sometime."

"I'll do that. I recently bought a house and I'm planning to renovate in the spring."

"How exciting! Isabelle must be thrilled."

Scott froze. Gina didn't know. He'd assumed everyone in their crowd had heard that Isabelle had rejected him. Or he'd rejected her. Honestly, it was a bit of both. They'd parted ways, and there was no going back.

Or did she know something he didn't?

"I think *aghast* was more her reaction when she saw the house. Of course, it was dark and she couldn't see it in its proper light. Lucky thing, too."

Gina took his arm and they tiptoed toward the door. "Oh, don't worry," she whispered. "Isabelle is a sensible girl. Creative. But sensible. You'll see."

Dinner was winding down as Scott finally made it to the buffet table. Toasts were being made. Cake was cut and the string quartet played the first dance for the bride and groom.

Scott had just polished off a stuffed shrimp when he noticed Isabelle at his side.

"Dance with me?"

He couldn't discard his plate fast enough. "I thought that was my line," he said, taking her in his arms and pulling her a bit closer than usual.

"I figured you owed me a dance after our New Year's debacle," she said, tilting her head back to look at him.

Till the day he died, Scott didn't think he'd ever come to a point when a mere glance from Isabelle wouldn't send him to his knees. For so long he'd played his cards close to his chest. He'd waited patiently, hoping she would one day see what was right in front of her. Hoping that maybe, just maybe, she could share her heart with him. But some part of him had always known that her heart was in her painting.

The fact that he was dancing with her was a shock.

Because they'd gone their separate ways, Scott spent a lot of time rehashing the past and what they'd been to each other. They hadn't actually been a couple, though he'd wanted that. He supposed in his mind, he'd been guilty of possessiveness toward Isabelle. He wondered if his presumption had perhaps kept Isabelle at arm's length.

Had he unconsciously sabotaged their relationship?

He'd given her space when she needed it, and even when he felt it was the worst thing for him. But right now, holding Isabelle was a miracle. A Valentine's miracle.

"I got you something," she said.

"No, you didn't. We don't exchange gifts. Remember? One of your…"

She put her fingers over his lips. "It's not like that." She reached under the sash around her waist and pulled out a folded card.

"What's this?" He opened it up. "An invitation?"

"To my showing. It's by invitation only, and I want you to come. You have to be there, Scott."

"I do?" *I do. And I don't.* As her friend, he'd

always supported her. But she had chosen her world of art over him and he couldn't deny that he was heartbroken. He was surprised she'd invited him. He would have thought that Wes would have been enough for her.

Then again, there was a chance that Isabelle was confused. Her invitation told him that she wasn't ready to discard him completely.

"Say you'll come."

"I will." He smiled at her and this time he leaned down and fulfilled a tiny part of his earlier fantasy. He kissed her lightly. It was only a few seconds that their lips met, but it was a strategic move.

"Oh, Scott," she sighed and put her head on his shoulder.

He looked up at the crystal chandelier overhead and smiled to himself.

It had been a good move.

CHAPTER EIGHTEEN

"WHAT BAD TIMING," Scott grumbled under his breath as he held his cell phone in one hand and brushed Bella's hair with the other. "Mom, you can't have the flu. I'm leaving in twenty minutes for Chicago."

"I'm sorry. But I don't want the kids to get this and neither do you."

"You're right, of course."

"Why don't you call one of Isabelle's sisters and ask if she can stay with the kids? Didn't Sadie watch them last Saturday when you had to work?"

"Mom," he replied with exasperation. "All of Isabelle's family will be there. In fact, I think everyone we know in Indian Lake is going."

"Isn't that wonderful? All her friends showing their support like that?" The last word was lost in a fit of coughs.

"It is, Mom. Well, I'll figure something out. Take care of yourself."

"I will. Love you."

"Love you, Mom."

Bella took the brush from Scott's hand before sliding a black velvet headband onto her head. "Gramma's not coming today?"

"No, honey. She's sick."

"Like my mom?" Bella's eyes grew wide with the old fear he hadn't seen her express in two months.

Scott gathered her into his arms and hugged her. "No. She just has the flu. She'll stay in bed, drink hot tea and honey and she'll be fine."

"Promise?"

He tweaked her nose. "I promise." He slapped his thighs. "Well, I guess there's no way around it. I can't miss this show."

"Is it a movie?"

"It's Miss Isabelle's showing of her art. She's worked a very long time on her paintings and she wants me to be there. And since Gramma can't take you, both you and Michael will have to come with me to Chicago."

"Really?" She jumped up and clapped excitedly. "I get to spend the day with you and see Miss Isabelle again."

"You like her, then?"

"Yes."

"Why?"

"A lot of reasons."

Scott glanced at his watch. "We need to hit it.

You get your coat. I'll get Michael. You can tell me the reasons why you like her on the way."

"Okay. And you tell me yours," she said, rushing off to the closet.

ISABELLE DIDN'T KNOW whether to panic or to pray. Her churning stomach was making the case for the former, but she chose the latter.

And staring at her reflection in the bathroom mirror of her Chicago hotel room, she prayed hard.

The day before, she'd driven into the city with her paintings, and despite Malcolm's compliments and assurances that he was pleased with her work, Isabelle knew the jury was still out. She wouldn't be able to relax until she'd sold something.

Isabelle had expected to see Wes yesterday, but he hadn't shown up. He'd called Malcolm several times explaining that he was still tweaking his pieces for the show. She blamed her nerves about her first gallery showing for the excitement she felt each time she heard Malcolm pick up his phone and say his nephew's name.

She was almost surprised at her disappointment when she realized she wouldn't see him before the show. Almost.

A nearly sleepless night of checking the

clock every hour and overthinking every one of her paintings hadn't helped with her emotional state.

She clamped her hands to her cheeks. *Isabelle, what is the matter with you? Terror of critics? I get that. But why does not seeing Wes bother you?*

She blinked. Over the past two weeks, immersed in painting, holed up in her apartment, she hadn't thought about Wes once.

Yet when she hadn't been painting, she'd seen more of Scott these past two weeks than ever before. Well, she hadn't actually spent much time with him, but she'd talked to him on the phone. Run to the grocery late at night for children's cough syrup and more diapers. She'd made macaroni and cheese for the kids. Baked a turkey breast and two vegetable casseroles.

Her empathy for Scott and his situation went deeper than she'd imagined. It had rallied her to action and at the very least she'd proven she wasn't as self-centered as she'd thought.

But here in Chicago, everything reminded her of Wes. His openness with her about his past. The way he was able to focus on her and no one else in the room. The way he made her feel that her passion for her art was a legitimate path in life. She was getting in deep.

She turned on the cold water and splashed some on her face, but it didn't stop her cheeks from burning. She leaned on the sink and pressed her forehead to the mirror. "Isabelle! Get a grip, girl. Wes is a famous artist. You're a beginner and quite obviously untested in the market. Who knows how many protégé types he's met and found uninteresting." Yes, she'd bonded with the man, but she didn't know him. Not really. And mapping uncharted territory made her uncomfortable.

She'd no more than gotten the words out when the vision of Scott's face rose before her.

Scott had told her he would come to the show, and Isabelle realized how much she'd counted on him.

She was torn between her best friend and the man who could offer her a future.

At a time when she should be filled with excitement and even pride for her accomplishments, she'd never felt more adrift. No matter which direction she chose, she would lose something.

"You're here!" Wes swept Isabelle into his arms and kissed her forehead the moment she stepped into the Whitestone Gallery. Just like before, the touch of his lips seemed to brand her. She could no more stop her imagination from going to the next step—a kiss on the mouth—than fly. As she struggled to regain her composure, the door opened and a bevy of fashionably dressed men and women breezed into the gallery as if they owned the place.

Wes dropped his arms, stepped around Isabelle and extended his hands to them. "Consuelo! I can't believe you made it in from Buenos Aires! You said there was a problem with the airlines."

Isabelle stepped aside, hearing French, German and Spanish accents around the room. The entourage apparently all knew each other, and from Wes's gregarious demeanor and the way Malcolm rushed from the back room to the front like a bolt of lightning, Isabelle inferred that they all bought art together.

Clearly, the party had begun.

Waiters, all handsome men in their early twenties, carried silver trays bearing elegant morsels of smoked salmon on toast points, cucumber rounds filled with feta cheese and spicy crab meat and lots of champagne.

Over the next half hour all of Isabelle's family arrived, much to her surprise. "Mom!" Isabelle hugged Connie and rolled her eyes at Violet and Sadie, whose attention was on the waiters and not the art. "I was hoping you'd be here, but I didn't expect you *all* would come."

Connie put her hand to Isabelle's cheek. "That makes me a bit sad. We all love you very much, Isabelle. We wouldn't miss this for the world. This is what you've always dreamed of, and you've worked so hard. I'm so proud of you." Connie hugged her again.

"Thanks, Mom."

Christopher, tall, dark and more handsome than anyone in the gallery except for Wes, perhaps, said, "I suppose your pieces are out of my price range, huh?"

"Just a little."

Ross walked up, wearing a tan sports jacket, camel cashmere sweater and dark khakis, every hair precision cut; he looked every inch the forensic CPA he was. "It wasn't a bad drive up from midtown. I can't stay long. I have a meeting with a client."

"On Saturday?" Isabelle asked.

"It's a divorce case. He's in Vegas for the weekend. My client found a second set of his business accounting books behind the freezer in the garage. Apparently, he didn't think she'd clean back there. Oops." He laughed.

"I thought people kept all that stuff on Quick-Books," Christopher said.

"Not if you're hiding twenty-seven million dollars," Ross replied, taking a sesame thin piled with coconut ceviche off a silver tray. "This is good. Try some," he urged Isabelle.

"I'm too nervous."

"Yeah?" Dylan said from behind her. "So how much is your least expensive piece?" He chuckled, snagging a flute of champagne as a waiter passed.

"Three thousand," she replied. Her brother nearly spat out his drink, and his eyes watered.

Connie's eyes rounded. "I had no idea."

"That's for the watercolors. The oils are more."

"How much more?" Sadie asked.

"A bit." Isabelle didn't want to sound smug, but she felt it. She'd waited for this moment forever.

"Great. When you're rich, I'll get to charge you more for your taxes," Ross joked.

"I do my own, thank you very much," Isabelle shot back, enjoying the camaraderie their newfound respect for her brought. For once, her family wasn't asking her to do something for them. Wait on them. Care for them. They were here to show solidarity. They were proud of her and sincerely hoped she'd succeed.

Or perhaps she was the one whose eyes had opened. Had they always been there for her and she just hadn't seen it? Flashing back to family holiday parties and dinners, she couldn't remember anything but the pressure to get the meal to the table while it was hot. Making sure everyone else was happy.

This time, she was making herself happy.

Violet took Christopher's arm. "Come on, let's go see what three thousand dollars looks like."

"Mine are in the room over to the right." She gestured toward the doorway.

Then she saw Scott enter the gallery. He caught her eye and smiled broadly. Bella held his right hand and Michael had hold of his left.

"Scott." She walked over to him. "You brought the kids."

"I'm sorry, Isabelle. My mom got sick and everyone else I knew to call was either here or on their way. Don't be mad."

"I'm not," she replied and bent toward Bella. "How do you like the gallery?"

Bella's eyes were on everything except Isabelle. "It's a lot of people."

"It is." Isabelle chuckled. "Just ask them to move out of the way so you can see the paintings."

"Did you paint all these, Miss Isabelle?"

Isabelle's smile stretched from ear to ear. "No, sweetie. Just the ones in the art nouveau room. Would you like me to show you?"

Scott unzipped Michael's Cubs jacket and hoisted him into his arms. "Lead the way."

As they headed toward the room, Malcolm intercepted them. He put both hands on Isabelle's shoulders. "Hello, everyone. Scott. Good to see you again. And who is this pretty girl?"

"This is Bella," Scott said. "And Michael."

"Wow, Isabelle, they look like the nymphs in your paintings. But listen, the *Tribune* is here. They want to meet you." He nodded conspiratorially at Scott. "Photos, too." He grasped her chin between his thumb and forefingers. "You look fine. Let's go."

"Bye," she barely got out before Malcolm whisked her away. She felt like she was being led to the gallows.

Five dour faces stared at her as they approached, taking in her apparel, jewelry, shoes, the expression on her face and her manner of walking. She'd read their interviews in past copies of their respective magazines and newspapers. They didn't miss a tick of an eye or a blundered sentence. They were psychologists and investigators and some were embittered artists who couldn't paint but could ruin the lives of those who were brave enough to try.

Isabelle's mouth was a desert. Her brain had crashed ten seconds ago. She could barely remember her own name, much less the brilliant phrases she'd rehearsed to explain her work.

The fact was, Isabelle didn't know what

drove her. She painted because she saw things in her head.

Banal statements like that could kill a career.

She could only hope Malcolm would do the talking.

Malcolm performed the introductions with practiced manners that reminded her of a Regency drawing room scene she'd read in a novel.

No one broke a smile, though they shook her hand. Isabelle wondered if they were as acutely aware of the power they wielded as she was.

Just then Wes walked up and whispered something in Malcolm's ear before rushing away. Malcolm turned to Isabelle. "We have the first sale of the day. It's your boy sailing through the stars."

"Really?" One of the critics, a scrawny man with a drawn face, perked up. "Do we know the purchaser?"

"Yes. Rudolph Gethsman. From Munich."

"Gethsman is here?" the critic asked, finally taking out a pad and gold Cross pen from his lapel pocket.

Now he was going to work. Isabelle took it as a good sign. If her family or friends had pitched in to buy a painting to make her look good, these reporters would have discovered it immediately. Malcolm wouldn't lie in front of them; if he did, both their careers would be shot.

Malcolm rocked back on his heels. "And Jacqueline Dubois is here from Paris. She's redecorating her Île de la Cité apartment and, supposedly, a new seaside pied-à-terre. She's looking at several of Isabelle's works for the new place."

Three more critics reached into their purses and briefcases for recording devices, cameras and iPads to take notes. Suddenly, they broke ranks and scattered.

Isabelle hadn't said a word.

Malcolm leaned in. "Go mingle and get in that room. I expect you to help sell. If anyone wants to commission anything…agree. Got it?"

"Got it," she replied as Malcolm whooshed away.

ISABELLE COULDN'T BELIEVE the number of people who came and went from the gallery in the next hour. Wes and Malcolm introduced her to so many collectors and dealers, the names and faces blurred and her hand was sore from all the congratulatory handshakes she'd received.

Best of all, her friends from Indian Lake had come to the viewing. Sarah and Luke drove up with the kids plus Trent, Cate and Danny.

They all planned to go to Maddie's Cupcakes and Cappuccino afterward.

At one point, Sarah took Isabelle aside.

"There's something I need to tell you," she whispered.

"Is everything okay?" Isabelle asked, suddenly anxious for her friend.

Sarah burst into a huge smile. "Yes, more than okay. Isabelle...I'm pregnant. Not everyone knows yet. Luke and I are planning a celebratory dinner party to make the announcement next week. Will you come?"

"Of course, I'll be there." Isabelle wrapped Sarah in a hug. "When did you find out?"

"Just the other day. I've suspected for several weeks, though. With the holidays and then the new medical clinic we just designed, I've been so busy. I've barely known what day of the week it was, much less the time of the month." Sarah laughed.

Isabelle hugged her again. "Make sure you get approval from your doctor to scull with us this spring."

"I will." Sarah beamed.

"I'm really happy for you, Sarah. This is what you wanted."

Sarah put her hand over Isabelle's. "It is."

Together they walked to the door as Mrs. Beabots arrived. She'd ridden up with Katia and

Austin McCreary in Austin's Rolls-Royce Silver Cloud. Austin promised to take them all to Spiaggia for an early dinner.

Mrs. Beabots lifted a flute of champagne from a waiter's silver tray. "I like the orchids on the trays. Nice touch. Anyway, Isabelle, all I did was tell Austin that I wanted spaghetti and meatballs. He insisted we go to Spiaggia."

"It's the best in town," Wes interrupted as he came up and placed his hand on Isabelle's elbow. "Sorry to intrude, but we just sold two more of your paintings. We need you," he said.

Mrs. Beabots beamed at her. "I'm so happy for you, Isabelle. You go. This is your time. Drink it in!"

Isabelle slipped away and introduced herself to a small group of Belgian buyers. Wes explained that they owned a small shop in Brussels not far from the art nouveau house of architect Victor Horta.

A man in a colorful vest that reminded her of a Van Gogh painting handed her a business card. "We're interested in more pieces—for the future."

"Yes. But our buyers have specific requests sometimes," his colleague put in. Her black mink coat gleamed in the soft gallery lighting.

"I'd be happy to discuss them with you," Isabelle assured her. "Here's my card with my email."

The ringing of a bell drew everyone's attention to the center of the room, where Malcolm stood.

"May I have your attention, everyone."

The chattering died down.

"As you know, Whitestone Gallery is always on the lookout...some would say prowl..." He laughed.

Twitters of amusement rose and subsided as if on cue.

He continued, "...for new talent. This season we are showcasing three artists. My nephew, Wes Adams, some of you may know. Certainly, our friends from the *Chicago Tribune* and *Art World* magazine know him." Malcolm gestured toward the critics. "Thank you for your support. I'm happy to announce that Wes provided us with five paintings for this show, and as of fifteen minutes ago, they have all sold."

Applause erupted. Oohs and aahs rumbled across the room.

Isabelle searched for Wes in the crowd, and spotted him accepting hugs and slaps on the back, absorbing the good news. Then she spotted Scott leaning against the door frame leading to the room that housed her pieces.

He wore that neutral expression she was

coming to dislike. He didn't take his eyes off her—not even as Malcolm spoke.

"Another artist, Saul Grover from New York, sent one painting that arrived at the last minute. Though it's not in the program, it has sold, as well. Lastly, we are introducing Isabelle Hawks from Indian Lake, Indiana. We are proud to announce that four of her paintings have sold. Congratulations, Isabelle."

A cacophony of applause filled the room. She assumed most of it was from her family and friends. Christopher actually put his fingers in his mouth and whistled. She couldn't help but laugh. He'd always been such a goofball. She was stunned at how much her heart swelled seeing their smiling faces.

Tears filled her eyes and her throat burned with love for her mother, her brothers and sisters and her friends. She was speechless.

Mrs. Beabots walked over and handed her a white handkerchief. She dabbed her eyes and noticed the Coco Chanel logo on the corner. She handed it back.

"Keep it. To remind you of this moment. These tears."

Isabelle hugged her. How was it that Mrs. Beabots always knew exactly what someone was thinking at the moment they were thinking it?

"Thank you."

When she straightened, her eyes went to Scott. His bland expression had been replaced with defeat and loss, though he still kept his eyes on her. As if he had realized, like her, just how much the roads they'd chosen had diverged.

Malcolm cleared his throat and hushed the crowd again. "I've only done this once before, as many of you know. And because it was Wes, many of you—" he nodded toward the critics "—thought it was because he's my nephew. Not true. I believe that when I see talent and it needs a bit of nurturing, it's my job, my honor and mission in this life to encourage and support it. That said, Isabelle, would you come over here?"

"Uh, sure," she replied, threading through the crush of people to stand beside him.

"I'm making the formal announcement that I've selected Isabelle Hawks to be my protégé. Isabelle, I will provide a studio and housing for your use on the weekends. You will have everything you need to hone your craft to the utmost of your talent."

The reporters snapped photos and made notes. The buyers and crowd applauded. Isabelle's family stood stunned and then clapped. Her friends smiled and cheered.

"What do you say to my proposal, Isabelle?" Malcolm beamed.

Unprepared for a total life change in a single afternoon, Isabelle swallowed hard. *This is how it happens. In a nanosecond. Just like Scott's decision to foster the kids...*

There was only one answer that would make her dreams comes true.

"Yes," she replied.

Malcolm wrapped her in a fierce bear hug.

Over his shoulder, she watched Scott put his empty flute down on a folding tray with other discarded glasses. He caught her gaze then lifted Michael into his arms and gave Bella's shoulder a tap. He pointed toward the door. Looking back at Isabelle, he gave her a two finger salute and left.

CHAPTER NINETEEN

"I NEED YOU," Scott said into the phone several days later.

Isabelle knew that her answer to Malcolm's offer had surprised Scott, judging by his abrupt departure from the show. She would never forget the wounded look on his face, as if he'd lost her as a friend. Once all the guests had left that evening, she'd taken the first opportunity to call him and assure him she would only be in Chicago on the weekends. All he'd said was, "That's good news."

After that response, she was surprised he was calling her now.

"You do?" she answered, looking down at the perfect, dusty green color she'd just blended for a new painting. She still had her easel set up in her apartment; though Malcolm had provided a studio and small living space for her in Chicago, she only had access on weekends. A student at the Art Institute of Chicago lived there during the week. Malcolm certainly used his assets to their full extent, she thought.

She stood back to examine her work. She was in the middle of painting a woman lying in a spring forest glen, with tiny plant faeries peeking out from moss, lily of the valley and daffodil leaves. The dewdrops she painted as pearls. "Scott, I can't."

"You're the only one who can. I've got two truckloads of toys, books and games. I've got kid furniture, an indoor wood slide and I don't know how to arrange it all so it doesn't look like a junkyard."

She dipped her camel hair brush in the green paint and dabbed at the canvas. "It's for kids, right? They won't care. Trust me. They'll play on whatever you have, wherever you place it."

"Isabelle. You have special skills. You're an artist. You have an eye."

"I have a deadline, Scott," she replied, putting the brush down.

"Hey! Bella! Don't touch that." She heard a commotion in the background. "Put it down. Now!"

"What's going on?"

"She just picked up the box cutter."

Isabelle sighed. "I'll be right over."

ISABELLE PRACTICALLY FLEW in the front door of Scott's store and came face-to-face with a six-foot-high stack of boxes.

"Scott?"

"Back here! Michael had to be changed."

She maneuvered through the maze of new deliveries and found Scott crouched on the floor and pulling a new pair of pants onto the toddler.

Michael stood up and pointed at Isabelle while gripping Scott's sleeve. "Issa."

"Wow. He called you by name," Scott said.

Isabelle cocked an eyebrow. "But still wary of strangers, I see."

"He just woke up from his nap. He'll come around in time," Scott said, getting to his feet.

Bella raced over to them. "Miss Isabelle! You're here." She glanced at Scott. "Good. Dad needs help."

Isabelle couldn't agree more. There was hardly room to move in here. Except for the front counter area, which was still cleared so that Scott could wait on customers, the shop was stuffed with boxes, furniture and inventory. "You need more than my help. Scott, this is a disaster."

"I know. I bit off more than I could chew. I thought I was doing great and then the play yard things arrived."

Bella looked up at Isabelle with expectant blue eyes. "He bought a slide. Like at McDonald's."

"No," Scott assured Isabelle, whose eyes had grown wide. "Not like that. This is a little kid's slide. Waxed and sanded. Guaranteed not to splinter. And it's not steep enough to cause injury. But I bought a cushion to put at the base— to be safe." He grinned sheepishly.

"Good thinking," she said, taking off her jacket. She was still wearing her painting smock.

"You did rush over," Scott remarked.

"Frankly, I was expecting blood." She put her hand on Bella's head. "Thank goodness that's not the case."

"I wanted to see the slide," Bella said remorsefully.

"I told you it has to wait until I get these other boxes unpacked. I have to move things around." Scott raked a hand through his hair. His eyes were pleading when he took Isabelle's arm and pulled her aside. "I'm sorry to drag you into this. I know how busy you are, but I'm drowning."

She supposed it had to happen sometime. He was crashing. He looked tired. She remembered all too well her sleepless nights with teething toddlers. She was impressed he'd done as well as he had, adjusting to the kids and their needs, the new house and now this bookshop redesign.

She looked at her watch. "I'll give you two hours, but that's all. I'm behind myself. Okay?"

"Deal," he said and kissed her softly. "You're the best."

She studied him. "You really think so?"

She was amazed at how she pinned so much hope on the look in his eyes, his smile. His words. He'd made a monumental life decision without her, but now she understood so much more. She'd already come to care about the children, and she knew in her heart that becoming a dad was the right thing for Scott. He was happy—even happier than she was.

She was a bundle of nerves most of the time, but at moments like this, with Scott, all her concerns melted away.

And the chasm they'd dug between them, which had only seemed to widen since New Year's, had healed.

He lifted his hand to her cheek and traced her jawline. "I do."

"When you left the gallery, I was afraid you were angry with me."

"I shouldn't have done that," he said.

"No?"

"It was my insecurity. You belong there, Isabelle. All those critics raving over your work. I'm proud of you."

Her breath caught in her chest with a spreading warmth. His words had more impact than all the reviews and accolades she'd received for the show. "Thank you, Scott. That means a lot to me. So much."

"Good," he said and kissed her again, only this kiss lingered. She got the impression he didn't want to stop.

Neither did she.

"Dad?" Bella was standing right below Scott's elbow.

"What?" Scott's eyes reluctantly left Isabelle's face.

"Are you still mad at me?"

"No," Scott replied. "And I wasn't angry. I was afraid you'd hurt yourself."

"Oh."

"I'm sorry for yelling. Sometimes adults seem mad when they're actually scared," Scott said, putting his hand on her shoulder affectionately. "I don't think I could ever be angry with you, Bella."

Bella's lips trembled. "I used to make my mom mad all the time."

Isabelle knelt next to her and put her arm around the little girl's waist. "That wasn't your fault, Bella. And now we have happy things to work on. Like getting this slide out of the box and put together for you. Right?"

Bella nodded.

Michael clapped his hands together. "Yay! Toys!"

Isabelle looked up at Scott. "He catches on quick."

While Scott unpacked the furniture, new bookcases and, of course, the slide, Isabelle took stock of the space.

She helped Scott put the slide together, and mercifully it wasn't difficult. The little chairs came preassembled. The shelves took a bit longer, but soon they had everything ready to place.

Isabelle showed Scott her layout of the new children's area, which she'd drawn on a piece of paper. "You can divide the room in half using the bookcases to distinguish between the play area and your storybook section. The slide will go here, closer to the back wall. Do you have an easel?"

"No. What for?"

"I'll bring you one of mine. Kids love to draw. All you need is one of those huge pads of drawing paper and some crayons or cheap watercolors. I've got a couple aprons to get you started. Could we take a couple of the kids' tables you already have and put out coloring books and crayons? Not the expensive coloring books you sell, but something they can tear out the pages from and take home."

"I like that," he said. "I've got a supplier for those. I hadn't thought of it before."

"Great. Then the little chairs we'll put in a

semicircle around an adult chair, which will be where you or whoever reads to the kids can sit. Too bad you don't have a crown to wear for that."

"I don't need a crown," he argued. "It's too much."

Bella, who had been reading a Cinderella pop-up book, looked up at Scott. "She's right. You should have a crown."

Isabelle scrunched her nose at Scott. "I can order one online."

"Forget it. I'm not wearing a crown."

Isabelle put her fist on her hip. "Fine. Then order small crowns for all the kids."

"Will you forget the crown thing?"

"No. And why should I?"

"It's dumb."

"It's not. It shows that you're special and the kids need to be made to feel special, too. Kids like hats and crowns."

Michael was playing with a set of blocks. He stopped mid-motion, hearing their argument, and started crying. Bella scrambled away from her book and went to her brother. She put her arms around him and drew him close.

"Stop fighting. Please. It upsets him when people fight. Me, too," she said sharply, kissing Michael's cheek.

Isabelle glared at Scott. She cocked her head toward the kids. "Apologize."

Scott sighed and sat on the floor next to Bella. He took Michael from her and put his palm on Bella's cheek. "I'm sorry. I don't want to upset you or Michael." He met Isabelle's eyes. "I guess I'm tired. And all this—" he gestured with his free arm "—was getting to me."

"I understand," Isabelle said. "The kids are tired, too."

"I'm hungry," Bella sniffed.

"I'll get you a snack." Scott put Michael back on the floor and rose.

Isabelle glanced at the clock on the wall over the front windows. "Scott. It's past lunchtime. They have to be starving."

He shook his head. "I guess we lost track. I made peanut butter and jelly sandwiches."

"What else?"

"And milk." He shrugged. "Since Mom's had the flu, I haven't gotten to the grocery store like I normally do. I was planning…"

Isabelle put her hand on his arm to stop him. "Listen. I'll keep working here and stay with the kids. You go down to the deli and ask Olivia for some cut-up fruit. A banana for Michael. Ask her if they have their chicken noodle soup and get a quart. Then you'll have leftovers for dinner tonight."

He tapped his temple. "Good thinking." He went to the coat rack by the front door and took his jacket. "Back soon!"

After Scott left, Isabelle began moving the bookcases into place. Empty as they were, they were easy to slide across the floor. "Bella, would you move all those little chairs over to this side of the room? I'll let you arrange them for me. I think four to a table would be good."

Bella just stared at her. "I don't know what you mean."

"Do you know how to count, Bella?"

"Uh-huh."

"How far can you count?"

She held up both hands. "Ten."

"Okay. Then four are the fingers on one hand minus your thumb, right?"

"Yes." She looked down at her hand.

"Then I want you to count out four chairs and put them at the tables. Here, I'll show you. We'll do it together."

Isabelle took Bella's hand and walked over to a stack of little plastic chairs. She showed Bella how to place the chairs.

"I can do that," Bella replied confidently.

"Good. Then I'll leave that task to you while I move the slide into place."

Bella finished placing all the chairs.

"Excellent job, Bella. Give me a fist bump."

"What?"

"I'll show you," Isabelle said. "This is what kids do when they really like something. Adults do it, too. Mostly men."

She curled Bella's fingers into a fist and then with her own fist she "bumped" Bella's hand.

Scott returned with the fruit and two salads for Isabelle and himself. They set up their lunch at one of the larger "adult" tables. Scott had invested in two wood high chairs for the shop and he put Michael in one.

"This is amazing, Isabelle," he said, opening a small container of milk for Bella and inserting a straw. "It's like you're one of your elves or faeries. I walked to the deli and when I came back—poof!" He munched on a carrot. "The shop is all in place. It's magic."

"Well, there is still all the inventory. That's your expertise," she replied, cutting up the banana into bite-sized pieces and putting them on Michael's tray. The baby picked them up expertly and ate them, smiling after each bite.

"He's a fan of banana, huh?" Isabelle asked.

"Yeah. Loves them. DCS gave me booklets about food for the kids. I took a nutrition course at night in addition to my required parenting class. Mom watched the kids," he added. "Speaking of Mom, she constantly tells me she is the world's foremost expert on babies. She had me," he teased.

"Well they both look healthy," Isabelle said, wiping her hands on a paper napkin.

Scott smiled humbly. "Since he's twenty months now, it's time for him to start transitioning to table food. He needs to learn to eat what we eat."

"Even peanut butter and jelly?" Bella asked.

"Yes," Isabelle put in. "He will love it. But Scott, go easy on the jelly," she instructed.

"Deal," he replied.

"After we finish lunch, I have to go," Isabelle announced. "I'd planned to be here two hours and it's been four."

Scott stopped chewing.

Isabelle had seen this look before. His brown eyes were as innocent and guileless as a child's. She read hope and hurt, longing and need…and something deeper, something that sent a zing straight to her heart.

Her heart was that dangerous organ that told her a life with Scott would make her happy. Her heart could so easily sabotage everything she'd worked for.

With Malcolm's support, she had the chance to spread her wings. If she allowed her heart to guide her decisions, she'd wind up coming full circle, returning to the life she'd had as a kid, taking care of her siblings.

There was a reason she'd stayed for four hours, she realized now. It was comfortable being with Scott and getting to know Bella and Michael. It was easy, simple, yet at the same time it was treacherous. It was too easy for her work to plummet to the bottom of her priority list. She couldn't let that happen.

She wiped her hands on a paper napkin. "I think you can handle just about anything now, Scott. Don't you?"

He held his fork just above the Styrofoam box of salad then sat back, still holding her with that look. "Yeah. I've got it."

"Good," she said. "Mind if I take this with me?" She closed the lid on her salad.

"No. Go right ahead."

Isabelle rose. She smoothed the soft cap of hair on Michael's head. This time he didn't duck away from her touch. Maybe he was warming to strangers. To her.

She turned to Bella. "You be a good girl, okay? And keep practicing your counting. Your daddy will need your help with the inventory."

She put on her coat. "See you," she said to Scott.

He didn't say a word. She could tell by his expression that he knew she was running away.

She knew it, too.

THAT NIGHT, AFTER Scott put the kids to bed he went to the living room and sat on the sofa looking up at one of Isabelle's faerie paintings, which she'd given him years ago. He'd always loved her paintings, but he knew she was driven by some inner passion to excel. Isabelle would never be satisfied with what she'd accomplished yesterday.

She was all about setting goals and pushing her limits.

It was one of the things that had drawn him to her. He'd been like that once, back at the *Tribune*. He'd pushed and challenged himself. He'd raised his own bar.

"That's why I want you to do this, Isabelle," he said aloud, raising his coffee mug to the painting.

Isabelle was right. This was her chance. And she'd been courageous to take it. He admired her for that.

He could also tell she was a bundle of conflict. He'd seen that today at the shop. She'd delayed going back to her easel because she'd wanted to spend time with him and the kids. She'd laughed and bonded with Bella and Michael and for a few precious moments, he'd slipped into that delusion that they were a family.

But we're not. Not yet.

Scott was aware that Wes was attracted to Isabelle, but did she see him as anything more than a famous artist? He imagined it was tough for a protégé not to be swayed by the lure of success. After all, that's what Isabelle had always wanted—to be the best she could be.

Wes and his uncle could give that to her. Scott couldn't.

He was just a guy who'd loved her for a long time.

He took a long, thoughtful sip of his coffee. When he'd kissed her today, Scott believed something significant had changed between them.

She'd looked at him with an appreciation he hadn't seen before.

When she interacted with the kids, she'd been kind and caring. For a woman who claimed she didn't want children, she certainly could have fooled him.

He'd always known she was giving and generous. He'd seen that with her girlfriends and her family. And with him. As much as he'd sometimes been frustrated by her lack of recognition for how much he did for her, he had to admit that she'd returned his favors in her own way. Like gifting him with her paintings. The times when she helped fill in at the bookshop when he was short-handed. Since the kids had come to live with him, she'd been even more generous.

It was possible that her new opportunity with her art was allowing her to look at every part of her life. And if he was part of that equation, so much the better.

These past months had been an eye-opener for him, too. He must have lost his mind thinking that becoming a father would fill up his life.

He loved the kids. They fulfilled him in a way nothing had before. But they hadn't pushed Isabelle out of his heart.

He finished the coffee.

He had a new house, children and a new perspective. But that place he'd carved out for Isabelle was still there, and it was cavernous.

He would never truly be happy until she came to stay. Forever.

CHAPTER TWENTY

Isabelle clutched at the collar of her white wool coat as she trudged through a strong March wind, lugging her wire cart filled with paints and a canvas toward Malcolm's studio.

It was a miserable slate gray day that wouldn't give her much in the way of natural light, she thought as she reached the red brick building. She guessed the place had been built in the late 1930s, before the war. The symmetrical square windows punched into the exterior walls looked like vacant, hopeless eyes. As she took out the key Malcolm had given her, she scoffed at herself for the grandiose images she'd had about what an artist's studio would look like. This was no more than an old workshop in need of rehabilitation.

She slipped her key into the lock and it spun. The door was unlocked. She pushed inward.

Loud classical music poured into the entryway. The energy of Wagner's *Tannhäuser Overture*, with vibrant violins that made her think of bumblebees, was familiar to her. She crept down the dark paneled hall toward the open door at the end.

Light flooded out, pulling her forward. She parked the wire cart beside the door and slipped into the studio.

She felt like an intruder on a sacred ritual as she watched a barefooted Wes, dressed in a black T-shirt and jeans, fling black paint onto a huge canvas on the floor, moving to the music. Floor-to-ceiling canvases reminiscent of Jackson Pollock creations hung on three of the walls.

She withdrew into the shadow of the doorway to watch him work.

He was in his element. As the music rose to a crescendo and the tubas boomed, Wes lunged at the canvas like he was a fencer and the paint stick was his foil. With a flick of his wrist, he sent the paint across the surface in a horizontal line.

Isabelle scooted down to a crouch and hugged her knees to her chin, trying to absorb all that Wes was creating.

He splashed vortexes of black, red, amber, blue-gray and tonal white that gave a luminance to the entire work.

Another classical piece began with a staccato movement that caused Wes to jerk and flick his paint onto the canvas. He changed colors as the violins, piano and other strings segued to a moderately fast tempo.

Amazingly, the crimson blotches were symmetrical, each forming a precise "tail" in perfect alignment with each other as a geometric pattern began to form.

Isabelle didn't dare announce her presence or the fact that she'd come here to paint, as well. Her work, her canvas would remain blank for today, but her mind would not. With each of his movements and the corresponding marks on the canvas, Wes was teaching her to think differently. She could almost feel her craft expanding. Wes was every inch the master and she was the pupil—even though he wasn't aware of it yet.

He grabbed another stick, this one coated with gray, and dipped it in a can of white. When he pulled it out, it revealed an interesting tone, like the smoky fog that whorled off Indian Lake in the winter. It was one of her favorite colors and sometimes if she looked closely between the lily pads and cattails, she would imagine a tiny water sprite waiting for discovery.

Isabelle cocked her head, content to watch and absorb. Time had no purpose in this place, she knew. This was the artist's dimension. The hours passed or they didn't. There were no responsibilities to others here, only the duty to art. To one's talent.

Few understood that duty, or what it meant to her. Probably not even Scott.

The light in the room changed, and Isabelle lifted her gaze to the ceiling. Long panels of glass stretched across it without any shade or blinds to cut off the light. She'd been watching Wes for so long that the clouds had drifted away, revealing a clear blue sky.

Isabelle let out a small gasp as she took in the beauty of it.

Wes froze. He stepped back and withdrew his arm from its position over the canvas so as not to dribble paint on a place it wasn't meant to be.

"Who's there?"

He spun around, his eyes glazed and unfocused, as if he'd just awoken from a dream. She knew that kind of disorientation. It would take him a minute to see her.

"Oh, my gosh, Wes. I'm so sorry." She rose from her crouch, her limbs stiff.

"Isabelle?"

"Hi," she said, stepping toward him. "Didn't Malcolm tell you I'd be here today?"

"Er. Uh. Yes." He put the paint can on a bench and laid the stick over it. He picked up a rag and wiped his hands. His eyes were still dazed. He stepped around the canvas. "I came in early to get a head start. I guess I forgot the time. How long have you been here?" He glanced down at his wrist but he wasn't wearing his watch. He ran a hand through his hair. "Guess I forgot a few things this morning." He chuckled.

"I see that." She looked around him at the painting. "It's magnificent." She gestured toward the canvases on the walls. "They all are."

"Mediocre," he grumbled. "I know I can do better."

"You're not satisfied?"

"It's a fault of mine, I know. Malcolm tells me that my critical eye will drown my creative eye and one day, I'll go blind."

Isabelle laughed. "I hate that he's so astute."

Wes moved up behind her, staring at his painting from over her shoulder. "What do you really think of this? Be merciless."

But she couldn't focus on the art at all. If she was honest, all she could think about was his spicy scent, the heat she could feel right through her wool coat. He was too attractive. And she had to put her attraction to him aside.

This is work, Isabelle.

He put his hand on her shoulder.

She wished he wouldn't do that. He wasn't helping the situation.

She stepped away from him. "I already told you—it's magnificent. But my opinion means nothing. Wes, seriously. This is what we do, isn't it? We throw our total selves onto a canvas." Turning, she tapped his chest. "It's what's in here that matters. And how it flows into the work."

Wes shoved his hands in his pockets. "When you put it that way…" He looked into her eyes. "You said magnificent." His voice was solemn and direct.

Isabelle knew he wasn't just talking about his art anymore. "Yes. The painting for sure, and from my limited experience with you, I would say you have a magnificent heart, too."

He folded his arms over his chest and smiled. Blindingly. She wondered if he could see her knees quake.

"Then there's one thing for us to do," he said.

"What's that?"

"Increase your limited experience."

She cocked her head. "I would think that with us working together in this studio, that's inevitable."

"And you'd be right." He laughed.

Isabelle took a deep breath. Wes was the kind of man she'd hoped would walk into her life. The fact that he was an artist and lived in the art world, breathed its air and consumed its energy had everything to do with it. She could learn so much from him.

She liked to think that being part of a team would enhance both their careers and their lives.

He raised his eyes to the skylight. The sun was gone. Dark clouds had moved in from the west.

"Tomorrow, I'll be better," he said.

She glanced at his painting. "I don't see how."

"I mean, about making a space for you." He gestured around the room. "As you can see, I'm messy, disorganized and—"

"A hog."

"Huh?"

Laughing, she said, "You're taking up the entire floor. I couldn't get an easel in here if I tried."

"An easel? Do you have one? I don't. Maybe I should ask Malcolm."

"It's okay," she assured him, holding up her palm. "I have a collapsible one in my cart. I have everything I need. Promise."

Wes rocked back on his heels. "I'm sure you do."

She cleared her throat. It was the oddest moment for her to think of Scott, to remember how it had felt to have his arms around her. His last kiss had barely grazed her lips, but she knew she'd remember it forever because she had wanted it to be more. She had wanted Scott.

A moment ago, she was feeling Wes's breath on her neck and now she was wishing she were back in Indian Lake helping Scott fix dinner for the kids. Looking into Scott's deep brown eyes.

"Actually, I can set up over there…" She pointed to the small space by the door to the office."

"Are you sure?" he asked.

"Absolutely." She gestured to his painting. "You continue with your work. I don't want to stop you."

"Okay. Thanks," he said and picked up his pail and stick. Within moments he was totally focused on the canvas.

Isabelle went to the hall, grabbed her cart and rolled it to the space she'd chosen. The light was good here; it would help her get the feel she wanted in the piece she was working on.

She listened to the music and watched Wes out of the corner of her eye as she set up. There was no disruption in his flow. If she'd wondered if he could paint on cue, she knew now that he could. He was like a machine.

She blended paints but her mind wandered away from the canvas and back to Scott. It was Saturday. Was he at the bookshop with the kids or had his mother taken them for the afternoon? He'd told her that one Saturday night a month he went to a DCS family function with the kids. He'd said the socializing with other parents was informative, but what he liked best were the games and activities that Zoey and the counselors organized. And if they weren't there, were they renting a movie or would he take them for a walk along the lighted trail at Indian Lake?

Isabelle took the top off a tube of paint. It was a tube Scott had picked up at the art supply store months ago. She remembered because it was a difficult color of gold-brown. She was still searching for the precise gold that shone in his eyes.

She missed him, she thought, chills spreading across her back.

How had she become so confused? What trigger had she missed?

And why would she start feeling this yearning for Scott at the precise moment when she had decided to move on? When he had, too.

Had she always been this foolish?

And now that she realized what he meant to her, was it too late?

She hadn't received a call from him for two days. She knew he was busy. So was she.

But why did she feel so hollow?

"How's it going there?" Wes shouted over the music.

She looked at her brush and moved it to the canvas. "Fine," she said, knowing already this faerie would look like Scott.

CHAPTER TWENTY-ONE

"LET ME SHOW YOU," Wes said, taking Isabelle's hand and dunking it into the can of blue-gray paint she'd spent over an hour mixing until it had the right tone and value. The day was cloudy and the light from the studio skylight played havoc with the saturation, which was why she'd gotten frustrated.

Experimentation was the hallmark of any artist and Isabelle was no exception. Her faerie paintings sold well, and she was confident that Malcolm liked them, but she couldn't shake the feeling that they weren't the extent of her talent. Of all she could be. She liked to be challenged, and if she was to embrace this new opportunity, this time in this studio, she wanted to push herself out of her comfort zone. Maybe she'd fail. Maybe she wouldn't.

She'd tried to explain her needs to Scott but he'd never understood. Too often, she'd felt like his admiration for her faerie paintings kept him from accepting her ambitions for growth in her art.

As much as she missed Scott and as much as

she was counting the hours till she drove back to Indian Lake, she also knew that she'd regret it if she didn't ask Wes Adams for advice.

Wes held his hand over hers, competent and strong. Was it possible for his talent to seep through her skin and transport her visions onto the canvas?

He'd taken her newly stretched canvas and laid it on the floor near his massive construction, like a fawn following a great buck. The mighty and the meek.

Isabelle had worked alongside Wes now for four days. Two weekends. And each day she'd studied him, marveled over him, encouraged him—though he didn't need it. He was a universe unto himself.

"Just remember, no one comes to expressionism easily. Pollock spent years painting realist murals in the thirties." His fingers were warm and caressing. Each time she gripped the painting stick too tightly, he nudged her to relax.

"I started out with surrealism myself. It's a pathway to the unconscious. Or subconscious. I don't know which, but for me it turned on the fire I feel now. Cubism can teach you the understanding of space. I saw a bit of cubism in your butterfly painting. Malcolm saw it, too."

She barely heard the words he spoke. She was aware of his breath on her neck. The feel of his strong chest against her back as they leaned over the canvas.

"Is this right?" she asked.

She felt the undertow of him, his energy and charisma. It was impossible to believe he didn't have a dozen women breaking down that door out front to get to him. Yet, here she was, in this studio with the incomparable maestro of expressionism. The next "Big One," *Art World* magazine had dubbed him.

She was living every moment of the dreams she'd scripted all her life.

"Just about," he said. "Ease up on the pressure here and let your mind guide the paint from the stick to the canvas. Will the paint to perform the dance you're choreographing? Don't let it stray. Control. You have power over that dribble, splotch or trickle."

The paint fell. Dangled. Then swished and swayed and undulated into a line that resembled the eddies in the lake she was hoping to interpret.

"Now," he said. "Again." His fingers pressed against hers, demanding. Eliciting a response.

She flicked the paint this time, channeling the power of a roiling lake.

He twisted her wrist so that the last bit of paint rushed off the end and met with the canvas.

"More paint," he said, dunking the stick so it held twice as much paint as last time.

His movements now were more energetic.

"Close your eyes," he commanded.

They painted together as if they were one creative force.

"Feel your thoughts travel down through your arm. You're using your will to make the paint dance from the stick to the canvas. It's like telekinesis."

"That's impossible," she guffawed and opened her eyes.

"Shut those eyes!" He was nearly shouting.

Isabelle jumped. "Okay!"

He laughed. "You're so much fun."

"I am?"

"Mmm-hmm," he said. "I'm watching those eyes. Now, do as I told you. Command the paint."

"I am."

"No you're not. Your mind is someplace else."

If he only knew.

Though she was surrounded by art—by Wes—she still found her thoughts fleeing back to Indian Lake and Scott. Bella and Michael. She wondered what Scott would think of this new direction her work was taking. She wanted to feel the energy of the paint and the canvas the way Wes did.

"I'm trying," she objected and squeezed her eyes tighter. "I'll concentrate."

"Okay. Get some more paint on there."

He was so different from dependable Scott. He had a certain power over her, when Scott usually asked for her advice or deferred to what she wanted.

Though not so much lately…

Why did that thought sting?

Wes grasped her hand, bringing her back to the moment.

Each time he refilled the paint stick, his bicep flexed against her arm. Between thoughts of Scott and this closeness with Wes, she had no hope of focusing on her painting. She had to get her head on straight, or she would blow this opportunity—maybe even her whole career. She'd be back in Indian Lake with her tail between her legs, admonishing herself every day till she died.

"This lake you're painting—it exists?" he asked.

"Yes. At home. I went there often as a child. Now I work at the Lodges which are at the north end of the lake."

"Ah, so it inspires you?" He whisked her hand rapidly over the canvas as if cracking a whip. The paint slashed across the former stripes and waves.

"Yes, though I paint in my apartment. But I get ideas there, at the lake."

"We need some aquamarine here." He pointed at the top of the painting.

"That's exactly how I saw it." She marveled. She gestured toward the bottom half. "This is the underside of the lake, where the light can't penetrate."

"Much like a tomb," he mumbled.

"Yes."

"Then the sunlight streams down, creating the gradation of color. Azure to cerulean to navy."

Isabelle shouldn't have been surprised at his acuity. "Pretty mundane stuff for you, huh? After all, it's just a lake."

He went over to the bench and shuffled several cans of paint around before plucking one from the group. He held it aloft like a prize. "Add some white to this. When you mix, think of what's in your heart and mind. Fear? That will be the blue-black of the lake bed. Where people drown. Fish die. And life is renewed. What kind of renewal do you want for yourself, Isabelle?"

He walked over to her and put the can on the floor. Without flourish or hesitation, he placed both hands on her cheeks and pulled her face to his. He pressed his lips gently to her mouth. She expected him to pull away quickly, as he'd done in those first days after they'd met. A hello kiss. A friendly kiss.

That's not what she got.

He increased the pressure and drew in a deep breath as if he were about to plunge underwater. He traced the edge of her jaw with his thumb, then placed a hand on the small of her back, pulling her to him. She felt his heart pounding inside his hard chest and she wondered if he could feel hers, too.

Isabelle felt dizzy, weak. Her body seemed weightless, as if she could float to the moon and back. Sail away to the stars like the boy in her painting.

The boy. Scott.

She couldn't help thinking about him now, probably with Bella and Michael leaving the bookshop for the day. She wondered if he thought about her when she wasn't around.

Lately, Scott had been so busy with the kids that she'd felt displaced from his life. She was the one texting him. She stopped by with macaroni and cheese for the kids. She made excuses to see him.

For too long she hadn't admitted that Scott took up a large place in her heart.

How could she even consider kissing someone else?

"Sorry," she said, pulling away from Wes.

"Isabelle?" Wes whispered. He rested his forehead against hers.

"I... I suppose there's some rule about kissing the protégé?" She scrambled for a diplomatic exit. She was flattered that he found her attractive, but she was confused by the tumult of emotions inside her. She couldn't get Scott out of her head.

"No. Thank God."

"Oh."

"Not unless you didn't like it. Then we'd make one up."

"I didn't say that," she replied, tilting her head back. She'd just kissed the one-way ticket into the world she'd dreamed about. She should be elated. But Wes wasn't a prize to be won. He was gifted and talented and she liked him a great deal.

But he wasn't Scott.

"I thought it was...lovely."

"Is that all?" He smiled.

"Now you're teasing me."

"I am. Sorry. But you're fun to tease. And instruct," he said. He brushed her cheek with his thumb. "Ordinarily, I'd suggest that we try it again."

She dropped her eyes and glanced toward the door.

"But I'm guessing there's someone else in this painting."

"Uh, huh."

"But he's not here, is he?" Wes asked.

"No, he's…moved on."

"I see." He dropped his hands and bent down, gathering his paint can and stick. "Then there's still hope for me."

CHAPTER TWENTY-TWO

SCOTT TWISTED THE cap off a bottle of beer and sat down at Luke's kitchen table across from Trent and Luke.

"Are you sure you want to go see her this weekend?" Luke asked, taking a sip from his own bottle. "I mean, I was at that gallery, man. I saw the way that guy was moving in on her."

Trent tapped his bottle on the table and stared at it thoughtfully. "He impressed me as the sophisticated type. He knew all those clients and he's obviously been to Europe and Argentina to see their galleries. What woman could resist a guy like that?"

Scott snorted. "Thanks for the support, guys."

"Just saying." Luke spread his hands.

"Listen, both of you. This is a big break for her. I wish Isabelle nothing but the best," Scott said sincerely. "And I've moved on."

"Blah, blah, blah." Trent rolled his eyes. "You can't tell me that just because you're a foster dad that all of a sudden you don't love Isabelle."

Scott dropped his chin.

"What were you thinking?" he pressed. "That she'd come running? It doesn't work that way."

"I... I thought the kids would make a difference for me," Scott confessed. "I thought they'd be enough."

Luke blew out a heavy breath. He clutched Scott's shoulder. "We've known each other for a long time. You were there when Jenny died. I did the build-out on your coffee shop. I've never seen you this...resigned. You don't think you've lost her, do you?"

"I'm getting that feeling, yeah."

"Dang, buddy," Trent said. "What can you do to stop it?"

"I'm doing it. I'm staying close. I want her to know I'm still here. If it turns into a train wreck, I'll be there to pick up the pieces."

Luke and Trent shook their heads glumly.

Scott knew what they were thinking. They had both gone through a great deal of challenges to be with the loves of their lives. Trent had nearly lost his life in the process. But right now, his friends were glad they were where they were and not walking in his shoes.

When they'd finished their beers, Scott rose from his chair. "Well, guys, I'm heading back to the shop to check on some inventory before I call it a day. Great shooting today."

"Yeah, your aim is definitely improving," Luke said.

"Thanks—" Scott slapped both their backs and left.

It was Sunday evening and the sun was just going down. The sidewalks were clear and patches of grass showed in the yards where the snow had melted. Most folks in town didn't like March. It was gloomy, gray and you never knew from one day to the next if spring would wander in or if you'd wake up to a blizzard. Scott liked the unpredictability of the month, though. The promise of spring was pervasive, even in a snowstorm.

Hope. That's what Scott needed when it came to Isabelle.

Not to mention a strategy.

It was strange not to have Isabelle calling him for help. But ever since he'd taken in the kids, he hadn't had time to take her for coffee or meet her for dinner. The tables had completely turned. He'd been the one doing the asking.

He stopped cold. *That's it.*

He took out his cell phone and hit her name.

The call went to voicemail. "Isabelle. Hi. It's me. I know I've been leaning on you a lot lately, but this is a woman thing. Or a girl thing. Easter's coming up and I want Bella to have her first Easter dress. I was thinking I'd drive into

Chicago and we could all go shopping. Macy's or Carson's. We can meet you on State Street. Then, maybe—if it's okay, I mean—we could see this studio where you work. Call me back." He paused then added, "Miss you."

Scott felt a surge of confidence. He had to make sure she knew that he was still here. Still her rock.

SCOTT STOOD ON the corner of Randolf and State Street holding Bella's hand, with Michael lodged between his knees as they stared at the Easter display windows at Macy's. The floor of the display was covered in lush green grass that Scott could swear was real. Tall Ficus trees were strung with lights and adorned with pastel eggs. Masses of potted tulips and daffodils filled the foreground near the window's edge. But the main attraction was a six-foot mechanical rabbit dressed in blue-and-white-striped overalls, which stood at a tall, white pedestal holding an artist's palette and paintbrush as he decorated a giant Easter egg. The motorized bunny nodded toward Bella and Michael, and each time he did, Michael squealed with delight.

"He's funny!" Michael clapped his hands.

Bella was all smiles. "I've never seen anything like him before. What is it?"

"That's the Easter Bunny I told you about."

"I thought he was a rabbit." She looked from Scott to the big bunny. "A little one."

Chuckling, Scott said, "Everything is big and wondrous in Chicago."

"I couldn't agree more," Isabelle said from behind him.

Scott whirled around. He couldn't hold back a grin. He was happy to see her and she looked radiant. "Hi!" He kissed her cheek. "How long have you been standing there?"

"Oh, a bit," she teased with a smile sweet enough to kiss.

"Miss Isabelle," Bella said softly. "Dad said you're going to help me pick out a dress." Her eyes traveled warily up to the enormous bunny. "For Easter."

"I'm happy to help," Isabelle replied, putting her hand on Bella's head.

Scott lifted Michael into his arms, and as he did Michael reached out, grabbed a hunk of Isabelle's long caramel hair and pulled her toward him. He gave her a kiss on the cheek. "Issa!"

"Hello, Michael. I'm happy to see you."

"Yeah." Michael buried his face in Scott's collar as if he was embarrassed.

The moment felt like a dream come true to Scott. He was here with Isabelle. Two kids. And they were going shopping for Easter outfits.

But his dream was an illusion. He was far from making all this real.

Scott nodded to Bella. "You take Miss Isabelle's hand and don't you lose her."

"I won't, Dad."

Scott didn't know what he expected from the kids' department other than racks of tiny outfits, and clearly, neither did the children. They all paused at the entrance, staring up at shelves brimming with enormous, colorful baskets tied up with cellophane, streamers and huge bows. Michael scampered from a stuffed bunny to a chick to yet another bunny, snuggling each soft and cuddly toy for a moment before moving to the next.

Bella was overwhelmed by the sight. She stood stock-still, her eyes tracking from the pink wheelbarrow filled with toys and candy to the lilac teeter-totter with a kid-sized bunny on either end. Mechanical bunnies painting Easter eggs were stationed all across the floor.

"Bella, the dresses are over here," Isabelle said, but Bella didn't budge. Isabelle looked at Scott expectantly.

"Bella?" Scott leaned down. "Are you okay?"

"It's so beautiful," she sniffed.

Sensing that this moment was an emotional one for Bella, Scott signaled to Isabelle with a slight jerk of his head for her to leave them alone.

"I'll get Michael before he knocks something over," Isabelle said and left.

Scott put his hand on Bella's shoulder. "What is it, sweetheart?"

"I didn't know all these things. My mother never told me," she whispered as tears filled her eyes. "She should have told me."

"Sweetie, the thing is, well, the Easter Bunny is like a story. A fairy tale. He's not really real."

"No?"

"He's a myth."

She wiped her eyes and looked at him with a crinkle at the bridge of her nose. "A what?"

Scott considered the marvelous display. He thought of the hours of work it had taken the designers to create this scene. "The Easter Bunny is a symbol of spring. The renewal of life. A long, long time ago, a storyteller used symbols like the bunny and the egg to explain that spring always comes. There's always hope. Then in America—" he eyed the pyramid of gold-wrapped boxes of candy "—the manufacturers kept the story going so they could make the day more special." He frowned. "I think."

"I thought you wanted me to have a new dress."

"An Easter dress for a little girl is very special. And I want you to have something nice. That's why I asked Miss Isabelle to help. She's good at picking out dresses."

Bella leaned closer to Scott. She put her hand on his collar and fidgeted with it, pulling it out from under the neck of his sweater. "Nuh, uh. That's not why she's here."

"It's not?"

"No, Dad. She's here because you like her very much."

"How do you know that?"

Bella leaned even closer. "Because you smile a lot when she's around."

Scott pulled her into a hug. "You know something, Bella? You're very observant. Maybe someday you'll be a journalist like me."

"I want to be like Miss Isabelle." She turned back toward the display. "And the bunnies. A painter."

Scott felt his heart leap and then crash. Isabelle had made a strong impression on Bella without even trying. That was one of the things about Isabelle—she was unforgettable. He wanted so much for Isabelle to want what he had. To want him. If she didn't, not only would Scott be heartbroken, so would the kids.

WITH ISABELLE'S HELP, Bella chose a pink, sleeveless dress with appliqued daisies around the hem, waist and neck. Scott insisted on white patent leather shoes, tights, a purse and a straw hat.

"I don't want all that stuff, Dad."

"Why not?"

"It's too much," she said shyly.

Scott shook his head. "Isn't this what girls wear for Easter?" he asked Isabelle.

"It is," Isabelle agreed. She lowered her voice. "But she's never had an Easter like we did as kids. She doesn't understand. Sometimes less is more. You know?" Isabelle leaned down to Bella. "Did you find something else you want instead?"

"Yes," she replied cautiously. She held out a pair of pink glittered high-top sneakers. "I like these."

"Oh, my…" Scott wiped his face with his palm. "St. Mark's will never be the same."

Isabelle laughed. "I think they're terrific, Bella. What a fashion statement!"

"My mom will kill me," Scott said.

"Please, Dad?"

Isabelle jumped to her defense. "Honestly, Scott. She can wear the sneakers to school. By fall, she'll have outgrown them. The dress is adorable. And these are better for running in the lawn during the egg roll. The white shoes would get grass stains."

"What's an egg roll?"

"It's a game we play every Easter at my mother's house," Scott explained. "This year it will be at our house, though. I was going to surprise you kids with it."

Isabelle winked at Bella. "We'll get the sneakers."

"Yay! Michael, look at my—" The excitement drained from Bella's face. "Dad, where's Michael?"

"He's—" Scott turned to the spot where the toddler had been playing with the stuffed bunnies. "Not here."

Isabelle gasped.

Alarm bells rang in Scott's head. "Michael? Michael?" he called.

Isabelle grabbed Bella's hand. "Stay with me."

Scott looked underneath the pink wheelbarrow and around each of the mechanical bunnies.

No Michael.

Isabelle and Bella were over by the racks of clothing. "Michael? Come see Miss Issa, sweetie."

Ice ran in Scott's veins as fear took over. Images of several worst case scenarios flew through his mind. "MICHAEL!" He shouted loud enough to be heard three floors above them.

"Da!"

Scott halted. "Michael?" He spun around. "Da."

Scott followed the sound to a corner cabinet piled with clear plastic boxes filled with delicately painted chocolate eggs imported from Belgium. "Michael?"

"Da."

Scott opened the cabinet door and inside sat Michael, still in his spring jacket and jeans, his light-up sneakers flickering brightly as he ate a chocolate egg. He smiled at Scott with chocolate-covered teeth.

Scott reached into the cabinet and pulled him out. Not until he had the boy in his arms did his heart start beating again.

"Michael!" Isabelle and Bella came running up.

"He ate the chocolate!" Bella gasped.

"I think he was hungry," Scott said.

Isabelle nodded. "I'll go pay for Bella's shoes and dress…and this box of chocolates. Maybe we should take the kids to the cafeteria upstairs before I show you the studio."

"Good idea," Scott replied, taking a packet of tissues—something he never traveled without anymore—from his pants pocket. He wiped Michael's face. "Here's my credit card."

"Scott." Isabelle put her hand on his arm, her thumb caressing him. "Are you okay?"

He couldn't get over the love he saw in her eyes. Did she feel it? Did she know it was there? "I thought I'd lost him. I was so…"

"I know, Scott," she replied with a sigh of relief. "But you didn't. We're all still here. Together."

"We are," he said. His heart pinged. Just once. It was all he would allow.

CHAPTER TWENTY-THREE

ISABELLE UNLOCKED THE studio door and proudly stood aside as Bella and Scott, who was holding a sleepy Michael, entered her new world.

Isabelle couldn't describe the elation she felt as she ushered them toward the magnificent room that vibrated creativity.

Wes's canvases hung on the walls around them, dwarfing her own paintings. But they were hers. For that alone, she knew Scott would appreciate them.

"So, it's been going well?" he asked.

"It has," she answered as they walked toward the easel where her most recent piece was covered with a cloth. She wanted a proper unveiling. A bit of drama. One day there would be a red carpet gallery showing for her art—a solo exhibit. One day.

Scott's eyes roamed the room, taking it all in. "This is all Wes's work, right?"

"It is."

"Wow," Bella said, reaching for Scott's hand. Michael was wide awake now, squirming in

Scott's arms. Isabelle watched both the children taking in sights she guessed they'd never seen.

"Wow," Michael echoed, though Isabelle guessed he was more impressed with the sky-light than he was the paintings.

Scott was equally impressed. "His work is massive."

"It's for a commercial client. He's meeting with them all day today."

"What does somebody pay for that much commissioned art?"

"I'm not sure," she answered honestly. "But it's a lot. Malcolm told me that much. Wes's interviewed with another client in New York and one in Milwaukee. He's hoping to land them both. He said the work would take him over eighteen months to complete."

Scott was looking at her intently.

"What?" she asked.

"You seem know a great deal about him and his work."

"Of course I do. We're together every week-end, you know. I've learned a few things, even if he doesn't talk much. He blasts his music and paints and shouts and whoops. You should see him in action. It's really something."

"I should." His voice was flat. "And what do you do?"

Her eyes lit up. "That's what I want to show

you. Besides Wes and Malcolm, you and the kids are the first to see it."

"Well, come on, then," Scott said. "Take that rag off your masterpiece."

Isabelle walked over to the easel and whisked off the cloth. "Ta-da!"

"What in the…" He pointed at her canvas. "You did that?"

"What is it?" Bella asked. She cocked her head right. Then left. She blinked and stared.

"Purdy." Michael grinned.

"It's an expressionist vision of Indian Lake," she explained.

"Ah! I see that now. Interesting. I like the colors," he replied. Something was off about his smile. "Everything here is amazing."

He scanned the room, and Isabelle imagined he was taking in every detail, like the journalist he was at heart.

Bella's head was cranked all the way back to stare at the ceiling. "What is that?"

"It's a skylight, sweetie. The roof was taken out and they put a window in there," Scott said.

"Why?"

Scott sent Isabelle a gentle smile, and this time it felt more familiar. Genuine. Warm, friendly and so very Scott.

"Bella, do you remember what I told you about the light in your bedroom?" Isabelle asked. "How light looks different depending on which side of the house it comes in from?"

"Uh-huh."

"Well, this skylight helps illuminate our paintings. It's important for us to see exactly what colors we're using."

Isabelle took Bella's hand. "Come. I'll show you."

She went to an enormous box of oil paints and opened the lid.

"There's so many, I can't count that high."

"You'll learn. Tell your Dad to help you with your numbers. In the meantime, see this tube? This is crimson. This is burgundy. This next one is a blood red. This one is coral." Isabelle picked up other tubes. "With white, black, blue and brown, I make other colors. There's no end to the colors I can create. Then I use those colors to make a picture that I hope no one has ever seen before."

"What picture?" Bella asked.

Isabelle smiled from her heart. "The pictures in my mind. I see all kinds of things. I see the world the way I wish it was. Filled with peace and harmony. Love and gentleness."

Isabelle heard Scott suck in a breath and she turned to him.

"I never knew that," he said, his voice filled with respect.

"I thought I told you," she replied.

"No." His tone was sad, as if she'd cheated him. Maybe she had. Suddenly, she felt guilty. How many other things had been left unsaid between them? It was mostly her fault. She'd kept her emotions locked away so they wouldn't interfere with her goals. If she spent hours focusing on her needs and wants, other than the pursuit of art, she'd never get her work done. She might never have picked up the first paintbrush.

She remembered Wes's instructions to her and how he painted from the heart. He infused his energy, his passion, into his paintings and channeled his most inner self.

That was what Isabelle had been doing with her faeries, and even more so in her expressionist interpretation of Indian Lake.

Wasn't it?

"Miss Isabelle's painting is very pretty," Bella whispered to Scott. "Do you like it, Dad?"

"Actually, I do. It's different from what I expected, but it's very good," he replied though Isabelle noticed that he barely glanced back at the painting. His eyes were on her.

Isabelle rubbed her arms, suddenly chilled. Funny. She'd never once felt uncomfortable in Scott's presence. But there was a distance between them now that she'd either been too preoccupied or too naive to notice. Maybe her attraction to Wes, her immersion in her work, had caused this. Or was it Scott's decision to move on with his life, to foster the kids? They had been traveling down different paths for a while now. Would they ever find their way back to each other? Did she want that?

"Isabelle, I was hoping to talk to you for a second," he said, glancing at the kids. Bella was enthralled by the art in front of her. She picked up a brush. "Is this what you use?"

"Yes," Isabelle said and gently took the brush from her. "But it's my best one and not a toy."

"I know," Bella said, eyeing the tubes of watercolors.

Michael was on the floor untying his shoes. He pulled one off and tossed it on the floor. It skidded too near Wes's painting.

"Maybe we should move the kids over to the corner where they won't cause any trouble," Isabelle suggested.

"Better still..." Scott reached into the miniduffel bag he carried and pulled out a coloring book and a sticker book. "This will keep them quiet for a few minutes. Michael is getting good with sticker art."

He handed the book to Michael, who shoved it away. "No."

Isabelle looked at Scott. "I think the day downtown has been too much for them."

"I'm seeing that."

"Let's get them away from the paintings. We can sit on the bench back there."

Scott handed Bella the books, some crayons and a plastic bag filled with stickers. "Bella, you and Michael play in the back of the studio out of the way of these paintings. Okay? I'll only be a minute. You watch out for Michael, okay?"

"Where are you going?" Bella asked with a catch in her voice. Isabelle realized that the little girl still clung to old fears. It might take months, even years, for Bella to learn to trust Scott completely and heal from her old life.

"Bella," Isabelle answered softly. "We're not going anywhere. Just moving away from the paint and canvases." They walked the kids to the back of the studio. "You and Michael can play with your books. You can see us and we can see you. Okay?"

"Oh, okay. When you finish talking, Miss Isabelle, would you show me how to paint like you?"

Isabelle hadn't been prepared for the warmth she felt at Bella's interest. "Of course I will."

"Okay." Bella sat down next to Michael and opened the bag of stickers.

"What is it, Scott?"

"I wanted to say that what I've seen here today—I think I understand more about you than I ever have. This is your world, Isabelle. You belong here—in this studio, with this enormous energy around you."

"You feel it, too?" She gasped.

"I do. And I can't compete with it, Isabelle."

"What are you saying?" She began to tremble. She felt as if she was losing him.

He took her hands and squeezed them, smiling gently. "Maybe all I want to say is that I get you like I never have. Your art isn't just a career for you, it's your passion. Your soul. You wouldn't be you if you weren't painting and that's never going to change. It shouldn't change. I want you to do all you can to learn and better your skills, to seize every opportunity that comes your way. You deserve it. You're an amazing woman, Isabelle. I'm so lucky to have been part of your life."

"Scott, are you trying to say goodbye to me? That's not what I want."

"No, I'm not saying that. But I am saying that I can see how easy it would be for us to drift apart. More than we already have. We're both busy and things get away from us, you know? I've got the kids and you—you have all this.

And you should have it. I'm really happy for you, Isabelle."

She didn't know when the tears had come, but there they were, filling her eyes, sliding down her cheeks. Everything he said was true. He was just being realistic. There was a strong chance that in the months to come they would be so consumed with by their separate lives that they wouldn't have time for each other. Scott had been a constant in her life for so long, but now it seemed like their relationship had to be all or nothing.

She'd overheard Wes talking to Malcolm on the phone about her progress. She'd received good to great reviews thus far. Wes had predicted "rave" reviews for her at the next show. Malcolm was pleased with her ability to produce on deadline. And he'd told Wes that he was impressed with the experimentation she was doing. As long as she still produced art nouveau paintings that sold, he supported her desire to spread her wings. She was measuring up.

Isabelle put her arms around Scott's neck. "Thank you for that, Scott. It means a lot to know you believe in me."

"I always have. Always."

"I know."

The edge of his mouth quirked up. "But I'm

not a *Tribune* art critic, so my opinion hasn't got the weight—"

Bella's squeal of delight interrupted their conversation.

Scott's eyes shot over to the spot where the kids had been one second ago.

"What?"

Bella was twirling like Isabelle had seen her do at their house. She had a tube of watercolor paint in her hand and squeezed a huge dollop into the air as Isabelle and Scott watched. Michael ran around her legs, coming dangerously close to Wes's mural.

"Bella!" Scott shouted.

Bella stopped twirling and sat on the floor wide-eyed. The paint plopped on the floor, making a puddle of blue. She burst into tears.

Isabelle was instantly on her feet and darted over to Michael, grabbing him under the arms and lifting him off the floor just as his feet were about to come into contact with the canvas.

Scott went to Bella and hugged her. He looked up at Isabelle. "Maybe coming to your studio wasn't such a good idea."

"Definitely not the place for children," she said. This was a good reminder. As cute as kids could be, they still got cranky and were full of mischief. And at least until they were a little older, they required constant attention.

They couldn't be a part of her new world. At the same time, her heart went out to Bella, who looked up to Isabelle. It wasn't the kids' fault. They were just being kids. She smiled at Bella. "Though I am an advocate for teaching children to paint."

Scott took the tube of watercolor from Bella's hand, passed it to Isabelle and then pressed Bella's head to his shoulder. "It's all right, sweetheart. You guys are tired. I think it's time to go."

Isabelle got a rag and wiped up the smear of blue.

"But I wanted to look at Miss Isabelle's other painting."

Isabelle held Michael as Scott stood and gathered the sticker book and crayons. "Well, I don't know…"

"It's okay," Isabelle said. "It's right over here on the easel."

The painting was covered in a cloth, and Isabelle pulled it away. She was proud of her blonde woman lying in a forest meadow, dewdrops glistening on her moss green gown.

"It's beautiful," Scott said.

Bella stared but remained silent.

Isabelle watched her as she took in every delicate detail.

"I want to be a painter like you, Miss Isabelle," Bella said.

"What a lovely compliment," Isabelle replied.

"Would you teach me?"

"I would love that," Isabelle said, looking over at Scott, realizing he hadn't taken his eyes from her.

Bella slipped her hand into Isabelle's. "Then I know I'll be good."

"Of course you will, Bella," Scott said. "Miss Isabelle is going to be really famous someday. People will come to see her paintings hang in galleries all over the country."

Isabelle gaped at him. "You think so?"

"I most certainly do," he replied confidently. "You have to see that."

She followed his eyes as they studied her painting. It was good. Very good. Even as she'd painted it, she'd felt herself transitioning to a new phase of her talent.

With each brushstroke she'd moved away from the world she'd known into uncharted artistic territory.

"Bella, let's get your jacket," Scott said as he took Michael from Isabelle. "It's time for us to go. Miss Isabelle has a lot of work to do. We're in the way."

Scott's words stung because they were the truth. She didn't see how she could weave both her worlds together.

They'd started to walk out. Bella held Scott's hand while he carried Michael, who was already drowsy.

Isabelle followed them to the curb and helped buckle Michael into his child seat. Scott closed the door.

The look he gave her was steely. "Tell me the truth, Isabelle, do you love me?"

"You've never asked me that before."

"It's time I did."

She drew in a deep breath. "Yes." She couldn't believe that it had come out so easily. Why hadn't she seen that before? She did love Scott.

"But?"

"But…" She glanced inside the minivan at Bella, who had closed her eyes. "I can't be tied to a family. I adore the kids, I do. Love them, in fact." She gestured toward the studio. "You saw what happened. They were right in front of us the whole time and it wasn't enough. What if they'd knocked over a can of Wes's paint and destroyed his work? What if they'd hurt themselves? And trust me, I'm not blaming them. What I don't want is to be that person that stifles them in any way. I want them to feel free and childlike. They've certainly earned it."

"And loving me?"

Her heart felt like it was shattering. Tears

burned her eyes and her voice caught. "I do love you. But I don't see how this can work."

Scott's brown eyes were filled with pain. Pain that she'd put there. Lost hope. Lost love.

"There it is, then," he replied and turned away.

He walked around the van and got in. He started the engine and when he drove away, he didn't look back.

She hadn't expected him to.

CHAPTER TWENTY-FOUR

SCOTT UNLOCKED HIS bookstore door. "Well, if it isn't the *Law and Order* duo," he joked as Sadie and Violet walked in. He closed and locked the door behind them. "Thanks for taking me up on my offer to man the store. I've found I can't run the shop seven days a week and take care of my family."

"I need the cash," Violet said bluntly. "I've only got six weeks till finals at the police academy. And I'm broke. Neither of us wants to ask Mom for any more money."

"Yeah, we already have plenty we have to pay back," Sadie agreed. "I want to get through law school as fast as I can, which means summer semesters. That's expensive. Working weekends for you will help us a bunch."

He rubbed his hands together with a bit of glee. "Then this could be the answer for all of us."

"Yeah, Isabelle said you've got it rough with the kids," Violet said. "At first I thought you wanted to spend your weekends with *her*. Up in Chicago."

"Nah, she's busy painting and I'm trying to get the house renovated. I'd thought I'd have more of it done by Easter."

"Easter's only a couple weeks away. Isabelle said your house was…er, needs a lot of work."

Violet's candor reminded Scott of himself when he first started at the *Tribune*. She was raw and intense like a litigator, prosecutor or an unpolished journalist. One thing he suspected, Violet would be a good cop.

"It does." Scott's thoughts flew back to the last time he was with Isabelle. She'd refused his proposal once before, and though she'd essentially told him "no" again, he wasn't buying it.

For the first time, she'd admitted that she loved him. For a split second he'd let his hopes expand.

That was a fault of his when it came to Isabelle. He would forever look on the positive side.

And for Scott, positive meant waiting for her to realize that his love and the life he offered her was as valuable as a show in the Metropolitan Museum of Art.

He didn't care that she spent her weekends with iconic Wes. She'd told him that she loved him—Scott.

And that meant something. He'd sent her text messages every other day or so and kept them simple. *Good morning. Have a good day. Hope all went well for you.* That kind of thing. He didn't want to pressure her because he felt that if he did, he'd lose her for certain. Her messages back to him were equally shallow. *Fine. How are kids? How's the new store lay-out look?* Stuff like that. Even during the days when she was back in Indian Lake, she didn't make time to stop by and see him.

He knew what she was doing.

She was hiding out. She'd made a declaration that he'd waited years to hear. Now that she'd blurted it out, he wondered if she actually believed she wanted her life in the art world more than him.

He couldn't be sure of anything.

They were tiptoeing. All he could do was get the house fixed up and throw one heck of an Easter brunch for the kids, Isabelle's family and his mother. She'd texted him that she'd attend. That gave him another chance to see her. Perhaps it was foolhardy to hope, but Scott didn't know any other way to be. He loved Isabelle and he would always love her.

"So, let's get started," Scott said to Sadie and Violet. He went around the display counter to the register. "Let me show you the cash."

Scott went through the mechanics of the digital register and chip reader.

"I'm really glad you don't have one of those monster cappuccino machines like Maddie has over at her café," Violet said. "I don't think I'd ever get the hang of steaming milk. Isabelle would be great at it, but not me. I'm all thumbs."

Scott couldn't help scoffing at her. "You? All thumbs? I heard you took top honors in the police marksman course."

Her green eyes flashed, reminding him of Isabelle. "I did. What I meant to say is that kitchens and I don't mix."

Sadie nodded. "Yeah. I'm with you on that one. I'm gonna marry a guy who can cook."

"Good for you. But in our family, Isabelle does it all."

Scott felt a surge of defensiveness for Isabelle. Her family always expected her to do the work. "And what does Isabelle want?" he asked, hand on his hip.

"Huh?" Violet scrunched her nose and tossed him a quizzical look. "What are talking about?"

"Have either of you asked Isabelle if she likes to cook?"

"Sure she does. She's great at it."

"Hmm." He pursed his lips. "I think she's good because she doesn't do anything that isn't perfect. I've seen the stack of cooking magazines she references when a holiday is coming up. But she hardly cooks for herself at home. I think she does a lot of things to please others. Especially her family." *But is she pleasing herself? Maybe that's what she's doing now. Finding Isabelle.*

"I never thought about it," Sadie replied. "I always assumed she liked taking over. Being the boss."

"She was bossy when we were little," Violet agreed. "I resented her for it, too."

Scott leaned against the counter and folded his arms over his chest. "She had to be the boss. You lost your father, and your mother was at work trying to make a living. Raising the family fell on the shoulders of a ten-year-old girl who never got a chance to finish out her childhood. If that had happened to me, I'd be pretty angry."

Violet and Sadie shared a private look. Violet swallowed. "So we were a burden to her."

"All I'm saying is that in the future, maybe you and your brothers could help her out a little more. Show your appreciation. I know I'm trying to understand her in a way I never did before."

Sadie put her hand on Scott's shoulder. Her

voice quaked slightly, reminding him of little Michael's whimper. "Thanks."

"Yeah," Violet chirped, but Scott saw the mist in her sparkling eyes.

Sadie and Violet loved Isabelle. So did he. They all thought they knew her well, but did anybody ever really know the person they loved?

SCOTT'S RELENTLESS TEXTS finally convinced Isabelle to agree to go to dinner with him on Wednesday night. Maybe if he went about his relationship with her as he always had, somehow, some way, she might realize that the only thing in life worth living for was love. His love.

He was dead tired from plastering and painting his dining room, taking care of the kids and managing the bookshop, which was busier than ever.

"There's only one remedy for this level of exhaustion," Scott said to Isabelle as he parked his minivan outside the restaurant and pointed to the sign. "Thai food."

After being seated at a table with a white cloth and a jar of spring tulips in the center, Scott ordered glass noodles, tom kha gai soup, crispy mango fish and a bottle of chilled Chardonnay.

Halfway through their meal, he realized Isabelle had done most, if not all, of the talking. She rhapsodized about Wes's ability to "will" the paint onto the canvas in the exact form and position he envisioned. Scott didn't know much about expressionism, but he was certainly going to order a book from one of his vendors on the subject. If this meant so much to Isabelle, he had to be able to talk to her about it.

He poured them each a second glass of wine while Isabelle kept talking. About Wes.

She'd always used her hands a lot when she expounded on her art, but never quite this much, he thought.

Though the lighting in the restaurant was low, he noticed distinct, dark circles under Isabelle's eyes.

When she finally took a breath and ate a piece of fish, he asked, "Are you sleeping?"

"Huh?" she answered with her mouth full and held her napkin to her lips. "Yeah. Sure." She sipped her wine. "Why do you ask?"

"You look tired."

"Thanks," she bit back as she twirled noodles onto her fork.

"I'm only concerned, Isabelle. I'm not criticizing."

She nodded and continued twirling the noodles. "Okay. So, I haven't been sleeping all that much."

He put his fork down. "Talk to me about you. Not about Wes, but you."

"I have been talking about me."

"Uh-huh. Here's what I see. For over a month before the gallery showing, you worked night and day on your paintings to get ready for the show. Now you tell me that Malcolm is having another show on Wednesday before Easter, which causes you to work doubly long hours both here and in Chicago to be ready for this thing in a little over a week."

"Right. So?"

"So, you have no time for your life. Your sisters say they never hear from you. Not even a text. I text you, but you don't reply—much. That's why I was surprised you agreed to come out tonight." He watched her shovel another forkful into her mouth. He held up his palm. "Don't tell me. You were hungry."

"I am," she mumbled through the glass noodles. "And how do you know about my sisters?"

"They work for me now. If you talked to them, you'd know that. And you'd know that your mother just won the bid on a new commercial building in South Bend."

"She did?" Isabelle's eyes widened. But she didn't smile. He could guess why. Guilt.

"Are you going to Mrs. Beabots's Palm Sunday party?"

"Her what?"

"Oh, come on. We go every year. It's tradition."

"I forgot, okay? Come on, Scott."

"And you'll be at my house for Easter Saturday brunch?"

She looked at him sheepishly. "Easter."

"Yeah."

He put his napkin on the table.

"Scott. Please. All I've thought about is this show next Wednesday. Not parties. This is important."

"I'm...we're concerned about you."

She tossed her napkin over her food and took a long slug of wine. "You can all stop."

"You've changed."

"No, I haven't. I'm the same Isabelle. Just a better artist."

Scott felt like a first responder trying to save a drowning man in a flood. "Isabelle, my mother is making your favorite French toast and that egg frittata thing you love. The kids are decorating Easter eggs for you. And Mrs. Beabots made a special trip to my shop to invite us for Palm Sunday. She'd love to see you. All your girlfriends will be there. They're very anxious to hear from you."

Isabelle carefully laid her fork on the rim of her plate. "You don't understand. No one understands. This is my time. I have to work around the clock and push and push. I have to get better. I just have to."

Her voice was calm, but her hands shook as she spoke. Scott could tell she was overtired, overworked and judging by the way she'd gulped down her food, she wasn't eating regularly, either.

"I can't take the time to see you all. I can't."

"Can't or won't?" he said, losing his patience.

"Won't," she replied resoundingly.

"Fine." He rose from his chair and took the bill that the waiter had left on the table. "I'll tell the hostess to call a cab for you. Then I'll make your excuses to Mrs. Beabots. But don't be surprised if you don't get an invitation when the next holiday rolls around."

"Scott…"

He heard her say his name, but it dissipated into the sounds of clashing dishes, customers talking and the piped-in music.

Scott went to the register, handed the woman the cash and stomped out the door.

He'd imagined dozens of scenarios when he'd made arrangements to see Isabelle tonight, but this wasn't one of them. He especially hadn't figured on her rejection of Easter. The Isabelle he remembered adored Easter. It was opening weekend at the Lodges, and Edgar's Easter brunch was tradition for most of the families they knew in Indian Lake. Isabelle had never missed Mrs. Beabots's party, or the brunch he threw on the Saturday before Easter Sunday. It was during those early spring mornings that Isabelle used to walk on the cold sand and look for her faeries.

But this new Isabelle didn't believe in faeries or family traditions or friends.

"Scott!" She yelled, as she rushed out the restaurant door. "Stop!"

He kept walking toward the spot where he'd parked his van.

"Wait!" she shouted. He felt a hand on his arm.

He spun around. "Why? So you can tell me one more time that you don't need any of us anymore? Look, our seeing each other when you're so preoccupied was a mistake. A big one."

"That's how you see this?"

"I do."

Her face crumpled. Her eyes glistened like cool, green waves, and he felt a fissure open in his heart. "I'm sorry, Scott. I'm truly sorry. I hate it when we both get upset with each other. That's not what I want."

"It's not?"

"No, Scott. Never."

It was all he could do not to pull her close. He'd heard of guys like him. Fools for love.

"I don't want to hurt your feelings. I don't. And you're right. I have been totally immersed in this new…life. I haven't been engaged with my friends or my family. And that was wrong of me."

"So what are you saying?"

"That I'll find the time for Palm Sunday and I'll do what I can about Easter brunch. The show is on Wednesday, and I don't know what will happen after that. You know?"

"Yeah." He could imagine how the picture would change if she did well. He might lose her forever.

She continued. "I'll call Mrs. Beabots and accept her invitation. Oh, Scott…" She started crying. "I feel like the worst person in the world. And I do miss you all."

He put his arms around her and hugged her.

Isabelle never lifted her head from his shoulder as he walked her to the minivan and opened the door for her. Outside La Bellevue, he kissed her goodbye. She didn't cling to him, but she also didn't push him away. He slipped his palm around her neck and pulled her closer. He meant this kiss to make her think.

"Good night, Isabelle," he said softly, touching her cheek as he stepped back.

"Night," she said, lifting her eyes to his and

pausing long enough for him to see the yearning there.

He kissed her forehead. "Sleep well."

"I will. Promise." She smiled gently and then walked into her building.

He sat in the minivan for a few moments after she'd gone. He'd felt it—that same electricity that had zinged him before. She was tired. He got that. Her mind was on her work, but her heart beckoned to him and he'd heard it.

Scott believed in their love and he wasn't about to give up on them.

CHAPTER TWENTY-FIVE

ISABELLE PRESSED HER fingertips to her pounding temples. She couldn't remember the last headache she'd had. Maybe in high school. This Palm Sunday headache was promising to be one she wouldn't forget.

Mrs. Beabots came around the kitchen island and stood next to her. "Are you all right, dear?"

"I'm fine." Isabelle forced a smile, but judging by Mrs. Beabots's piercing sky-blue eyes, she wasn't fooling anyone. Still, she had to try. "Your cream puffs are amazing. They're my favorite."

"I made them especially for you. The sugar pie is Sarah's favorite and Maddie likes my tropical layer cake."

"You went to a lot of trouble for us." Isabelle sighed, looking at the array of desserts piled on silver caddies and the sterling service for coffee and, no doubt, Mrs. Beabots's mint- and bourbon-laced tea.

"I love doing it." She beamed. "All you girls—" She paused.

Isabelle couldn't believe it. Mrs. Beabots's eyes had misted over. Not tears, exactly, because she'd never seen Mrs. Beabots cry. No one had, at least to Isabelle's knowledge. Isabelle reached for her hands. "Mrs. Beabots. You aren't getting sentimental, are you?"

"Good heavens, no! That would mean I'm getting really old. I'm not ready for that yet. There's too much to be done."

Isabelle was intrigued. "What precisely? I should think you'd want to rest these days."

Mrs. Beabots grasped Isabelle's chin between her forefinger and thumb. "First, I'm anxious to see this art you're now creating. It must be joyous to discover a new facet of yourself."

Isabelle sighed again. "I wish."

"What? It's not going well?"

"I'm trying and working very hard, but I'm missing something. And I can't figure out what it is."

"Oh, don't worry. It will come at the right moment. Revelations always do."

Tilting her head to the left, Isabelle frowned. "I thought revelation always came late. When hindsight can't help much."

"That's a negative way of viewing life," Mrs. Beabots countered. "I prefer to look on the lighter side. That's where you find miracles.

You do that, Isabelle. With your faeries. You always show such lovely dimensions in your work." She patted Isabelle's cheek, picked up a tray of pecan tarts and left.

Isabelle carried the heavy silver coffee service to the dining room table. The room was jammed with all her friends, chatting and laughing. Down the center of the table, Mrs. Beabots and Sarah had assembled narrow pottery planters to resemble a grassy meadow studded with spring flowers. Tall six-armed silver candelabras held pink candles that flickered merrily. From Maddie's lemon curd–filled cupcakes, to peach pie, sugar pie, four-tiered tropical citrus cake, cream puffs and éclairs, there was something for every sweet tooth.

"Here, let me help with that." Scott was at her side the moment she entered the dining room.

"Thanks."

Scott placed the tray at the end of the table. He fussed with the napkins to the side of it. "Did you talk to Sarah?" he asked.

"Yes. The doctor says she's doing well. She's going to keep working right up till the moment the baby comes."

"She's a trooper." Scott took a plate and piled it with two cupcakes and a pecan tart.

Isabelle heard her phone ring from inside her purse.

"You need to get that?" Scott asked, taking a bite of cupcake.

"Not now. I'll check it later." Isabelle guessed the call was from Wes. Her family was in the front parlor visiting with Maddie and Nate Barzonni, and all her girlfriends were accounted for. Practically every person who would ever call her was in this house.

It could only have been Wes.

"Can I get you a glass of wine?" Scott asked.

"I'm fine."

"Okay." He kissed her cheek. "I want to talk to Luke about the renovations on my house. See you later."

"Sure." Isabelle watched him walk away, the dull pain in her chest sharpening. She'd been feeling it since the day he and the kids had come to the studio. She'd told him that being together was impossible. Yet, here he was, being the friend he'd always been.

The look he'd given her had always been there. He loved her. She just hadn't seen it.

She wondered how her life, their lives, would be different if she had.

Loving Scott should be so easy. And it would have been if she'd pinched herself long ago, woken up from her self-induced dream of an art career. Everything was moving so quickly now that she didn't have time to look back.

She'd made her choice, hadn't she?

She'd chosen a life that didn't include Scott.

Isabelle moved over to join Sarah, Liz, Cate and Olivia, who were huddled near the entrance to the library. "It's a lovely party, isn't it?" Cate was saying. "Mrs. Beabots is so creative. And these desserts!"

"Yeah, I wish she'd stop raising the bar." Liz chuckled. "Each time I think it's my turn to host a holiday, she beats me to it and then dreams up these fabulous decorations. Have you ever seen a table like that?"

"Only in a magazine."

"Well, Isabelle could top it, I bet," Olivia said. She sighed. "I adore your paintings. It must be wonderful to be there in Chicago—painting."

Their words grated. Rather than feeling triumph or even joy in her work, she felt inadequate. They knew her as the old Isabelle. Painting for tourists. Selling on the cheap.

"It's wonderful." It was easier to lie.

"And the studio. What's it like?" Sarah asked.

"An old warehouse, really, but the skylight is amazing. Scott and the kids saw it. I'm learning expressionism."

Olivia stared at her. "Expressionism? Isn't that, um, a departure for you?"

"What's expressionism?" Liz asked.

"You know, Jackson Pollock and all that," Sarah said. "I have a small one in the dining room."

"A Pollock?" Isabelle asked.

"A copy. My father liked it," Sarah clarified. "I didn't know you were veering so far afield."

How could she explain all the changes in her life these past few months? "I've wanted to try my wings and this is the opportunity I've prayed for. I have to go for it."

"Well, whatever you do, you'll be great." Sarah gave her an encouraging smile.

"Thanks."

Cate beamed at Isabelle. "I want one of your pieces for my house. That way you and your spirit will always be around me."

"What a lovely thing to say." Isabelle managed a smile. "And how are your wedding plans coming, Cate?"

Cate was glowing, and Isabelle was certain she'd never seen that blissful expression on her own face. "Trent and I have been so fortunate." She lowered her voice. "I wasn't going to tell until after the party, because I didn't want to take away from Mrs. Beabots's moment, but we're getting married here. In Mrs. Beabots's house. Next month."

Isabelle gasped. "So soon?"

"I can't wait," Cate gushed. "It seems like

forever for us. But May is the most beautiful month in Indian Lake. Not too hot. Not too cold. Flowers everywhere."

Sarah put her arm around Cate's shoulder and laughed. "And I should definitely be over this morning sickness by then."

Cate rattled off the menu they intended to serve. Liz talked about her baby's teething and how he kept her up all night. Isabelle was surprised Liz could laugh about it. She'd hated walking the floors with Violet and Sadie, when they were teething, so her mother could sleep. On the other hand, she hadn't been as averse to quieting Michael when he cried.

After her Wednesday night Thai dinner with Scott, she'd realized, brutally, that she had been remiss in not texting her sisters, seeing her friends. Most important, Bella and Michael didn't understand why she wasn't coming around as much lately. She liked being with them more than she'd anticipated.

She realized with surprise that she'd only seen the kids twice this past week. She'd wandered over to Scott's bookshop with the excuse that she needed a break from painting. Scott had been busy with customers—in fact, he had more business than ever with the new child-focused shop—and she'd been happy to spend time with Bella and Michael.

Even more surprising was that Isabelle missed the kids when she went home.

I miss them. I really do.

The changes in her perspective were subtle but clear. She had taken to heart what Scott had pointed out. Her life was not solely about her art. It never had been.

Her phone buzzed again in her purse. She ignored it. She didn't want to tell any of her girlfriends about Wes. He'd sparked too much curiosity at Olivia's wedding as it was. She knew if she mentioned him she'd get a thousand questions and none of them had an answer. He was her mentor. That was all she could honestly say about him right now.

Isabelle excused herself and eased her way into the front parlor where Scott was entertaining the group with a story about one of his tourist customers. Her mother was there, and winked when she saw Isabelle. Sadie gave her a finger wave. Their eyes went quickly back to Scott.

Isabelle had forgotten how good a storyteller Scott was, and how easily he could entrance people with his wicked sense of humor. He was both observant and insightful. She leaned against the doorjamb and listened.

As Scott finished the story, everyone laughed and some applauded. Just then, Isabelle's cell phone rang again. If she didn't answer it, Wes would not leave her alone all night.

She went to the kitchen, where she could be alone to take his call. "Hello?"

"I miss you," Wes said straight off.

"Really? Why?"

"I'm working in the studio and for the first time ever, it feels empty. I like it better when you're here with me."

"Wes. I don't know what to say."

"Say you're coming back tonight."

"Um. Not tonight. But Tuesday. The art student won't be in the apartment this week. And I'll be there bright and early on Wednesday for the show."

"That's too long."

"Two days?"

"That's what I said. Long time." His voice was hushed. Sensual. She could hear loneliness in his tone.

Wes had worked alone all his life, he'd told her. In fact, in the beginning, he'd been concerned that their situation wouldn't work out. He was afraid Malcolm had been too hasty in offering her part of his space.

"Wes," Isabelle began. "I promised my mother I'd spend some time with her. I'll be there Tuesday afternoon before the show."

"Oh, okay. I get that. Seeing your mom. I guess."

She put her hand on the island counter. Whether to steady herself from the idea that Wes actually missed her or to help her concentrate, she didn't know.

"I'm so surprised you miss me," she said.

"Yeah. Shocker." He laughed. "Well, have fun with your family. Ciao."

"Ciao." She ended the call.

She turned around to see Scott standing in the entryway. He was watching her, but didn't say anything. "How long have you been standing there?"

"Long enough to know that Wes misses you." His face was expressionless, but she saw pain in his eyes.

"Oh." Once again, she felt as if she were suffocating. Her friends talked of little besides weddings and babies. Subjects that made her uneasy. Clearly, none of them understood her completely. But how could they when she was only now discovering all that was Isabelle?

He took two strides and stood next to her. He took the cell phone out of her hand and put it in her purse. "You won't be needing that. At least not for a few minutes."

"Why—"

"Isabelle," he whispered and lowered his

eyes to her mouth. He pressed his lips against hers and pulled her close. She closed her eyes and let his kiss take her away. He obliterated her feelings of inadequacy and all her misgivings about her art, the frustration she felt being at home with her friends who lived in a universe so separate from hers. She felt his breath and the beat of his heart. The warmth of his hands on her back gave her strength.

She was falling—

She snapped her eyes open.

That was it. She was falling into a trap. Love's trap, the one that had captured all her girlfriends and made wives and mothers of most of them. She couldn't let that happen to her. She had goals to achieve. Interesting artists to meet. Honors to receive. Her future was golden, and if she allowed Scott to mesmerize her like this, everything she'd done, all her hard work would have been for nothing.

She had to be very careful.

"Scott, I think I should go."

"I'll drive you home."

"No."

"Why not?"

She took a step back, forcing him to drop his arms. "Because if you do, we'll keep kissing. I'm too vulnerable right now. You know I need to make this next showing the best of my life. If I get off track…"

He put his fingers over her lips. "Stop talking. Connie will take you home. Okay? That better?"

"Yes." She exhaled.

"But I'll pick you up Tuesday, about two. That way you'll be there for the show on Wednesday."

"That'd be great. Mom has to leave for work and my sisters will be off to school by then."

"Well," he said, placing his fingers at her temple and brushing back a long lock of hair. The soft satin light in his eyes went straight to her heart. "I assure you, you'll be in no danger from me."

What was happening to her? One minute she couldn't wait to be away from him and the next she thought she didn't want to spend a moment apart. Was she sabotaging herself? How could she want something more with him when she knew what it would cost her?

Each time she was with Scott, she forced herself to think about her future and not the sense of belonging she felt when she was with him. Even now, when she believed they'd come to an understanding that their lives would never mesh, she'd begun to want him more. Want what he wanted.

Her art fulfilled all her childhood dreams. But did she truly hold the same dreams now? Was she guilty of clinging so hard to one part of herself that she hadn't explored her own potential for more?

She forced herself to think about a future without Scott in it and the prospect was icy and hollow.

She felt like she was inside an impressionist painting where the light was fuzzy and objects difficult to discern. She was woefully conflicted and confusion didn't begin to explain the web of emotions inside her heart.

"I'll see you tomorrow," she said.

"Okay," he replied and brushed his lips against hers.

She closed her eyes, expecting more, but when she opened them he was gone.

She started to go after him, but stopped herself. That would go against her plan. Her goals.

Wouldn't it?

CHAPTER TWENTY-SIX

ISABELLE WAS ALONE with Connie in the open kitchen–living room of her house. Outside the wraparound glass walls flowed rivers of pink, yellow, orange and purple tulips, resembling a Monet painting. "How many bulbs did you plant last fall, Mom?"

"Oh, five, six hundred. The boys helped me," Connie said, pouring a fresh cup of coffee for Isabelle. She handed it to her with a stern eye. "How much weight have you lost?"

Isabelle shrugged and took the coffee. "I dunno. A few pounds. It couldn't be helped. I've been working so hard."

Connie put a hand on her hip. "Don't kid me. Art has nothing to do with this. I watched you with Scott yesterday. You're not yourself. Not by a long shot. Now, do you want to tell me what's going on, or should I drag it out of you like Sadie is learning to do in law school."

"Oh, Mom." Isabelle allowed a smile to lift the corners of her mouth. "She was always like that."

"Don't change the subject," Connie ordered.

Isabelle let out a deep breath but it didn't stop the sting in her eyes. "I think I'm falling in love with him."

"I thought that was a given." Connie lifted the coffee mug to her lips then lowered it when a tear slid down Isabelle's cheek. "Isabelle. We're not talking about Scott, are we?"

"No. Yes. Yes and no."

Isabelle watched her mother's expression switch from bewilderment to confusion to revelation.

"There's another man?"

"Mom. I don't understand myself at all anymore. I'm on the verge of becoming everything I ever wanted to be. Malcolm is planning another gallery showing next month, and my new paintings will be in it." Isabelle stared into her coffee and saw nothing but darkness. No silver linings. No glimmer of hope. Only paradoxes and difficult decisions that she didn't want to make.

Connie leaned back against the sofa cushions. "This is about that handsome artist. Malcolm's nephew?"

"Wes. Yes." Isabelle leveled her eyes on her mother. Maybe if she told her the story, her mother would know what to do. Maybe her mother had the answer. "I paint with him every weekend in the studio. He's working on an enormous commercial project. Mom, he's the most talented artist working in Chicago right now. *Art World* has done two articles on him in the past three years. This project could put him on top."

"On top?"

"Of the world. Er, the art world. He'll be immortal."

"Immortal?" Connie cleared her throat. "Isabelle. Be honest with me. Is that what you really want for yourself? Fame that's so immense, so permanent, that you would achieve immortality?"

Isabelle stared at her mother's shocked face. "Would that be so bad?"

"Uh, no. I just had no idea." She put the coffee mug on the glass tabletop.

"Mom, be honest with me. Isn't that what you're striving for?" She gestured to the bookshelves high on the walls where Connie had placed her architect models of skyscrapers and innovative commercial buildings. "If you got the chance to build one of your dreams, you'd be lionized. And if it rose above Wacker Drive in Chicago, people would know your name for decades. Centuries, maybe."

Connie glanced at the shelves and then looked at Isabelle. "And you grew up with my dreams sitting on a shelf, urging you to go for yours. Didn't you?"

"Yeah, chip off the old block, huh?"

"I'll say so." Connie reached for Isabelle's hand. "But sweetheart, where does Scott come in? And this Wes?"

"Mom, that's the really hard part." She put her coffee down. "Scott's been there for me for years. And lately, he's been, well, more romantic. When I'm with him, I feel… I feel…" Isabelle wiped away another tear or four. "And then there's Wes. He's everything I ever wanted for a life partner. He's an artist. He's handsome and charming and so talented. I feel like a sponge taking in every word and action of his. I've learned so much from him, I don't even know where to begin."

"And how does Wes feel about you?"

"That's the thing," she choked out, feeling her throat burn with the heat of truth. "I think he's falling in love with me. At Mrs. Beabots's yesterday he called and told me he misses me. He felt lonely because I wasn't there."

"I see."

Isabelle threw her hands in the air. "What? What! What do you see? Mom, I don't see anything. I feel torn in two. Yesterday, when I was with Scott, I felt… I don't know. Good. Safe. Appreciated. Then when Wes called, I wanted to be with him. Mom, help me." She reached for her mother's hand again. "I don't know what to do."

"Do nothing."

"Oh, thanks," Isabelle groaned. "That's wisdom?"

"Hey, I'm an architect. Not a counselor." She rubbed Isabelle's shoulder. "I'm sorry, sweetie. There's nothing worse than watching your child go through heartbreaking times. But the one thing I do know is that you are in a place that demands patience. You need to see this through to the end. I admire your tenacity and dedication to your art. You do have what it takes to make it someday. As for Scott and Wes, let them make the moves. Stand still. See which one rises to the top. Then you'll have your answer."

"Rises to the top? When does something like that happen?" Isabelle asked.

Connie picked up her mug as her lips crept into a puckish smile. "Usually after an explosion. Life has a way of shaking things up just so we can see how they're supposed to settle."

"Sounds harrowing to me." Isabelle gulped.

"Life changes usually are," Connie replied. "But don't worry, you have your whole family as a safety net. We love you, Isabelle. We always have."

Isabelle couldn't hide her skepticism. "But

everyone is always so busy. They hardly know what I'm doing. They—"

Connie speared her with a resolute gaze. "This family, each and every one of us, will always be grateful to you, Isabelle, for all you sacrificed when you were young. You never got to have a childhood and we all know it. I've kept everyone from calling you so you could have time to concentrate on your art. The boys call me several times a week asking about you. They were thrilled about your showing. Weren't we all there?"

"Er, yes. I was surprised, really," Isabelle confessed.

"We all know this is your time. We don't want to do the first thing to stand in your way. If Scott loves you, and I believe he does, even if he's been too chicken to say so, then eventually, when you've reached that star you've picked out, he'll be there, too. I can't vouch for Wes. But I will say this—if he loves you, he'd better treat you like the princess you are."

"Oh, Mom. I love you so much." Isabelle flung her arms around her mother and rested her head on her shoulder. This time, she didn't pluck away her tears. She let them flow.

SCOTT DROVE EAST down the country road to-ward Connie's house the next morning. Isabelle had told him that Connie had insisted she spend the past two nights there, instead of her own apartment. It was so rare for Isabelle to stay there, Scott wondered why Connie had been so adamant.

"Hi, Scott!" Connie waved as she came out the front door carrying an insulated bag. Isabelle was behind her, suitcase in hand. Purse and small tote over her shoulder. The woman never traveled light.

He got out of his van and offered to help. "What's in here?" he asked Connie as he hoisted the bags into the back seat.

"I went to the deli and got some things for Isabelle. She won't have to cook for a week," Connie said, glancing back at her daughter.

"Bye, Mom. Thanks for everything." Isabelle hugged her mother. "This was a good visit."

"Yes, it was," Connie replied, smoothing Isabelle's caramel hair from her cheek and placing a long lock behind her shoulder. "Once that food is gone, you let me know. I'll have Ross or Dylan drop some more off for you when they head your way."

"Mom…"

"You're not eating. Take it." Her voice dropped an octave; even Scott shuddered when Connie gave orders like that.

"Okay." Isabelle hugged her again. "I love you."

"I love you, too. Be careful on that train," Connie said.

Scott closed the door. "Oh, I'm going to drive her to the city."

"What?" Isabelle spun to look at him.

He grinned. He wondered if it seemed sincere or phony. "My mom's got the kids. Violet and Sadie are taking care of the bookstore. You can save your ticket for another time. And you'll save the Brown Line fare."

"I take the bus."

"Better still." Today, he wasn't taking no for an answer.

Connie hugged him. "That's so kind of you, Scott. I always worry about these trains and buses. Isabelle isn't a city girl, and well...you know."

"I understand." He held the passenger door open for Isabelle. "We should go."

"Bye again, Mom."

"Bye, honey. I'll call you tonight." Connie waved.

Scott honked the horn as they drove away and Isabelle waved one last time to her mother.

"Well." She turned to him, her voice devoid of the warmth it had held a moment ago. "That was pretty slick."

"I should've called you beforehand and given you some warning, but I had a lot of loose ends to tie up before we left."

"Take me to the station anyway."

"No."

"Scott!" She was mad. Good and mad. And he hadn't even hit her with the albatross he carried around his neck.

Relentlessly, she pushed on. "What, are you kidnapping me now? This is ridiculous. I'll be fine on the train."

"I know you will, but I need to talk to you about something."

"I know what you want to say."

"Is that so?"

"I do. You want to talk about me and Wes." She folded her arms across her chest.

Scott shifted in his seat. He hated feeling this on edge. But then, when hadn't he been in the dark when it came to Isabelle? She'd turned him down twice for the sake of her art. He supposed he understood that. Sort of. But she wasn't talking about them anymore. She was talking about another guy.

"Wes." He said the name flatly, shoved his anger into his foot and hit the gas. It was time they had this talk. He needed to know if she was falling for Wes. If she chose a life with Scott, he would support her artistic side—as he had throughout their friendship. But if Isabelle had chosen her art *and* chosen Wes, this was Scott's moment of truth.

"I have to be honest with you, Scott. You've always been honest with me."

He thought of his overnight decision to become a foster dad. The lightning-quick idea to buy a house and redesign his shop. All done without consulting Isabelle. He hadn't been exactly dishonest. But he hadn't been open, either.

"Honest." Scott wondered why the word felt so acidic on his tongue.

"I want you to know that there hasn't been anything between Wes and me...except for that one kiss."

"*What* kiss?" He spun his head to peer at her. *The guy was kissing her?*

He gripped the steering wheel so hard his fingers turned white. He should have figured on that one. Maybe he just didn't want to paint that picture in his head. Wes was in Chicago with her. Painting in a studio all day on Saturdays and Sundays. Maybe half the night.

"It was just the one time."

Apparently, once was enough to turn her head. But what about her heart?

Scott stomped on his temper. He took a deep breath to calm himself. "Look, Isabelle. You're a free agent. I don't have a say in your love life."

"Scott, I don't want to hurt you. I don't want anyone to get hurt. I had a long talk with my mother about all this—"

He cut her off. "You told your *mother* about Wes?"

This was serious. Very serious.

"Yes and she told me not to make any decisions about my personal life right now. I need to focus on my art. I need to learn all that Wes can teach me."

She went on about Wes and her art and Malcolm's next showing, but all Scott heard was that she was conflicted about him and another guy. Six months ago, she was sharing pizza with him regularly, painting faeries which looked astoundingly like him.

Isabelle kept rambling and Scott remained silent, trying to make sense of what she was saying.

He drove through town, circled around the lake and drove up to the Lodges, finding a space in the far parking lot reserved for employees. The lot was nearest to the thickest grove of lily pads and cattails. Spring daffodils poked their heads through the weeds and reeds.

"What are we doing here?" she asked.

"I have to drop off a big order of coffee that

Edgar wanted. Just be a minute." He turned off the engine, but didn't move.

He crossed his arms over the steering wheel, laid his chin on them and gestured out the windshield with his forefinger.

"I remember the first time you showed me this place. It was spring then, too. We were young—just teenagers. You said it was magical and I didn't believe you."

"I'd been going there since I was seven."

"You told me that," he said.

She stared out the window but remained silent.

He hoped she was remembering.

"You told me how you would walk out there barefoot and peek between the lily pads and reeds. You said you saw a water sprite just the day before. You took my hand and showed me where to look, but I didn't see a thing. But you did. That's when I knew that the magic was in you, Isabelle. You were born with that gift."

"I've seen them since I was a child," she said softly, not taking her eyes from the view.

"I know. I never doubted you for a minute."

She turned slowly to face him. "And now?"

"Nothing's changed. Whatever you've wanted to do, you've done. I still want you to stretch and grow like you always have. And yet, everything has changed. Now another man is encouraging you, too. Maybe he knows more than me—I mean, I know he knows more about art. But I'm not sure he knows more about Isabelle."

Scott realized he'd been wrong not to press her for a commitment years ago. He hadn't told her how much he wanted a family and then he'd made huge life decisions without including her. His actions had broadcasted one thing to Isabelle: she didn't matter to him.

But nothing was further from the truth. He wanted her, loved her more than ever, and now she was slipping away. One brush stroke at a time. "Isabelle, all I ask is that you remember who you are." He gestured to the lily pads. "You're a part of Indian Lake that no one else can claim."

"I know." She lowered her head. "But I'm better than this. You'll see. I can be so much more."

"I believe in you, Isabelle." Without another thought in his head he placed his hands on her either side of her face and kissed her. He wanted this to be the kiss that seared through her dreams at night. If she ever kissed Wes again, he hoped it was *this* kiss she'd remember.

When he pulled back, she kept her eyes closed.

"Scott…"

He kissed her again, as if he were going off to war and might not come back alive. It was a kiss filled with all the love in his heart. A kiss that words could not describe.

This time when he withdrew from her, she pierced him with her smoky green eyes.

"Scott. Take me to the station. Please. I need to clear my head."

You need to clear your heart of Wes.

"Sure. I'm very happy for you, Isabelle. This show will be your ticket to stardom." He started the engine. "Maybe it's best I do take you to the train station," he said.

"It would be best," she agreed.

Scott had meant what he'd said. He would always, always want the best for her. He loved her enough to let her go. If she came back to him, then he would know she would never stop loving him.

He pulled up to the South Shore.

"Isabelle, there's one last thing."

"What's that?"

"Promise me that I'm the last guy you'll kiss today."

She smiled softly, leaned over and kissed his cheek. "What a silly promise," she said, opening the door. "Bye, Scott."

"Bye," he replied and watched her race to meet the incoming train.

She got on board without looking back. The train pulled away quickly. It had schedules to keep.

This train was taking Isabelle toward her future. He sensed that the gallery show would be successful for her. She was about to achieve all she'd worked so long and hard for.

The train had sped away and was now a speck disappearing into the horizon.

Scott felt the moments of his life with Isabelle funnel into the hollows of his heart where they would become memories of what he once had. And had lost.

CHAPTER TWENTY-SEVEN

TUESDAY AFTERNOON MALCOLM made a surprise visit to the studio, interrupting her work. As far as Isabelle was concerned, nothing good could come from an unscheduled critique.

"Isabelle. Lovely to see you." Malcolm rushed toward her, his suit coat open and flapping in the wind he created with his always-theatrical entrances and exits.

"Malcolm. How was Barcelona?"

"Enchanting. Paris was riveting and Florence—ah!" He clasped his hands in front of him. "I lost my shirt on the Florence deal."

"I'm sorry."

"Not as sorry as I am." He walked around her. "Now, Wes tells me you've been busy. By the way, where is my nephew?"

Isabelle had just started a new piece, one she'd felt a particular inspiration to paint.

Spring fever had caused Isabelle to think about her faeries again. But she wanted to push open that door to her own mind and communicate the love and freedom she'd felt when she first envisioned her water sprites years and years ago. She wanted to capture their green-and-blue eyes. Happy eyes. Hope-filled eyes. That's how she liked to look at life, but she'd lost that perspective lately. She hoped the painting would help her regain it.

"Wes is with his prospective client," she replied, placing a tube of azure blue paint on the bench. "We didn't expect you."

"I like to surprise my protégé." He smiled greedily as he looked from the canvas to a half dozen wooden painter's palettes smeared with the oils she'd been combining. "Did you mix these?" he asked, walking over to the bench and inspecting them.

"I did." Isabelle felt the same barbed nerves she'd experienced the day of the gallery showing. Malcolm was not there as her friend, but as her investor and her biggest critic. She braced herself.

"Interesting hues. You're painting water again?"

"No. The eyes of the water sprites."

With his hands clasped behind his back he straightened. The gaze he leveled on her felt like a blast of autumn wind off Indian Lake. "I love it already," he cried. "*L-O-V-E*! My nephew has helped you turn a corner, hasn't he?"

"Yes. He has," she said, the joy of accomplishment leaping inside her. The last time Malcolm had inspected her work, he hadn't been all that pleased. Of course, at this point he was only looking at the colors she'd mixed. Not the finished product. It was probably best not to let her joy go to her head.

"Wes suggested that I concentrate on surrealism for this piece rather than expressionism. And I'm doing it in oil. I have a raw sketch—"

Malcolm waved his palms in the air as if warding off a swarm of gnats. "Goodness no. I have to experience the finished product. Let your genius flow. Hmm?" His eyes were round with anticipation.

He put his hand on her shoulder and with a grave expression, he said, "Isabelle, I'm counting on you tomorrow. I have clients who are known to support emerging talent. They can't afford Wes anymore, and honestly—" his chuckle was laced with arrogance "—who can?"

Realization struck her like a strange kick in the head as she listened to Malcolm talk. So, this was what he had in mind all along? For her to be a poor man's Wes? She was intended to be his clone. Was it like this for other unknown artists in her position? It didn't matter. She'd seen through the illusion and now she had to make a choice.

She was here. All she had to do was bring

the vision in her head and the emotion in her heart together in a symphonic blend of color on a canvas.

She could do this, and she didn't give a hoot if the buyers were looking for rummage sale bargains; she'd give them prestigious collectors' items.

"I won't disappoint you, Malcolm." She flashed her green eyes confidently.

"I believe you won't."

FIRST SHOWINGS WERE nerve-wracking, Isabelle realized, but this second show was a mindbender. The first time around, she'd displayed work she'd been creating for years. This show was all about her advancement and her ability to produce on deadline. Unfortunately for her, Malcolm had been praising her abilities to clients, critics and the social media. She felt like a monkey in a zoo.

She was about to jump out of her skin.

She wore a pearl gray sheath dress with a chambray duster over it. In her ears were long narrow slivers of Arizona turquoise and sterling silver. She'd washed her hair twice and conditioned it with a protein pack. She wanted it to shine like one of her faerie's tresses. But all her attention to her attire did nothing to quell her nerves.

It didn't help that Wes was late. She could have used some encouragement.

Malcolm was reserved as he, too, wove through the crowd of art buyers, explaining Wes's new commissioned paintings, expounding on the bargain prices for his smaller canvases at only ten thousand dollars each.

"Oh, Isabelle," she grumbled. "You are so naive. This isn't about you. This is about you making money for them. They care about the overall show. Get a grip. Toughen up."

This time, Malcolm had allowed her to hang her new work in the same room, but to display them as she pleased. She was happiest with the painting of lifelike swirls of blues and greens that depicted the ripples in the lake on a summer day, a dragonfly darting over the surface. The artistic stretch was groundbreaking enough that, even now, chills shot down her spine.

Malcolm had pressured her to produce as many pieces as possible, and when she'd first started, she'd been so unsure of herself. Wes had told her he actually couldn't work without deadlines. Now she knew what he meant. She'd painted five works. Four were in acrylic. One in oil. The oil would command a higher price and was the one Malcolm had the most enthusiasm for. However, Isabelle knew that in the very commercial art world, acrylic paintings like hers could sell well over a thousand dollars. Granted she didn't have a name in the marketplace yet, but she would.

She cocked her head as she inspected her painting of a water sprite swirling inside a funnel of aquamarine water as she rose above the lake. This painting was important to Isabelle because the faerie's heart was broken.

Just like mine.

Each time she'd seen Scott, and then left him, their parting had been bittersweet. She knew she'd come back for his party or see him again around town.

Wouldn't she?

What if this new life didn't allow her to split time between Chicago and Indian Lake? What if she was offered an opportunity that would take her to the East Coast? The West? Would she go with it?

Or would she stay?

Right now, she felt like her faerie, dancing on slippery rocks, with high winds of change swirling around her.

Yes, she'd been painting her broken heart.

And Scott had broken it.

Or had he?

Up till now, all she'd focused on was a gallery showing. She hadn't explored the possibilities for her life after her acceptance into the art world. That was the rock that tripped her.

"Don't you look anxious?" Wes said, slipping up behind her. He put his hands on her shoulders and looked at her display. "Great job. They'll love it."

"Do you think so?"

"I do."

She turned to face him. He was handsome as ever, dressed in a dark blue suit, blue shirt, navy silk tie and black cowboy boots.

"How did it go with the client?"

"Bagged 'em."

"Everything you do, Wes, is brilliant. It's no wonder you got a new contract. Malcolm must be over the moon about it," she said.

"He is."

"Everything that Malcolm has promised about you, you've been able to deliver. I admire that. You work better under pressure than anyone I've ever seen."

He touched her nose and winked. "I was until you came on board. Now I feel I have to keep up with you."

"Don't start your flattery—"

"It's the truth. You're amazing, Miss Isabelle." They both turned at the sound of Malcolm's voice calling them.

"I better go."

Miss Isabelle. How odd.

Even when Wes said her name, all she heard was Bella's voice, as if the child were calling to her. But that was crazy.

She looked around the gallery at the increasing number of patrons. The place was packed—even more than the spring show—and yet, no one was buying. True, Wes's works were pricier this time. Hers were up two hundred dollars a unit from the last show. She gnawed her lower lip. Was Malcolm being too aggressive? Had he priced them out of the market? This was a different crowd, he'd said. Unlike last time, this was an American group. No Europeans or South American collectors had been invited. Malcolm said he was saving them for the summer and autumn shows.

With a shock, Isabelle realized that other than Wes and Malcolm, she didn't know a single person here. Her entire family had come to her last show. All of her friends. Mrs. Beabots.

Scott and the children.

Bella had been intimidated by the experience, but obviously enthralled.

Isabelle remembered their trip to the studio and the kids' overactive behavior. Scott had been frustrated, but Isabelle had understood their enthusiasm.

It was second nature to her—being a mom. Being the mother Bella and Michael needed.

She looked back at her painting of the faerie on the rocks. She'd always known how to walk through the shoals over slippery rocks. She'd always known how to give love to a child when he or she needed it. She knew how to put her heart and soul on a piece of canvas and stick it on a wall in a gallery for all the world to see… or for a critic to deride.

She was stronger than she'd ever realized.

Malcolm walked up. "Ah! Isabelle, my beautiful protégé. You look fabulous. Like one of our master paintings," he said, loud enough for the well-dressed couple nearby to hear him.

She knew he was playing to the crowd. It was a bit overdone, but he was a genius at selling art. They air-kissed.

"How's it going?" she asked. "The sales I mean."

"Nothing yet. But it's early." He raised his hand in answer to the elegant couple's signal. "I'm wanted."

Hmm. It's not all that early, she thought.

A waiter passed Isabelle with a tray of champagne flutes. "Can I get you something, miss?"

"A water, please. Tall. Very tall." She smiled. Something told her it was going to be a long afternoon.

For the next hour, people came and went, buying little. Wes spent an abnormally long time with a couple who owned a gallery in New York. The woman was fashionably dressed in current Coco Chanel with more jewelry than Isabelle had even seen on Mrs. Beabots. Isabelle guessed her to be around forty. Her hair was professionally colored with four shades of blond, each swirling into the next like spun gold and honey. She was beautiful and she didn't take her eyes off Wes from the moment they entered the gallery.

Wes laughed and joked. He seemed unaware of the woman's interest in him. Isabelle wondered what the man with her thought of her intense focus on Wes.

After another ten minutes, the two men were slapping each other on the back and still laughing. Finally, the man turned to the woman and she nodded.

Isabelle lowered her water glass. The woman held the purse strings. Wes beamed as the woman gave Wes a slow and brazen wink.

As if on cue, Malcolm appeared at their side and shook their hands. Closing the deal was Malcolm's forte. He was overly enthusiastic and laughed along with them all. They walked to the back hall that led to Malcolm's office as Wes turned and introduced himself to two male buyers who were admiring the gray-and-blue masterpiece he'd named *Odysseus* because he felt the pain of a solitary man battling life like a sailor in a maelstrom.

As Wes threw himself into his next sales pitch, Isabelle saw a man walk up to her paintings, which were displayed in a group. "Can I tell you anything about the works?" she asked sweetly.

"No." He twitched his head from side to side, up and down as if he needed bifocals and was too cheap or afraid to seek an ophthalmologist's help. "I'm not here to buy."

Though disappointed she said, "Admiring is fine, too."

He shifted his gaze to her. "I'm observing, yes. Admiring? Not so much. I'm writing an article on this show."

"Oh." Isabelle swallowed hard. She'd been wondering where the critics were. For Malcolm's last show they'd come early for the food and wine and left late. This time, she hadn't been able to pick any out. "And you write for...?"

"Arttoday.com," he replied haughtily.

"I'm so sorry, I haven't heard of you."

He eyed her like she was a goldfish in a bowl and he was considering flushing her down the toilet. "I haven't heard of you either, Miss Hawks."

She swallowed twice. Once to keep her mind focused so that she wouldn't sink right through the floor and once to bite back the searing retort on the tip of her tongue. She couldn't say it if she ever wanted to sell anything again. "I'm...just getting started," she managed and then regretted her apologetic tone.

She should have walked away. She should have killed him with kindness, but she didn't. She stood her ground and squared her shoulders. "What can I tell you about the paintings? I'm sure you have questions."

"I don't. Not about these, er, yours. But I was wondering if you would introduce me to Wes?"

Isabelle felt as if she were the usher in a large theater, taking tickets and pointing out the proper aisles. She wasn't the main attraction. She wasn't even the pre-show. This man wasn't from *Art World* or *The New Yorker*. She'd have to look up the number of followers he had online. He could be a hack himself. And he wanted a favor from her?

She was Malcolm's protégé and she owed him a great deal. Even if she'd like to escort this man to the front door and kick him to the curb, she could not. "I'd love to," she said. "What's your name?"

"Gerard Tate."

The only Tate Isabelle knew was the famous

Tate Gallery in London. "Is Malcom expecting you?"

"Not exactly." He patted his slacks and jacket pockets. "I left my business cards at the hotel."

"No problem. Come with me, Mr. Tate."

Isabelle led the way to where Wes was discussing his crimson, gray and amber work. At a break in the conversation, she introduced Gerard Tate.

"Thanks, Isabelle," Wes said with a nod, indicating she should go back to her station to talk to buyers. Isabelle went back to where her paintings were hanging.

Or had hung.

Two were missing.

Two men rushed up to her. "Are you Isabelle Hawks?" the taller one asked. "Wes said you were here."

"I am." She blushed, sensing their enthusiasm. This was a new experience. Someone had asked for her by name.

"We just told Wes we want these three paintings," the taller man continued. "I love this woman on the rocks. There's so much movement. I almost can feel the spray on my face."

"Yes. We're designing a mid-century modern house in Ogden Dunes overlooking the lake," his companion added. "We need something incomparable. Something extraordinary. And these colors! You have quite a talent. Your work is perfect for us."

"I'm flattered," she replied. "Mr.—"

"How rude of us. Sorry. I'm Andrew Fitzwilliam and this is George Ducaine. We own F&D Design House here in Chicago." He looked at her as if she should recognize the name.

"Friends of Malcolm," George added. "We were in St. Moritz during the last show. We heard you sold everything then, as well. What we want to know, Miss Hawks, is whether you'd be willing to create for our clients on demand."

Isabelle's jaw dropped open. She wanted to jump for joy, but somehow she managed to keep her feet on the ground. "I could do that," she said casually, clasping her shaking hands behind her back.

"Here's our card," George said, handing a heavy cream business card to her. "Malcolm has all our information." He took out his iPhone. "Could you give me your cell phone number so we don't lose touch?"

"George, you're too aggressive," Andrew chided.

Isabelle laughed and gave him the number as two of the gallery crew came over and took down the last of the three paintings Andrew and George had just bought. "You're taking them today?"

"Absolutely. I know Malcolm. If someone offers him more money, he'd give us the boot."

"No," Isabelle scoffed.

"Yes." Andrew cocked his eyebrows.

They finished exchanging information and Isabelle chatted with them as they finalized their purchases.

After saying goodbye, she noticed that there was only one of her paintings left and none of Wes's.

An hour later the show was winding down. Malcolm walked the last group to the door, making certain they each had one of his business cards and his private cell number.

Wes came up to Isabelle. "I have to run. I'm meeting my new buyers across town for a drink."

"The man and woman from New York?" she asked, knowing full well which buyers he meant.

"Uh, yeah. Madrigan and Charles are brother and sister and have a place in Soho. They bought three of my pieces. They want more." He leaned over and air-kissed her cheek. She didn't feel a thing. "See you later."

"Ciao," she said, but he'd already darted out the door, slapping Malcolm on the back as he went.

How odd. He didn't congratulate me on my sales or my success.

Scott would have.

Malcolm strode toward Isabelle with a brilliant smile across his face. "We should talk, Isabelle. In my office?"

"Certainly," she replied, following him down the hall.

The gallery was quiet without the phone ringing and the receptionist's welcoming voice, the clink and clang of dishes and glasses. The busy caterers had vanished and the last of the buyers' conversations had faded. The party was over.

Oddly, Isabelle's heart felt like iron in her chest as she lowered herself into the chair opposite Malcolm. This was her moment. She had achieved success, glory. But she didn't feel like she was on top of the world.

That rush of joy and elation she'd felt when she was painting was nowhere to be found now. The pull of the subjects she intended to paint that kept her awake at night had abandoned her.

"Malcolm," she said brightly, clasping her hands in her lap. "The show was a success. Wes said he sold three paintings to the people from Soho."

"We sold everything Wes produced and commissioned several more. I expected that," he replied, drumming his fingers on the desk.

"I only met one critic this time. A man..."

"Oh, the critics were here. In the first hour. They left early."

"I didn't see them. I'm sorry."

"Me, too." Malcolm clasped his hands and leaned back in his chair smiling up at the ceiling. "What I do know is that they loved your work. And they're touting me for finding you. Isabelle," he said, sitting straight up, "you've made me even more famous."

She blinked in astonishment. "I did that for you?"

"You did, young lady. I told you I have an eye for talent." He puffed his chest. "Must be my genius."

"I'm certain." She smiled back.

"So, Isabelle, as to what this means…"

This could mean something more? What more could there be? She'd paint on commission for George and Andrew. Produce pieces for Malcolm. Beyond that…

"I want to move you to Chicago full-time. I'll get you a nice apartment, like I did for Wes. I may look around for a studio all your own."

"Malcolm?"

He held his palms in the air to stop her. "There's more. I have a feeling that Wes might pull off this sale this afternoon and wind up with a studio in New York. Now, I know I'm getting ahead of myself here, but if that happens, I want you to consider living there, too. Part-time at the beginning, of course. Then there's the fact that I haven't been blind, you know."

"Blind?"

"I've seen the way Wes looks at you. Like there's no one else on earth but you."

"Yeah. He does that a lot," she said.

"No, Isabelle. He doesn't. You're special to him. I think he's in love with you."

"That's not true. He's never said a word." But then again, Scott hadn't exactly swept her off her feet, either. Other than New Year's Eve, when he had told her that he wanted a family and he wanted her help. But he hadn't gotten down on his knee. There hadn't been a ring. He hadn't made her feel loved. He'd needed her to be a mother...but not a wife.

"Perhaps he needs encouragement, Isabelle." He cleared his throat and his voice became stern. "Both of you have your heads in the clouds, if you ask me. You both think, breathe and live your art, which is great for me, but maybe not so great for you. Don't get me wrong. He's my nephew and I love him, but he can be difficult sometimes."

"I don't know what to say, Malcolm. This is a lot to think about. Moving here. New York. Even Wes. I'm going to need some time."

"I understand. And there's no rush." He chuckled. "Except for the paintings. I'll need more for the summer show."

"When is that?"

"June. It's a door-buster." He grinned.

Isabelle rose and walked behind his desk. She put her arms around his neck. "Thank you for all you've done for me, Malcolm. You gave me the world I've dreamed of. And then some."

He hugged her back. "You're welcome, Isabelle. You deserve it."

She went to the door and opened it.

"Uh, Isabelle. Am I too bold to ask—your hesitation, does it have anything to do with that guy from Indian Lake?" He snapped his fingers, unable to summon Scott's name.

She held the doorknob. She was passing through yet another door. But what future did it lead to?

She faced him. "It might."

He nodded. "Ciao."

"Ciao."

CHAPTER TWENTY-EIGHT

Isabelle put her brushes and paints in her tote, then stuffed her splattered smock in on top and zipped the bag. She looked around the studio, now devoid of all her paintings. Wes's murals would be placed in a few weeks. All his paintings had sold.

This studio, which had so much life in it when she'd first come here, seemed empty now. The energy she'd thought was Wes's and Wes's alone, she realized, might have been the energy of her dreams.

Maybe she'd been the one to give life to this old place.

Maybe she'd had it inside her all this time and the only one who had seen it was Scott.

"Hey, there you are!" Wes said, coming down the hall. He was still dressed in his suit, a broad smile on his face. "Malcolm said you might be here."

"Yeah. I'm going back home. Easter—this weekend."

"You have plans, then?"

"Yes," she replied cautiously. She hadn't heard from Scott since yesterday. She'd thought he might send her a text about the show, but he hadn't. Still, there was his brunch on Saturday. She hoped she was still invited. "I think so."

"Malcolm is excited and proud of you," Wes said, approaching her. "So am I."

"Thanks." She hoisted her tote onto her shoulder.

"He told me about his offer."

"Yeah, I'm still in shock."

"You should be. He's never done that before."

"Never?" She gasped.

"No. He said you didn't take it."

"I told him I had to think about it—"

"Look, Isabelle, I know I've been distant and we've both been under a lot of pressure to meet his demands, and believe me, he can be a taskmaster. But the truth is, I miss you terribly when you're not here, and that's never happened to me before. I look forward to seeing you every weekend—can't wait for Saturdays to roll around, it seems. You don't know what you've done to me."

What had Isabelle done to make this icon of an artist, this very pleasant and interesting man, actually feel that she added something to his mesmerizing life? "Tell me."

"You've changed everything. I don't want to go to New York without you."

"Pardon?"

"This deal for the Soho space is going to happen, and I want it for both of us. With you by my side, I feel, I mean I *know* I can be better than I have ever been. You bring out something in me that wasn't there before. I think it's heart. My uncle says I've fallen in love with you. I've never been in love, so you need to excuse my slow uptake on this. But I have to agree with him. I'm in love with you."

Isabelle felt as if she was in the middle of one of her surreal paintings. This was exactly what she'd scripted as the movie of her life. Her art would be renowned. A famous artist would find her irresistible and she would go on to awards and fame all over the world.

But as she looked into his blue eyes, she didn't see Wes. She saw brown eyes with gold flecks. She saw the man who'd stolen her heart years ago. For a person who was expected to see visions of other worlds and colors and sights that most humans miss, she'd hoodwinked herself.

She'd left Scott. She'd denied her growing love for Bella and Michael because she was convinced that children, especially Scott's, would weigh her down.

What she hadn't realized was that they would make her life worth living.

"Wes, I don't know what to say."

His smile dropped off his face. His blue eyes clouded. "I was hoping your reply would be obvious."

"You're wonderful, Wes. You are, but my heart…"

"Belongs to someone else."

"It does."

"If that were true, then why isn't he standing here next to you?"

"Because I'm a fool," she replied, feeling her eyes sting and her heart grow heavy with sadness.

"We're all fools, Isabelle. Certainly, I am. I should have realized that what I was feeling wasn't only admiration."

"I'm sorry, Wes."

"Yeah." He hugged her. "Isabelle, if it doesn't work out, would you give me a second chance?"

A second chance. Didn't everyone deserve another chance? Even her?

"I believe I would."

He smiled again. "Then you take care."

"Goodbye," she said and headed out the door.

Another door. Leading to uncertainty.

CHAPTER TWENTY-NINE

ISABELLE HAD ASKED her brother Ross to drive her home from Chicago since he was going home for the Easter weekend, as well.

When they reached her apartment, she thanked him profusely.

"I don't mind at all, Isabelle. You would have done the same for me. You've always been there for all of us. Now it's our turn to help you."

Her tears were unexpected. "I love you, Ross."

"I love you, too, sis."

After dragging her bags to her apartment, she collapsed on the sofa.

Probably an adrenaline crash after the show and the offer from Malcolm, she told herself as she pulled an afghan over her legs.

She didn't know what it was about making life decisions that caused this weariness, but all she could do was close her eyes and hope she would find answers in her sleep.

ON SATURDAY MORNING, Isabelle dressed for brunch in a soft pink dress and beige heels. Friday had passed in a blur of unpacking, laundry and dyeing Easter eggs for Bella and Michael. She'd bought Easter baskets for them at a children's shop in Evanston not far from the studio.

As she drove through town and toward the lake over streets strewn with pink and white pear and crabapple blossoms, she felt as if she'd been away for ages, not just a few days. Yet in those few days the landscape of her life had blown up like it had been hit by a tornado.

All her life she'd wanted to know if she was good enough, if she had real talent. The reality of it hadn't settled into her bones quite yet, but she liked her newfound confidence. It was a new feeling. A safe feeling.

For so long she'd been swimming in a riptide of uncertainty and doubt. And after all that had happened in Chicago, with Malcolm and with Wes, she knew she was back where she belonged. Indian Lake was paradise.

Without realizing it, she'd steered her car to the Lodges and not to Scott's new house, as if her heart was her GPS.

She realized she might never work here again, and the idea made her sad. She'd had fun working for Edgar. Seeing her friends on holidays, planning events and dances for special occasions. It had been a good life she'd built; she just hadn't always appreciated it.

She parked in the employee lot. Shadows of the last time she and Scott sat in his van in this very spot ghosted across her mind. She touched her lips, remembering his kiss.

She'd achieved her dreams and they exceeded her expectations. Yet, without Scott, the void inside her grew.

She turned back to the car and opened the door. The sun glinted off the window, and she blinked. Then she saw the reflection of the lily pads bobbing in the lake.

Mesmerized by the vision, she shut the door, turned and walked toward the beach and the tiny inlet where she and Scott had so often ventured.

She crouched down, peeking between the ripples of lake water and the lily pads. She remembered Scott's words to her.

The magic was in you, Isabelle.

Her tears sprang anew, and through the iridescent veil they created across her field of vision, she saw a faerie. This one had green eyes like hers and long, thick caramel hair. Its wings were opalescent and shimmered brightly.

The faerie smiled at her.

In that split second, understanding shot straight to Isabelle's heart. All these years, she'd been painting herself. Isabelle had been robbed of a normal childhood to care for her brothers and sisters. She'd taken out her resentment and anger on them, her mother and even herself. She'd convinced her adult self that she didn't want a family or a home and that only her art could make her happy. She knew, now, that wasn't true.

She was not just good, but accepted by the art world. Her work would sell, whether she painted faeries or continued to explore the depths of her talent. She would always paint; her art was as much a part of her as her arms and legs.

Something settled down in her heart. She'd been fluttering around the truth for years, not seeing reality. Isabelle was no longer frightened by the idea of a family. In fact, she was warmed by it. Over the past months, she'd come to realize how much her brothers and sisters had supported and loved her. They'd thanked her for being there when they were so young.

She realized that if she had to do it all over again, she wouldn't change a thing.

She would walk the floor with her younger sisters and she would help her mother in every way she could—because she loved them.

She loved them.

And she loved Scott.

Scott, the wise one. The observant one. He'd seen all this time that the faeries she painted were depictions of the little girl inside her.

Through her art, these fantasy self-portraits, she'd been healing her broken heart.

"I've been so blind," she admonished herself as tears filled her eyes. The world she wanted had been at her fingertips all along.

Isabelle had taken the first steps into a world where her painting would be part of her life, but not all of it. Scott was her world.

CHAPTER THIRTY

ISABELLE HAD TO PARK A half a block away from Scott's house because his driveway and the street were filled with cars she recognized. All their friends were here.

As she approached the house, she did a double take. When he'd moved in back in February, the place had seemed stark and uninviting, but this picture-perfect bungalow with blooming hyacinths, daffodils and forsythia surrounding the newly painted front porch was lovely.

The pear trees were in bloom and the grass was thick and emerald green. Scott had placed a huge stuffed Easter bunny on a chair on the front porch. As she lifted her hand to knock, she heard dozens of voices coming from inside.

She turned the knob and pushed the door open. "Hello?"

She heard children laughing and a cacophony of pots and pans, dishes and silverware.

"Hello?" She walked past the empty living room, noticing that blinds and curtains had been hung. The bookshelves were filled and there were two toy boxes under the front window. A kid-sized rocking chair sat next to a new stuffed club chair, and Easter decorations filled the mantle.

Bella came running out of the kitchen with Danny Sullivan on her heels. She was squealing with delight, holding a chocolate bunny over her head. The second she saw Isabelle, she stopped. Danny ran into her back.

"Bella!" he chided and took the Easter bunny out of her hand. Then he, too, looked at Isabelle. "Oh, hello, Miss Isabelle."

Isabelle's eyes remained on Bella. "Happy Easter."

"Happy Easter." Bella heaved a sigh, as if she'd been holding her breath. She walked straight over to Isabelle and threw her arms around her waist. "I was afraid you wouldn't come."

Isabelle shifted the Easter baskets to her left hand and put her right hand on Bella's head. "Why wouldn't I?"

"Dad read all about you in the newspaper this morning. He said you were famous. It said you were moving to New York."

Bella lifted her face and smiled. Tears ran down her cheeks.

"It said that?"

"Uh-huh."

"Oh, Bella." Isabelle felt her heart bloom as she knelt beside the little girl. "I missed you too much. I would never move away from you."

"Honest and truly?" Bella sniffed.

"Honest. I told you I would be here for Easter. And I brought something for you and for Michael."

"That's very sweet of you, Isabelle," Scott said, stepping out of the kitchen as he dried his hands on a dish towel.

He wore black jeans and a spring yellow sweater with the sleeves pushed up. She'd never seen him look so handsome, not even in a tux. Yet his eyes were wary. He moved slowly toward her.

She didn't blame him. She'd thrown him nothing but crumbs for too long. She'd come here to apologize. To ask forgiveness for her thoughtlessness. Her selfishness. Blind ambition. For all the times she'd hurt him. She'd come to ask him for a second chance. Or thirteenth. Whatever number it was, she owed him a lot.

Danny tugged on Scott's arm. "Are we going to eat soon? Because my mom won't let me have this bunny until after breakfast."

Scott rubbed Danny's thick, dark hair. "Fifteen minutes. Okay? You go tell your mom."

Danny rushed back into the kitchen. "Mom! Miss Isabelle is here! Now we can eat."

Isabelle watched Danny go. "You waited for me?"

He put his hands on Bella's shoulders. "I was hoping…" He choked out the words. "I wasn't sure."

"I should have called, but I was so busy packing my things. Ross drove me home…"

"Wait. Back up. Packing? What are you talking about? I know congratulations are in order…"

Isabelle looked down at Bella. "Sweetie, could I talk to your dad for little bit? And would you take this basket to Michael?"

"Sure." Bella took the baskets and darted out of the room.

Scott watched her leave and then turned back to Isabelle. She got the feeling he was taking his time to sort through his thoughts. "I'm confused. I thought everything went well for you at the show."

"Better than well, Scott. I have commissioned paintings from a design firm and Malcolm, well, he'd be happy if I painted 24/7."

"Then, that's really great. That's what you wanted."

"It is." *Or I did.* She moved close to him.

"The art section said you have an offer in

New York. You told me once that if you got an opportunity like that, you'd be out of Indian Lake so fast—"

She put her fingers over his lips. "The old me said that."

"What's changed?"

"Everything has, Scott. Everything. You've changed. I've changed. Our lives are so…"

"Yeah, different, I know. You said that."

"They are marvelous and wonderful and I don't want them to be separate anymore."

He was speechless. She knew because he stared at her like he was trying to figure her out. She had to admit, she was probably not the easiest person in the world to deal with.

"You don't?"

"No."

"But I have children now. In fact, I'm thinking about adopting them permanently."

"Oh, Scott. I'm so happy for you. It's the right decision."

"It is for me."

"It is for them, too," she said.

"I thought that was a deal breaker for you," he said tentatively, his eyes floating over her face. "You told me…"

"I said a lot of things, Scott. I was pretty mixed up, and I confess I had my priorities badly jumbled. I don't think that anymore."

He took a deep breath. "I've wanted to talk to you about the adoption for a while now, but then I figured that since you'd fallen in love with Wes, and—"

"I'm not in love with Wes," she interrupted.

He pulled up short. "Sure you are."

"No, Scott. I'm not. I'm in love with you."

"But he's what you always wanted."

She wrapped her arms around his neck. "I want a life with you. And the kids. And my art. I came here today to ask you if you think you could fit all of it in."

He put his palm on her cheek, his thumb tracing her jawline. He peered into her eyes. "You blow me away, you know that, right? I read that article in the *Tribune* and I thought I'd lost you forever."

"It's not going to be easy, you know. Being married to an impassioned artist."

"Married?" His head jerked back and his eyes filled with surprise.

"Yeah," she replied decisively.

"Who said anything about being married?" he asked with an impish grin.

"Scott…"

He slid his hand into hers and said, "Come with me. I want to show you something."

"No."

"Why not?"

"You didn't answer me," she said.

He held up his forefinger. "You're so impatient. Come on."

Scott led her through the dining room, where the table was covered in a linen cloth with pretty pink plates and glasses. An Easter bunny sat in the middle of the table.

"Cute," she said.

"I stole the idea from one of your Easter brunches at the Lodges years ago."

"You remembered that?"

They went through the kitchen where Mrs. Beabots was dishing out baked pears with Theresa. Violet and Sadie waved to her as she walked through.

"Hi, everybody! Happy Easter," Isabelle said as Scott pulled her toward the back porch.

"Hi," they chimed in unison, continuing their work.

That was odd, she thought. Usually, they'd want to hug her. She could get lost in the kitchen talking for hours. *Hmm.*

They went out to the backyard where her brothers, Ross, Chris and Dylan, were playing bean bag toss with Trent, Luke, Timmy and Danny. Annie and Bella were sitting on lawn chairs with Cate, Sarah and Connie.

"Hi, Mom! Hi, guys!"

They all waved, but went back to their conversations.

Okay. This is really strange. They all knew about her success in Chicago; the newspapers and her texts to her family had relayed the news, but they seemed more engrossed in their own concerns.

"Wow. This yard is really big," Isabelle said. "And gorgeous."

The long narrow yard was surrounded on all three sides with blooming daffodils, tulips and hyacinths under tall spruce trees. A flowering pink crabapple tree filled the south corner.

"Yeah. I've been saving up for a riding lawn mower. It's a killer to mow."

Suddenly, she stopped dead in her tracks. "And what is that?" She pointed to a small house at the very back of the property, complete with flower boxes in the windows.

"It used to be a potting shed. The owner was really into the garden. As you can see. In the winter it was hard to envision, but I took Cate's word for it since she knew the woman who lived here before she died."

"So, are you going to make it into a playhouse for the kids?"

"No," he said, opening the door and letting her enter first.

Isabelle stepped inside. The sun poured down

from above. "What in the world?" She looked up at the skylight, which had obviously been installed recently.

"It's an artist's studio now," he said shutting the door and taking her into his arms. "Isabelle. Marry me? Stay with me forever. I don't think I could be apart from you ever again. I promise I'll never do anything without our mutual consent."

Isabelle put her arms around his neck and smiled. "So, I'm guessing that since I asked first, your answer is a yes?"

"Yes." He chuckled.

"Then I concur. Yes."

"We're mutually agreed?" he asked.

"Yes."

"I have one last thing." He bent down and turned over a clay pot that was sitting next to the door. He withdrew a black velvet box.

"Scott?" For the first time she saw that look she'd longed to see in his eyes—there was nothing and no one in the world more important to him than her.

Or perhaps it had been there all along, and she just hadn't noticed or understood.

He held the ring out to her. "Luke and Trent said I should take you to the jeweler's so you can pick out what you wanted. But I thought you might like a surprise."

Isabelle held out her hand so that he could

slide the pretty round cut diamond in the simple antique setting onto her finger. "It's beautiful. Just what I'd pick."

"See? I do know you very well."

She glanced up at the skylight where sunlight would shower her paintings for years to come. "Yes. Scott. You always have. You know me better than I know myself."

"I love you, Isabelle, and I'm going to say it dozens of times every day."

He kissed her, sending a thrill through her body and straight to her heart. She pulled him closer, wondering why she couldn't seem to get close enough. He held her face and kissed her cheeks, eyelids and lips a dozen times.

And then she felt as if she was sailing away to the stars with Scott. Finally, her dreams had come true and she had everything she'd ever really wanted.

* * * * *

For more stories from
THE SHORES OF INDIAN LAKE, *check out* PROTECTING THE SINGLE MOM *and* SOPHIE'S PATH. *Find more of Catherine Lanigan's titles at Harlequin.com, and don't miss the next book in this miniseries, coming soon from Harlequin Heartwarming!*

Get 2 Free Books,
Plus 2 Free Gifts—
just for trying the Reader Service!

Love Inspired®

YES! Please send me 2 FREE Love Inspired® Romance novels and my 2 FREE mystery gifts (gifts are worth about $10 retail). After receiving them, if I don't wish to receive any more books, I can return the shipping statement marked "cancel." If I don't cancel, I will receive 6 brand-new novels every month and be billed just $5.24 for the regular-print edition or $5.74 each for the larger-print edition in the U.S., or $5.74 each for the regular-print edition or $6.24 per the larger-print edition in Canada. That's a saving of at least 13% off the cover price. It's quite a bargain! Shipping and handling is just 50¢ per book in the U.S. and 75¢ per book in Canada.* I understand that accepting the 2 free books and gifts places me under no obligation to buy anything. I can always return a shipment and cancel at any time. The free books and gifts are mine to keep no matter what I decide.

Please check one:

☐ Love Inspired Romance Regular-Print   ☐ Love Inspired Romance Larger-Print
   (105/305 IDN GLWW)   (122/322 IDN GLWW)

Name	(PLEASE PRINT)
Address	Apt. #
City State/Province	Zip/Postal Code

Signature (if under 18, a parent or guardian must sign)

Mail to the **Reader Service:**
IN U.S.A.: P.O. Box 1341, Buffalo, NY 14240-8531
IN CANADA: P.O. Box 603, Fort Erie, Ontario L2A 5X3

Want to try two free books from another line?
Call 1-800-873-8635 today or visit www.ReaderService.com.

*Terms and prices subject to change without notice. Prices do not include applicable taxes. Sales tax applicable in N.Y. Canadian residents will be charged applicable taxes. Offer not valid in Quebec. This offer is limited to one order per household. Books received may not be as shown. Not valid for current subscribers to Love Inspired Romance books. All orders subject to approval. Credit or debit balances in a customer's account(s) may be offset by any other outstanding balance owed by or to the customer. Please allow 4 to 6 weeks for delivery. Offer available while quantities last.

Your Privacy—The Reader Service is committed to protecting your privacy. Our Privacy Policy is available online at www.ReaderService.com or upon request from the Reader Service.

We make a portion of our mailing list available to reputable third parties that offer products we believe may interest you. If you prefer that we not exchange your name with third parties, or if you wish to clarify or modify your communication preferences, please visit us at www.ReaderService.com/consumerschoice or write to us at Reader Service Preference Service, P.O. Box 9062, Buffalo, NY 14240-9062. Include your complete name and address.

LI17R2

Get 2 Free Books,

Plus 2 Free Gifts—

just for trying the Reader Service!

HOMETOWN HEARTS ♥

YES! Please send me **The Hometown Hearts Collection** in Larger Print. This collection begins with 3 FREE books and 2 FREE gifts in the first shipment. Along with my 3 free books, I'll also get the next 4 books from the Hometown Hearts Collection, in LARGER PRINT, which I may either return and owe nothing, or keep for the low price of $4.99 U.S./ $5.89 CDN each plus $2.99 for shipping and handling per shipment*. If I decide to continue, about once a month for 8 months I will get 6 or 7 more books, but will only need to pay for 4. That means 2 or 3 books in every shipment will be FREE! If I decide to keep the entire collection, I'll have paid for only 32 books because 19 books are FREE! I understand that accepting the 3 free books and gifts places me under no obligation to buy anything. I can always return a shipment and cancel at any time. My free books and gifts are mine to keep no matter what I decide.

262 HCN 3432 462 HCN 3432

Name	(PLEASE PRINT)	
Address		Apt. #
City	State/Prov.	Zip/Postal Code

Signature (if under 18, a parent or guardian must sign)

Mail to the **Reader Service:**
IN U.S.A.: P.O. Box 1867, Buffalo, NY. 14240-1867
IN CANADA: P.O. Box 609, Fort Erie, Ontario L2A 5X3

Get 2 Free Books,
Plus 2 Free Gifts—
just for trying the Reader Service!

HARLEQUIN *super romance*

KRISTINA KNIGHT
Famous In a Small Town

TARA TAYLOR QUINN
The Fireman's Son

YES! Please send me 2 FREE LARGER-PRINT Harlequin® Superromance® novels and my 2 FREE gifts (gifts are worth about $10 retail). After receiving them, if I don't wish to receive any more books, I can return the shipping statement marked "cancel." If I don't cancel, I will receive 4 brand-new novels every month and be billed just $6.19 per book in the U.S. or $6.49 per book in Canada. That's a savings of at least 11% off the cover price! It's quite a bargain! Shipping and handling is just 50¢ per book in the U.S. or 75¢ per book in Canada.* I understand that accepting the 2 free books and gifts places me under no obligation to buy anything. I can always return a shipment and cancel at any time. The free books and gifts are mine to keep no matter what I decide.

132/332 HDN GLWS

Name _____ (PLEASE PRINT)

Address _____ Apt. #

City _____ State/Prov. _____ Zip/Postal Code

Signature (if under 18, a parent or guardian must sign)

Mail to the **Reader Service:**
IN U.S.A.: P.O. Box 1341, Buffalo, NY 14240-8531
IN CANADA: P.O. Box 603, Fort Erie, Ontario L2A 5X3

Want to try two free books from another line?
Call 1-800-873-8635 today or visit www.ReaderService.com.

* Terms and prices subject to change without notice. Prices do not include applicable taxes. Sales tax applicable in N.Y. Canadian residents will be charged applicable taxes. Offer not valid in Quebec. This offer is limited to one order per household. Books received may not be as shown. Not valid for current subscribers to Harlequin Superromance Larger-Print books. All orders subject to approval. Credit or debit balances in a customer's account(s) may be offset by any other outstanding balance owed by or to the customer. Please allow 4 to 6 weeks for delivery. Offer available while quantities last.

Your Privacy—The Reader Service is committed to protecting your privacy. Our Privacy Policy is available online at www.ReaderService.com or upon request from the Reader Service.

We make a portion of our mailing list available to reputable third parties that offer products we believe may interest you. If you prefer that we not exchange your name with third parties, or if you wish to clarify or modify your communication preferences, please visit us at www.ReaderService.com/consumerchoice or write to us at Reader Service Preference Service, P.O. Box 9062, Buffalo, NY 14240-9062. Include your complete name and address.

HSRLP17R

Get 2 Free Books,
Plus 2 Free Gifts—
just for trying the Reader Service!

Love Inspired HISTORICAL

Get 2 Free Books,
Plus 2 Free Gifts—
just for trying the Reader Service!

HARLEQUIN *Romance*

Get 2 Free Books,
Plus 2 Free Gifts –
just for trying the Reader Service!